VALIANT
WITNESS

VALIANT WITNESS

A NOVEL OF MORONI

ROBERT H. MOSS

International Standard Book Number
0-88290-226-1

Library of Congress Catalog Card Number
83-81586

Horizon Publishers Catalog and Order Number
1954

Second Printing, January 1984

Printed and Distributed in the
United States of America
by

Horizon Publishers & Distributors, Inc.

———————————

50 South 500 West
P.O. Box 490
Bountiful, Utah 84010

Preface

The Angel Moroni, visible on temple towers throughout the world, has always intrigued me. Little is said about his life in the Book of Mormon, but from the time he first began his writings until he closed the book, thirty-six years went by. What would a man do, living alone for thirty-six years? Where would he go? What would he think about during those long days and even longer nights? Could he stand inactivity after an active life of serving his Lord as a disciple?

These questions bothered me as time after time I read his record. Then one day I read the book, *He Walked the Americas.* The book tells of stories and legends held by native North and South Americans concerning the visits to their peoples by the "Pale One." The supposition of the book is that the "Pale One" was Jesus Christ. This could well be so. However, the question could be asked, "Would Christ have spent so much time wandering on foot between villages across North and South America?" He only spent three years in His ministry in Palestine. His ministry to the people of the American continent after his resurrection was relatively short according to the account in Third Nephi. To me it was not reasonable.

We know that the Lord cares enough about all of His people that He would want to visit them and tell them of His gospel. But the obvious solution is that He would send His disciples. Moroni was an ordained Disciple. He had spent his life training for the ministry. His life was a life of service and dedication. He had much time available to him between the final battle in A.D. 385 and the end of his writings in A.D. 421. It is my theory that Moroni was the "pale one" which these legends speak of. I believe that he was Christ's emissary to the scattered tribes of North and South America.

Other questions sometimes asked concern the Hill Cumorah. "Was there only one?" "Where was it located?" *In Search of Cumorah* gives strong evidence to support the theory of two Cumorahs. If there were two, then it was Moroni's responsibility to get the plates from the Cumorah in MesoAmerica, where they were written, to a hill in upstate New York where a young prophet could be led to them 1400 years later. If Moroni made this journey, would it not be reasonable that he would make contacts with the people along the way?

This book attempts to to answer some of the above questions concerning this great prophet and his mission. As we read the scriptures, we feel the strength and testimony of the characters, but we don't read much about the wives and children—the problems and obstacles faced and overcome, the triumphs, the joys, the sorrows, or even the stories of love. In this story of the life of Moroni, using scriptural and historical sources, I have attempted to help us gain insight into Moroni as a man, as a husband and father, as a son, as well as a Prophet of the Lord.

In the writing of this series, I have used all applicable scriptures, either quoted or paraphrased, plus many additional references. The index of quotations and list of these references is found at the end of the book.

This book is the culmination of years of study and desire. I commit it to you, the reader. May you find within its pages something that will help you to become a hero to your loved ones. Moroni was and is a hero to me.

I dedicate this book to my father, Clarence McAllister Moss, who will always be a hero to me.

Contents

Prologue: Birth of a Prophet

Mormon nervously kicked the gravel in the path as he paced back and forth in front of his house. The path was lined with red and yellow flowers which threw a sweet smell into the air. Bees flitted between the flowers. He had been pacing since early morning, awaiting word from his servants that the time had come for his wife, Merena, to deliver their firstborn.

Old Leera, the midwife, had pushed him out the door, saying "You go do something. I will take care of Merena and will tell you when the baby is to be delivered."

He watched with concern as a maid-servant came from the house, went to the well, and returned with a basin filled with water. A loud cry came from the house. Mormon jumped forward, ran to the door and attempted to push his way through.

Leera, a large woman, firmly pushed him away. "The pains have begun," she said, "but it may still be a long time. Merena is young and small. Have patience, Mormon."

Mormon turned, muttering under his breath that patience was not one of his virtues. To fill his mind as he paced and waited, he thought back over his life with Merena. He loved her so.

He had met Merena soon after Ammaron, the scribe and keeper of the records, had approached him about becoming the new keeper of the records for the Nephites. As a boy of ten, Mormon was not sure just what that responsibility would entail. He only knew that it was a great honor to be asked by the aging Ammaron. He ran breathlessly to his father, telling him of Ammaron's charge. Father Mormon, knowing the significance of this calling, moved his entire family to Zarahemla so that young Mormon could receive the necessary training in order to carry out his mission.

Mormon had been awed by Zarahemla. It seemed as if the entire valley was covered with buildings. In Zarahemla he had been apprenticed to Natschal, the engraver, where he could learn the art of engraving the perfect word pictures onto the plates of gold and brass. The first thing Mormon saw upon entering the house of Natschal was his ten-year old daughter, Merena. Mormon saw Merena often during the years of apprenticeship to Natschal and later to Alphus, the goldsmith.

After his apprenticeship and military training, he had been called by the Nephites to be the general over all of their armies. He was only sixteen at the time, but Merena had waited until he was able to return and take her hand in marriage. Oh, what a happy time this was in his life. The days sped by as Mormon and his young bride exulted in each other, exploring those tender relationships as husband and wife.

And now here he was, a year later, with Merena lying there in the house, in agony with the forthcoming birth of his firstborn. Mormon could no longer wait outside. He was a man of action. He strode purposefully to the house, pushed open the door, and stepped inside.

The room was hot and oppressive. The acrid smell of wood smoke and pinesap made him wrinkle his nose. A brazier stood on the stone floor with red-hot coals glowing. Three young maid-servants stood near the window aimlessly rearranging the cotton curtains. Leera, moved over and dropped a few more wood chips on the small brazier. The room, modestly furnished, was dominated by the large wooden bed in the middle of the floor. In the bed, semi-reclining, lay his wife, Merena.

He quickly moved to her side and took her small limp hand in his large one. She was lying quietly, but he could see that she had been in pain. Her brow was knotted and beads of perspiration stood out on her forehead. Her fine brown hair was matted and plastered to her face. Just then she wrenched in agony, her fingernails biting deeply into Mormon's calloused palm. She moaned loudly, before sinking back into the blankets. New drops of per- spiration formed on her pallid cheeks. She smiled wanly at Mormon, seem- ing to feel his tender concern and helplessness. How frustrating it was to be there but to be unable to help.

Leera knowingly moved to the side of the bed. "Last night I dreamed of this baby," she said. "I dreamed that it would be a boy and that he would be a mighty warrior like his father." She turned away. "I also dreamed that he would be a man of loneliness."

Mormon gazed quizzically at her, realizing that many midwives were known for their gift of prophecy. He turned back to Merena without com- ment, trying to soothe her. "It will be over soon, my dear," he whispered in her ear. Merena didn't answer, but he could feel the gentle squeeze of her hand in his.

Another pain struck and again Mormon's hand seemed almost crushed by the small hand within it. The pains then seemed to come one right after another. Leera said, "The time is here."

One of the servant girls who had been standing by the window quickly brought a basin of hot water from the brazier. Mormon was hustled out of the way.

The child was born. As Leera had predicted, it was a boy. He was born on the day of Eb in the month of Chen, in the 337th year after the sign of the Savior's birth. Grandfather Mormon, even though quite feeble with age, christened the eight-day old boy. He named him Moroni, after that great Nephite general who had led the Nephites during the time of Helaman.

In his blessing he said, "Moroni, I prophecy that you will be a leader of men. Your life will be a life of service. Just as the first Moroni raised the title of liberty for his people, you will be an instrument in the Lord's hands proclaiming to the world the message that liberty comes only through obedience to the Gospel of Jesus Christ. Your mission will extend beyond mortality. Your life on earth with be one of joy and service, but also one of loneliness as you become a witness to the destruction of the Nephite people. Through it all you will maintain a closeness to the Lord, and will remain faithful to His message and teaching."

As the elder Mormon continued his blessing on the baby, Mormon pondered his words. He thought, "How wonderful it is to bring such a child to this earth. Thank you, Lord, for letting us be creators with Thee."

After the blessing, Mormon proudly took the little Moroni into his arms, holding him close, smelling the soft sweet baby smell of him. He whispered in his tiny ear, "Moroni, you are going to be a champion. You and I, no matter what adversity may befall us, will spend our lives in the service to the Master."

At that time, Mormon did not know just how closely his life would be intertwined with that of his young son.

PART I

The Early Years

"Welcome to my home," the wizened old man said, "and welcome to the city of Bountiful." Moroni looked at Amonihah. He was gnarled with age, chisel-featured, with a hawk's-beak nose. He greeted Moroni warmly as they entered the room. He was bareheaded and Moroni noted that his hair, though now perfectly white, must have been coal black at one time. Only the beetling eyebrows, coming together over the bridge of his nose, hinted at their former color. His eyes were warm, deep set and wearied with age, but bright with a cheerful inquisitiveness.

Moroni, an ordained Disciple of the Master, had come to Bountiful to strengthen the local Christian Church. Amonihah was the local church leader and an old friend of his father's. Amonihah led him into the study, motioning for Moroni to sit beside the soft flame of the gilded brazier.

"Thank you, the warmth feels good."

Amonihah nodded pleasantly and signalled a servant girl to bring in something warm to drink. Traces of mud and clay clung to Moroni's sandals, and it was obvious that he was weary from traveling.

The servant girl moved lithely between the old man and his guest, setting a goblet of sweet cocoa before each of them. Moroni sipped his drink slowly, enjoying its warmth and sweet taste. After some small talk he got right to the reason for his visit.

"Amonihah," he began, "my father, Mormon, has spoken of you and your strenghth in the faith."

"Thank you," Amonihah smiled. "Your father and I have fought the good fight together for many years." He paused. "But I'm afraid that the battle is just about lost."

"Why do you say that?" queried Moroni, a troubled look on his face.

"Those of the faith are few. Our faith is strong. Our desire is great, but the pressures become stronger against us each day. To be a Christian in this community is a sign of weakness. Our youth are rejecting the message. They don't want to be different."

15

Moroni nodded, encouraging Amonihah to continue.

"We are faced with public ridicule, which we can handle, but continuing harassments by the government have become more than some of our people can bear."

Moroni contemplated what the older man had said. He had found similar problems in Lehi and Mulek. The Christians could not proselyte and the youth were leaving the Church in order to stay popular with their peer group. The Church was losing numbers each day. In his mind he had gone over the possible solutions time and time again, but the problems remained. He glanced up from the dancing flames in the brazier to find Amonihah soberly watching him.

He raised his hands helplessly. "I know what is happening. I've seen it in our own city, but something can and must be done. The Savior would expect it of us. The people we have are strong. Persecution always strenghtens those who are committed and have a testimony. The key to our problem is to help our people gain stronger testimonies."

"Moroni," Amonihah shrugged, "I don't know if there is anything we can do other than being strong ourselves. The Lord has predicted the total downfall of his people. Perhaps now is the time."

"I know of the prophecies," retorted Moroni, "but we cannot just give up and let our precious beliefs become lost among mankind." His voice rose. "We have been commissioned by the Savior to spread the gospel, to bear our testimony to this people. We cannot give up, though it appears that the odds are against us. We must continue to do that which our Savior would want us to do."

"I'm not giving up," the older man replied. "I'm just trying to be realistic. Our people don't want to fight. They will continue to live their religion, but they feel the time is past when they can convert anyone else. The members of our congregation are old. They feel they have no talent for proselyting."

"I am not as concerned about talent as I am commitment," responded Moroni. "I find that there are many talented people who are failures. I would rather work with some of the untalented who have some drive and determination to serve. Even if we fail it is better than not trying. Amonihah, I am convinced that we can turn this problem into an opportunity. It gives us the chance to strive onward . . . to stretch ourselves. What we need is the big goal . . . the big dream . . . that will keep us moving forward."

Amonihah stroked his beard in contemplation. Finally he said, "Moroni, I am an old man. There is very little time left for me. My dream, though, is like yours . . . to strengthen the people and preach the word. I'm just not sure that there is time enough left for me to complete that dream."

Moroni laughed. "Maybe I'm too emphatic but we must believe totally in what we are doing. You say your time is limited, but is God's? Consider what resources He has! My father is still leading the Nephite armies when he is well past the age when most men would be dead. The truth is, my friend, we have unbelievable untapped resources within us.''

"I am not giving up," said Amonihah, "I'll admit I am discouraged, but I will continue the fight."

Moroni leaned over and put his hand on the older man's shoulders. "Thank you, my friend." He leaned back on his cushion and thought of the many times in his short life when he had faced severe problems. With the Lord's help he had solved all of them. He closed his eyes in thought.

"Are you sleepy?" Amonihah interrupted his reverie. Moroni shook his head. Amonihah leaned forward, offering him a plate laden with dried fruits and nuts.

Moroni picked up a few cashews and chewed them slowly. "No," he said. "Strangely enough I am not tired. I really thought I would be after my long journey to get here."

"Tell me about your life, then," his friend asked. "I am interested in knowing more about you. What of your youth? What experiences prepared you to be a Disciple?"

Moroni's mind drifted back through the years, recalling his youth. What really stood out was an experience that happened to him just before his twelfth birthday.

Chapter 1

The Nephite Youth

Moroni looked carefully around, waiting for the right time to sneak away. His head was full of plans for the day and he didn't want to be slowed down by staying with the other warrior youth. It was a bright cool dawn with a light wind humming in the bushes and tall grass carrying scents of wood and swamp. Parcels of ghost-like clouds lay against the mountains. It excited him to know that in a few minutes he would be hunting by himself.

After all, he was almost twelve and had hunted alone before. He had become familiar with every hill and ravine around the city of Desolaton, slipping away often for hunting and play. Many times he would fantasize that he was a leader of armies just like his famous father, giving commands to legions of imaginary warriors as they conquered hordes of Lamanites.

He inhaled deeply, drawing into his lungs the fragrant scents of the myriads of flowers which lined the path. He looked up, watching the gaily-colored birds in the trees. A smaller bird, shiny green and yellow, lighted on a low-hanging branch, filling the air with a warbling song that reminded him of the flutes the temple priests played on ceremonial days. He stopped and listened. The other boys kept walking and he took the opportunity to slip behind a tree. He knew that his mother worried about him going off by himself, but . . . He shrugged his shoulders and pursed his lips. It was just something that he enjoyed doing. As he moved further into the brushy hillside, his spirits soared. He carried a small obsidian knife, a bow and a quiver full of arrows. Walking rapidly, he made his way through the trackless brush. Brambles scratched at his bare legs and water from the dew-laden plants soaked his torso.

Soon the jungle became thicker. Tall trees stretched their tops towards the sky. Parroty birds and insects screamed about his head. Two macaws croaked at him from above. As he looked up he could see bigger birds, perched or making shadowy flights near the treetops. He hadn't seen them up close, but he knew they were giant vultures. He took careful note of the trees and boulders so he would be able to find his way home.

It was midmorning now, and the rays of the sun filtered in streamers through the thick tree cover. Coming to the bank of a small stream, Moroni knelt on one knee and scooped up a drink. As he did so, he saw in the mud the deep, freshly made tracks of a large animal. Water was still seeping into each print. They were bigger tracks than he had ever seen and the hairs on the back of his neck prickled. An eerie feeling of being watched came over him. He glanced all around, shook his shoulders to get rid of the prickles, notched an arrow in his bow and then moved quietly down the stream.

A whisper in his subconscious said, "Look up." He did, right into the malevolent eyes of a great black jaguar. The big cat was perched in the crotch of a branch just a few paces ahead of him. Its tail whipped back and forth as it watched the youth below.

It seemed as if the entire jungle became empty and still. The only thing Moroni was aware of was the black form of the jaguar. He suddenly realized that he had been holding his breath and he let it out slowly, gulping in new air. In the stillness he could hear his own heart beating and wondered if the cat could hear it, too. Sweat stood out on his forehead, his breathing was short and jerky and he was aware that his hand was sore from gripping his bow so tightly.

He stared at the cat but the huge yellow eyes just stared back at him without so much as a flicker. The cat, its tail twitching like a large pendulum, seemed to be waiting for his slightest indication of fear or panic. Moroni was frightened—more than he had ever been in his life.

His father's words came to him. "Son, whenever you need help, your Father in Heaven is there. All you have to do is pray. Live worthily to receive His help and He will help you."

Moroni prayed. He prayed as he had never prayed before. He pleaded, his lips moving silently, "Father, give me courage. Help me to know what to do. I promise you I will live move worthily in the future. Please help me."

A peaceful feeling came over him. The change from near panic to calmness was sudden and dramatic. He now knew that even though the situation was still critical, he was no longer alone. His Father was with him and would not let him down. The large cat suddenly took the initiative. With a breathy hiss it crouched, ready to spring. Moroni reacted quickly. Drawing his bow, he loosed his arrows. He was thankful for early training in speed and accuracy and he made every arrow count. He then dropped his bow, gripped his obsidian knife, and stood prepared to face the charge of the angered cat. As it leaped at him, jaws spread wide, shiny white teeth which looked so fearful, Moroni stepped aside and struck at the cat's throat with all his strength, he could smell the cat's vile breath. As momentum carried the cat past him, the knife imbedded in its throat, it swiped at Moroni with its razor-sharp claws. Four long red scratches appeared on Moroni's arm, oozing bright red blood.

As the cat hit the ground its legs crumpled and it landed in an inert heap of twisting body, head, legs, and tail. Moroni suddenly felt weak. As he looked at the bloody carcass his stomach contracted and he gagged. He recovered and knelt down to offer a fervent prayer of thanksgiving. Never before in his young life had he felt the power of God to such an extent.

Feeling stronger, he slowly rose to his feet. He jumped upon a stump, cupped his hands around his mouth and gave an earsplitting yell, silencing for a moment the chattering of the birds and monkeys high in the branches overhead. Almost in a daze he walked around the big animal. It looked much less fearsome now. Moroni felt that it was a significant lesson. Problems and obstacles are huge until they are met and conquered.

He was suddenly aware of the burning on his arm. It was covered with blood and starting to swell. He stepped over to the stream and washed off the blood. As he stood there, he realized that he was no longer alone. The other boys had come up behind him. They stared in open-mouthed wonder as they poked the dead cat with their toes. Even Ammah, the leader and oldest of the boys, seemed impressed. He quickly took charge of the situation and had the boys trim a long straight limb on which they tied the feet of the jaguar.

When it was securely tied, two of the larger boys picked up the pole, placed it on their shoulders, and with the cat hanging upside-down between them started back to the city. Moroni, as was fitting, took his place in front of the boys carrying the cat.

There was a great celebration that night at Moroni's home. Merena was tearful as she cleaned and bandaged his bloody arm. She seemed to be thinking of what might have happened to her only son and tears coursed freely down her cheeks. Mormon, the proud father, patted Moroni on the back asking him again and again to tell the story of killing the jaguar. Sophrista, Moroni's little sister, tagged around behind him her eyes shining with pride. Merena fixed some of Moroni's favorite foods for dinner; honey on corn cake, roast fish, and fresh beans from the garden.

After the meal Moroni was asked once again to tell his story. He spoke quietly about his prayer and how it was answered. A lump came in his throat as he thought of how good the Lord had been to him. He uttered a silent promise to the Lord that he would always be faithful and follow the commandments. He noticed his father wiping away his tears with his large calloused hands.

Mormon cleared his throat to speak. Moroni and the rest of the family waited expectantly. Moroni idolized his father and he listened carefully as Mormon spoke. "Son, you have done today what few adults have done. Because of your faithfulness the Lord has blessed you, and now, with your permission, I feel a desire to give you a father's blessing."

Moroni could only nod. Tears welled in his eyes. Today's happenings had been almost more than he could comprehend. Mormon took his place behind him, placed his large hands on his brown touseled hair, and began.

"Dear son, Moroni. As a disciple of our Lord and Savior, Jesus Christ, and in His holy name, I give you a father's blessing. I praise the Lord that He has seen fit to answer your prayers. I bless you that the Lord will continue to take a special interest in you because of the special mission which you will be called on to perform. . . ."

Mormon listened to his father's voice as many beautiful blessings were promised to him. He sat there, feeling the weight and pressure of his father's hands upon his head, trying to listen and comprehend all that was being said, feeling a warmth as power seemed to flow from his father's hands into every part of his being.

". . . and when you have completed this mission, Jesus Christ Himself will call you home to live with Him. This blessing I pronounce upon you in His holy name, Amen."

The family sat quietly and reverently as Mormon slowly removed his hands from Moroni's head. Moroni swallowed, noticing for the first time how dry his mouth was. He stood, looked up at his father, clasped forearms with him, and then threw himself into his father's arms—so choked up he could not speak.

Little Sophrista, not to be left out, ran and threw her arms around Moroni's waist. He reached down with one arm to hold her. He had never felt so close to his family and he felt as if his heart would burst—it was so full.

Mormon broke the silence to make an announcement. "On the morrow I travel to check out the defenses in our outlying cities. Since Moroni has demonstrated his manhood so well, I will take him along as one of my warrior escorts."

Moroni couldn't believe what he had heard! His father now accepted him as a man! He looked at his mother who was proudly watching him. Little Sopie was jumping up and down in excitement, holding both his hands.

That night he packed the few belongings which he felt he would need for the journey. Try as he would, though, he could not sleep. He was too excited. His arm hurt but he tried to ignore the pain. All night he tossed on his pallet.

Morning finally came. By the time the red sun rose over the horizon, Moroni was dressed and ready to go. Impatiently he waited while Merena fixed a breakfast for him and his father. She took time to pack a bag of dried fruits for them to take with them. Finally, they were ready. Merena bid them a tearful goodby then stood in the door looking after them as they walked together down the street. As they turned the corner they looked back once again.

Merena bravely waved even though she could hardly see her husband and son through her tear-filled eyes. She had said many goodbyes to her husband over the years, but this was the first time she had ever had to say goodbye to both husband and only son. She felt a tug on her dress. Reaching down she picked up Sophrista. Hugging her tightly to her, Merena turned and walked into the house. It was now in the hands of the Lord.

* * *

Moroni's senses were extra perceptive as they journeyed. Every sound, every smell, every sight was new and exciting to him. He picked out the soft sound of birds cooing, the feel of the gentle breezes on his face, the shimmering greenery around him. Mormon often strode beside him pointing out where historical events had taken place, or where certain battles had been fought. These were favorite times for Moroni to feel the closeness of his father, to be taught by the man he loved most of all.

They traveled in a southwesterly direction and by nightfall they had reached the outskirts of Mocum. Mormon called the people together and instructed them to pack what belongings they needed and to move to Desolation. The little towns had no protection against the Lamanites and Mormon well knew that there was strength in numbers. Each town received the same instructions from him.

On the evening of the third day they arrived at the city of Bountiful. By then, the three day hike plus his lack of sleep had completely exhausted Moroni. His excitement, plus his dogged determination not to slow down the march, were all that had kept him going. That night he slept soundly.

The next day, while Mormon was meeting with the city commanders, Moroni slipped away to explore the city. Bountiful was a boisterous welter of color, and heat, and smells. It was a crossroads city which brought people from all corners of the Nephite lands. The streets rang with profane and shouting voices, the shops teemed. He covered his ears as he passed through the market because of the deafening cries of the merchants. Smells of cooking meat, of rotting fruits, and the forges of the metalsmiths all fused together. The sharp acrid stink of the gutter assailed his sensitive nose.

The boisterous city excited him. He was caught up in the bustling, frenetic clamor of the market place. He loved the sweet, warm smells of the open-air bakeries and even the pungent smell of the swirling dust seemed to have an air of excitement in it. Nephite warriors flirted with maidens who wore brightly colored dresses. Occasionally the sounds of an argument or a fight rose on the tepid air. Beggars sat along the streets, their backs to the walls, their hands out imploringly, wailing in anguish.

By late afternoon he had completed his circuit of the city. He had not ventured beyond the city wall which was ancient and crumbling in spots, but had clambered up on the wall and looked out. Stretching to the west and north were lush fields of corn, squash, and other vegetables. On the east the city extended almost to the beaches of the East Sea.

As the evening light began to fade, Moroni hurried back towards the barracks. He was hungry and his stomach growled in protest. He suddenly realized that he had been so busy that he hadn't eaten all day. As he crossed the plaza the tantalizing smells of baking bread caused his mouth to water. He felt for his pouch but found he had no money. He was still far from the barracks and he was very hungry. Right beside him on the window ledge above the baking ovens was a long row of freshly-baked loaves of bread. The temptation was just too great. Looking around and seeing that no one was looking he snatched a loaf of bread from the ledge and slipped it beneath his tunic. A wave of guilt hit him and he was ready to put the loaf back when he noticed the large crowd gathered at the base of the temple pyramid.

High above the heads of the crowd, on top of the pyramid was the temple. In the archway stood a black-robed priest, chanting something indistinguishable to Moroni. He was drawn towards the crowd. He saw the priest holding both hands high above his head. In one hand he clutched a long black obsidian knife. The other hand held something of a purplish color. It was dripping what looked like blood. Moroni stood as if thunderstruck. It was blood—running from the heart that the priest held in his hand. He suddenly felt nauseated. He had heard of the cults of the sacrificers—but here in Bountiful!

He raced towards the barracks to find solace in the strength of his father. As he ran the bread fell unnoticed from his hand—his hunger forgotten.

At supper that night, Mormon listened intently to his son. He was sickened by the brutality and sinfulness of his people. It was sad enough for the Lamanites to be practicing idolatry, but for the Nephites— with their civilization and learning. He shook his head.

"My son, my heart is saddened by what you describe. The Lord condemns those things which you have witnessed. He cannot look upon any sin with any degree of allowance." As Mormon talked, a great feeling of guilt came over Moroni. He was as bad as the priest. He had committed a sin. In his remorse his head dropped to his chest.

Mormon reached over and lifted Moroni's chin in the cup of his fingers. "It is all right, my son. The robbers and priests will have to pay for their sins. The main thing is to keep ourselves from sin."

At this statement Moroni could no longer hold back the tears. Burying his head in Mormon's shoulder he sobbed as if his heart would break. Mormon was perplexed. This was the first time that Moroni had cried like this since he was an infant.

Controlling himself, Moroni looked red-eyed at his father. He straightened his shoulders resolutely. "Father, I have also sinned. I was hungry and took a loaf of bread from a market stall." He hung his head in shame, waiting for his father's reply.

Mormon hugged his son tightly to him. "My son," he softly replied, "you have done right in telling me. The Lord has provided us a way to repent and be fully forgiven."

Moroni listened, anxious to have forgiveness.

"The Lord told Alma that if a person confesses his sins and repents in the sincerity of his heart that we were to forgive that person and that He would forgive him also. I can feel your sincere regret for what you have done, but there is one more thing you must do to show full repentance."

"What is it?" Moroni asked. "I will do it."

Mormon continued. "It is necessary that you give restitution for that which you have done and then forever forsake those sins."

"Father, what is restitution?"

"In this case," Mormon replied, "it is paying the merchant for the bread that was taken."

Father and son walked back to the plaza. It was quiet now and the crowd had long departed. Moroni led the way to the baker's stall. Mormon stood behind him to give him support. Moroni, with a quaver in his voice, told the baker, "Sir, a little while ago, while walking past your shop, I was hungry and took a loaf of your bread."

The baker was amazed. No one had ever admitted such a thing before. Moroni continued, "I have brought the money to pay you for what I took."

The walk back to the barracks was accomplished in silence, with each engrossed in his own thoughts. Moroni made a silent resolve to never again transgress the commandments of the Lord. His father's arm on his shoulder made him feel good and when his father gently squeezed his neck he knew that he had done the right thing.

He lay awake for some time thinking of what his father had said. He had learned a great principle.

* * *

By daybreak the warrior group was on the march, heading west. They swam across a large river and moved through a long, fertile valley which was ringed by volcanic cones pointing to the sky. During the next few days they stopped often at small villages, giving instructions to move to the cities. In four days they came to the West Sea. Moroni gazed in open-mouthed wonder at the immense blue harbor. Even though he had lived near the sea most of his life he had never seen such a beautiful spot as this. They camped that night in a deserted fishing village near the harbor. At first light, Moroni was up and poking around the empty thatched huts.

The warriors, under Mormon's direction, found some abandoned long boats and began to repair them. Each boat had been cut from a single log with the inside burned and hollowed out. They were big enough for at least ten warriors to ride in each one. Since several days were needed for repairs they had time to rest and to prepare for the rest of the journey.

They caught fish and dried them. Moroni became quite skillful at using a line and net. He also roamed up and down the beaches, catching crabs, digging clams, and just enjoying himself in the surf. In time he forgot some of the fears he had felt in Bountiful, but he didn't forget the feeling of sorrow he had felt about stealing the bread—or the spirit of peace he had after he felt the Lord had forgiven him.

At last the boats were ready. Moroni could hardly contain his excitement. The baggage and food items were loaded on first, followed by gourds of fresh water. Finally, the men pushed the boats away from the beach, waded out from the shore, and clambered aboard. Moroni sat in the front of one boat where he could see all that went on. The men were awkward at first with their hand-carved paddles, but by the end of the first day they handled the oars smoothly.

Mormon headed his awkward boats out beyond the breakers. He had learned earlier not to hug the shoreline where the water's motion was more violent and unpredictable. Moroni was a little nauseated at first by the roll of the boats, but after he got used to it he had fun. He could look down into the clear water and see multi-colored fish swimming. Occasionally a flying fish, attracted by the swish of the paddles, would leap out of the water.

For four days they paddled up the coast riding in on the breakers each evening to warm, friendly beaches. Fresh fish were caught and roasted—a welcome change from the dried fish and dried nuts and fruit. Moroni's skin was sunburned and red from the sun's reflection on the water. The cool evenings were welcome to him. He often swam alone in the surf then lay on the sand where the waves slowly died on the beach.

On the evening of the fourth day they arrived in a beautiful lagoon where a sparkling river flowed into the ocean. Mormon instructed the men to beach the ships for the last time. After camping that night, they struck inland for the city of Joshua—the northernmost inhabited city of the Nephites. Joshua was the furthest city from the lands of the Lamanites and thus would be the last defense of the Nephites. Mormon spent the day with his commanders, inspecting the city's troops and defenses.

Moroni wandered throughout the small city. Finally tired, he sat to rest in the central plaza. It was peaceful there and he enjoyed watching the ladies moving from the market to their homes. Several women came to sit next to him talking of a new temple city being built to the north. One of the lady's husbands had just returned from working on it. He had told her of the huge

Temple of the Sun and a Temple of the Moon which was almost as large. The robber priests had also erected a huge temple to their bearded serpent god. His curiosity aroused, Moroni vowed that he would someday see this fabled city.

That night, before he slept, Mormon showed him on a crude map where they would travel on the next leg of their journey. Moroni looked with interest at the simple map, noting the places that Mormon's finger pointed out. They would travel east, passing by the Hill Cumorah, and then on to Teancum.

* * *

Moroni turned to Amonihah. "I must be boring you with my memories."

"Not at all," responded Amonihah. "It is a fascinating account." He smiled. "Besides, I am learning a valuable lesson in geography."

Moroni yawned. "The rest of the journey was somewhat uneventful. We followed the route that father laid out. I was impressed with the Hill Cumorah and the Hill Shim." He reflected for a moment. "I had a very funny feeling when we passed by the Hill Cumorah. I don't know what caused it. Even as a twelve-year-old I somehow was impressed that part of my destiny would be entwined with that mountain. I have never been back there since that time."

In bed that night, Moroni again wondered about the strange feelings he had had at Cumorah twenty-five years before. I wonder what the future will bring? he thought. In his mind he again saw that large mountain, surrounded by fertile plains. He was still thinking of it when sleep came.

* * *

Chapter 2

The Warrior Youth

Making the rounds the next day with Amonihah, Moroni heard the same story over and over: persecution and ridicule, a desertion of the Church by the youth and a general feeling of discouragement among the members. His day was spend encouraging, telling them to "keep the faith," to "not doubt." "Doubt and discouragement," he said, "are tools of the devil. Doubt destroys faith and assures your defeat."

That night, exhausted, he sank into the soft cushions at Amonihah's home. He felt drained. After giving all day his cup needed filling. From his leather pouch he pulled some carefully folded bark papers. He handled them reverently. On these were transcribed his favorite scriptures. They were invaluable to him, not only as a help in preparing sermons for his people, but, more importantly, in times like these to just read in order to raise his spirits.

He read again the dramatic and soul-piercing words of Alma: *"Oh, that I were an angel, and could have the wish of my heart, that I might go forth and speak with the trump of God, with a voice to shake the earth, and cry repentance unto every people! . . ."* [1]

As he read and reread the words, he wondered if Alma had faced similar conditions.

At the dinner table Amonihah was eager to have Moroni tell more stories of his youth. "Your father, Mormon, has told me of your prowess in the Pok-a-Tok arena. What led you from the athletic life to the ministry?"

Moroni contemplated the question. He had been very active in sports. It was a major part of his warrior training. Pok-a-Tok had been his favorite sport and he had excelled in it. He thought again of the day in the Temple City where he had met his greatest challenge.

*   *   *

Panting for breath, Moroni stood on top of the great pyramid. He had laboriously climbed ninety ladder-like steps to get to the top. He and his team mates had traveled for several weeks to get to the Temple City and now he was not going to let the opportunity pass to see as much of it as he could.

From this vantage point he could see for miles in every direction. Down to the right he could see a great stone palace set atop a terraced base. Next to it, distinctive in its beauty, was a magnificent temple. He marveled at the years of sacrifice and toil which must have gone into the building of these great structures. Surrounding the temple area he could see the beautiful stone homes of the nobility and priests. These were the descendants of the Gadianton Robbers. They had turned to priestcraft in order to control the lives of the citizens. As rulers and priests they could tax the people and live without having to work. Moroni shook his head sadly.

Stretching beyond the luxurious homes of the rulers were the homes of the peasants. They raised the food, served the armies, and during the off-season labored hard in building the temples and homes of the rulers. It was easy to see that those rulers lived in splendor. They had the knowledge of reading and writing but refused to share these skills with the peasants. By controlling the minds of the people they could control their lives. Ignorance is slavery, Moroni mused. Only knowledge brings freedom.

From the other side of the pyramid he could see the observatory from which the astronomers had studied the heavens. Moroni thought of how earlier generations of the Nephites had developed a very accurate calendar which was still in use. The astronomers had even tracked the movements of the planets and predicted eclipses. But now much of that knowledge had become lost because of the wickedness of the people.

Moving to the other side of the pyramid, Moroni looked straight down upon the vast stone athletic stadium. This recalled the purpose of being in the Temple City. He and his band of elite warriors had been challenged by the nobles of the Temple City to participate in a game of Pok-a-Tok. In Desolation they had played the game on a dirt field. This stone stadium was huge! Even from this height Moroni could count the rows and rows of seats which filled it. He could even see the stone rings which served as goals on each side of the court. They were decorated with an image of Quetzacoatal.

Enjoying the quietude of the pyramid, he stayed as long as he felt he could. Finally he reluctantly decided it was time. He descended the long steps to the bottom. The game was to begin when the sun was at its highest point overhead. He felt he would have about an hour to get ready. As he reached ground level, he hurried through the spectators who were already arriving.

His team mates putting on their cumbersome playing uniforms, were a quiet group. Little was said as Moroni entered the room. All were obviously concentrating on the contest ahead, knowing that this was to be more than a mere game. It would be the Christians against the Sacrificers. There was much at stake. It had been rumored around that the losing team could even become the sacrificial victims of the temple.

Moroni strapped on heavy leather pads for his elbows and knees. He wore a heavy quilted loincloth over which was belted a leather hip girdle. To protect his head he put on a green-colored padded leather band which covered most of his head and ears. As the leader he wanted to avoid all chance of injury. He was used to playing at home in just a loincloth but this was to be a different game entirely.

Some players sat quietly after dressing while others engaged in small talk. There was a general tension in the air. When all were ready they knelt for a final prayer. As voice, Moroni said, "Father, please bless us to represent Thee well. Please give us strength and stamina. Help us to have a spirit of love for those against whom we are playing. . . ." After the prayer the team moved to the playing field. The Nobles' team, in blue-colored helmets, was ahead of them.

Thousands of spectators were squeezed tightly together in the stands. Late-comers stood in lines clear back to the pyramid. The Nobles were awe-inspiring in their brightly colored robes, feather capes, and jeweled armlets.

A hush fell on the crowd as the two opposing teams took their places in the arena. The hair on Moroni's neck hackled as he became aware of the fierce looks of his opponents. Teeth were visible between stretched lips— like the teeth of wolves. His instincts told him that these men were not here merely to play a game but that this contest was to be a battle of life and death. He glanced at his teammates. They, too, were intensely aware of the blood lust of their opponents. There was an almost imperceptible moving together as the green team members, shoulder to shoulder, waited for the game to begin. Moroni, at age nineteen, was determined to win.

He became aware of the monotone voice of the temple priest as he made his special prayers. The smell of burning incense was in the air. As the priest's singsong voice wound down Moroni's breath quickened in anticipation of the start of the game. With the last incantation finished the priest turned and looked intently at both teams, raised his hands high above his head, murmured a final word, and threw the ball into play.

Both teams scrambled for the ball. The rules of the game stipulated that no hands or feet could touch it. The ball could only be propelled by the head and body. It hurtled back and forth moved by heads, hips, elbows, and buttocks, bouncing and angling from one wall to another. The object of the game was to put the ball through one of the goals high on the side walls of the court. A single goal won the game. The spectators were well aware of the difficulty of getting the ball through the curved goal. It was almost as big as a person's head and the ring was only slightly larger. Added to that was the goal's position, lined up vertically on the wall about ten feet above the players' heads.

The spectators were cheering and shouting but the team members hardly heard them they were concentrating so intently on the game. Moroni hipped the ball towards a wall but it was intercepted by the elbow of a blue player. Immediately one of Moroni's teammates raced in, attempted to field the ball, and collided heavily with an opponent knocking them both unconscious. A roar went up from the stands. First blood. Moroni saw that it was his friend, Bilnor, who was carried from the field. There was no slow-down in the game and Moroni dodged into a position where he might receive a pass.

Sweat dripped from the players' bodies. Moroni bent and twisted, dipped and parried. He caught the ball with his head, elbowed it high in the air towards the goal, then fought himself into the melee of bodies to attempt to rebound his own attempt. As play got rougher and more intense, fights broke out here and there amongst the players. Elbows smashed into faces, knees into groins. Moroni knew that unless they were able to score quickly they wouldn't have any able players left.

The teams played as machines with no words needed. Leather against leather, skin or leather against the rubber ball, or the grunts as players made contact were the only sounds. Concentration was intense.

A blue player, taller than Moroni, seemed to be assigned as his guard. Wherever Moroni moved he was there. Several times his elbow caught Moroni on the bridge of the nose bringing stinging tears to his eyes, and one time bringing blood. All of the players by this time were bleeding from one or more places. Suddenly, without warning, the blue player hurled himself at Moroni. He had apparently hoped to catch him off guard but he was doomed to disappointment. Moroni's size belied his quickness and he easily sidestepped several inches. His huge opponent brushed past him. Again he rushed, both huge arms flailing as he came. At the last possible moment Moroni moved again, this time ducking under his arms and aston-ishing the big man by ramming him hard in the chest with his head and shoulders. Blue hat completely lost his momentum and his breath. He stood doubled over and sucking for air.

Moroni took the opportunity to rejoin the team play which had con-tinued unabated. He saw his opportunity, signaled for a pass, received the ball with his knee, bounced it into the air, and with a mighty swipe of his elbow sent it toward the goal. The crowd was silent. It seemed as if time stopped as the ball hung in the air while everyone held his breath.

The ball balanced precariously for a moment inside the ring and then fell through to the other side. It was through! There was a tremendous roar from the crowd. The players stopped in the middle of their frenzy; the goalkeeper held his hands high; the black-robed priest stepped back into the arena. The game was over! The green team had won!

No one could be heard in the clamor. The cheering spectators, caught up in the drama of the game, leaped up and down. Moroni's teammates hoisted him onto their shoulders and paraded him around the inside of the huge arena amidst the rain of flowers and bits of feathers thrown by the wildly applauding crowd.

The blue team members huddled together in the center of the arena. They were fearful of what would happen next. Had they won, they knew what terrible consequence they had planned for their opponents. Winning teams had been known to do cruel things to losers. What would the Christians do to them?

Moroni directed his team to carry him to where the other team was standing. Reaching them he dropped down, stepped forward, and extended his arm. The other members of his team quickly followed suit. Soon all of the members of both teams were grasping forearms and slapping each other on the back. As the crowd left the arena the athletes returned to the dressing rooms. The stadium was quiet once again.

In the dressing room there was pandemonium. After all the excitement of the game the team had difficulty settling down. Moroni finally held up his hand for silence.

"Friends," he said, "I just want you to know that we were not alone today on the playing field." The team members nodded, looking at him expectantly. "I know our prayers were answered today. I very strongly felt the Lord's help. I feel we need to give thanks." Without further prompting players dropped to their knees. There was a warm feeling in the group. Moroni, taking charge, asked Bilnor to offer the prayer. After the prayer the players slowly got to their feet.

* * *

Moroni turned to Amonihah. "That's about it. We triumphantly toured the city and then returned to our homes in Desolation. The gentle Amonihah, touched by Moroni's story, said, "Thank you." He wiped a tear from his eye. "It thrills me to hear your stories . . . to know how the Lord has prepared you for the ministry."

They rose and arm in arm left the room. Moroni fell quickly into sleep. Amonihah, however, lay awake for some time thinking about this warrior-leader whom the Lord had prepared so well.

Chapter 3

Moroni Finds a Mate

After another frustrating day of visiting and exhorting Moroni once again rested in Amonihah's home. The dinner hour had come and gone and the two friends were reminiscing.

Finally Amonihah asked, "Moroni, tell me how you found your mate. I am always fascinated by the stories of how people fall in love."

Moroni laughed, glad to relax and talk. His eyes glistened. "That's a fun one to tell. In fact, it happened on the way home from the Temple City after we won the Pok-a-tok contest." Amonihah settled back in his chair, waiting for the story to unfold.

* * *

Tiring of the Temple City, Moroni and his team started for home. They were loaded with jade and trinkets as sendoff gifts plus the necessary food supplies for the long journey home. As there was no great rush, they decided to travel northward from the Temple City through the dense jungle until they hit the East Sea, then follow the shoreline west.

Several days were spent getting through the heavy jungle. The clear blue water of the sea was a welcome sight. The young men frolicked on the beaches, swimming, running along the water line, wrestling one another in the sand, even occasionally sitting and quietly building sand pyramids and temples. It was a time for relaxing, for letting down from the emotional buildup of the Pok-a-tok contest.

Moroni frolicked with the others. He raced along the beach, his hair flying out behind him. When they finally started westward their pace increased. They walked for short distances on the flat hard sand of the beaches, then with youthful exuberance would break into distance-eating jogging. Sometimes they ran in the shallow surf with the edges of the waves curling and bubbling around their feet.

They dined daily on plentiful shellfish from the sea. Occasionally desiring red meat, Moroni or one of his companions would venture into the jungle with bow and arrow. Sometimes they were successful in killing a small deer or tapir, sometimes not, but it didn't matter.

One afternoon, as they were jogging along the beach in a carefree mood, a shrill cry rang out from the jungle. Someone was in distress. Another cry rang out on the heels of the first; a cry of fear and anger. Moroni took off on a dead run towards the cry, the others in close pursuit. He dodged through the trees ducking under the hanging vines. He wondered if he were heading in the right direction when another scream rang out. Stopping his headlong rush through the trees he moved carefully in the direction of the cry.

Through the trees he finally saw them: Eight Lamanites and a bearded robber Nephite were dragging a young blonde Nephite girl. Moroni wondered if she were unconscious but suddenly she straightened up, writhed to one side with her face close to the arm of one of the men holding her, and bit him. He howled in anger and with his free hand slapped her hard across her face causing her to sag again. Moroni took a step forward in anger but then his better judgment prevailed. Better to wait for the others. He couldn't hear what the renegades were saying but their intent was obvious.

He heard his companions moving up behind him and was glad that the ruffians were so involved with their captive. He turned and signaled for silence.

The girl cried out again as her captors roughly dragged her by the wrists to one of the smaller trees. Her hands were forced behind her back and then around the trunk of the tree where they were bound with a braided thong. Squatting down one of the Lamanites laced another thong around her knees, dodging her kicks, and bound her legs tightly to the tree. Leering, he grabbed hold of her robe and started to rip it off. The bearded robber barked a sharp command and the man sullenly backed away.

Moroni turned to his friends. There was no way of openly attacking the men without endangering the girl. He motioned for three of them to circle quietly to the right and three to the left. He and Bilnor would sneak straight forward. When they rose to shoot, the others would commence their attack.

They crept forward, avoiding dry branches and keeping as many trees between them and the bandits as possible. Moroni suddenly realized he had been holding his breath and gently let it escape. He inhaled quickly, continuing forward. When they were within range of his bow, Moroni moved behind a large tree and prepared his arrows. Bilnor did the same behind another tree. From his vantage point Moroni could see that the other Nephite youths were in position. He notched an arrow to his bow.

The robber chieftan pawed at the girl who twisted away. Moroni was tempted to shoot him right then but he was too close to the girl. The man's pudgy, dirty fingers grabbed at her robe and tore it down the front. Then he stepped back, which was the opening Moroni needed.

He loosed the first arrow. Before it struck he had another strung. The twang of the bowstring startled the Lamanites. They stiffened, looked around and grabbed for their weapons. The bearded leader, a look of surprise on his swarthy face, pitched lifelessly forward on the ground in front of the girl. Before the others could move Moroni's second arrow found a target and the Lamanite who had tied the girl to the tree fell with an arrow buried to the feathers in his chest. The others, yelling and brandishing their knives, charged towards Moroni.

Bilnor and his teammates loosed a flock of arrows and four more Lamanites dropped. Moroni had his third arrow notched but by now two bandits were upon him. He dropped his bow, drew his knife, and crouched behind the tree. The two jumped at him, cursing and swinging their knives. He ducked under their thrusts and using the tree as cover, jabbed at one of them. His knife grazed the arm, causing the renegade to flinch back which gave Moroni time to plunge his knife in the other's chest. Bilnor, by this time, had leaped into the fray and had dispatched the wounded one.

Moroni made his way towards the girl. He cut her bonds with his bloody knife and, averting his eyes, stepped back. The girl quickly gathered her torn robe around her, dropped to her knees, and burst into tears. She was about the age of his sister, Sophrista, and even looked somewhat like her. It was frustrating to Moroni. Even when Sophrista or his mother had cried, he had felt utterly helpless. He had the same feeling of helplessness now. He reached down and gently helped her to her feet. She wiped away her tears with a grimy hand leaving smudge marks on her fair cheeks. She smiled thankfully at her rescuers.

Bilnor finally broke the silence. "You're safe now, but how did you get into that predicament?"

"Oh, those awful men," she moaned. "Thank you for saving me." She looked at Moroni and her blue eyes opened wide. "I shudder to think what would have happened if you hadn't come."

Moroni asked, "What are you doing so far from civilization?"

She looked at him then glanced at the others, still appearing to be somewhat in shock. "Some girlfriends and I were gathering clams on the beach when these awful men attacked us. The other girls got away but they grabbed me and dragged me into the jungle. They have pulled me along all day, until . . ." She again broke into tears.

Waiting for her to calm herself, Moroni noticed how beautiful she was. Even the smudges on her cheeks added to her comeliness. He asked, "Where is your village?"

She waved her arm in a westerly direction. "We came this morning from the city of Moroni. My father and his friends went fishing in their boat and left us to dig clams. We were to meet them tonight where the river flows into the sea."

"How far is that?" asked one of the men.

She only shook her head. Moroni could tell that she was exhausted and did not know how far the men had dragged her.

"We'd better be moving," he said. "It will be dark soon."

Bilnor glanced at the dead Lamanites. "What about these?"

Moroni shrugged. "We don't have time to bury them. We'll leave them for the buzzards. We will tell the father of . . ." His voice trailed off as he realized that they didn't know the girl's name.

He turned to her. "We don't know your name."

"I am Armora," she stated simply.

Hurrying back to the beach the men slipped their packs on and resumed their journey. It was slower now because of the tired girl. They had not traveled long when they saw men with torches coming towards them along the beach.

As they neared, Armora broke from them and ran forward. "Father," she called. A large bearded Nephite put his arms around her, holding her close. He and his group looked suspiciously at Moroni and his teammates as they came up.

Armora turned, "Father, these men saved my life."

Smiles lighted the men's faces. They stepped forward, arms extended. Everyone seemed to be talking at once. A little embarrassed, Moroni and his little band were swept up by the group of fishermen.

Apparently noting their discomfiture, Armora's father said, "I know not where you are going, but you will stay with us in Moroni." Hearing his name as a city seemed strange but Moroni listened as the father continued. "We will order a banquet for our new friends and celebrate the return of my daughter."

Walking arm in arm, talking and laughing, the men turned and walked westward along the beach. Three hours later they arrived at the place where the River Sidon poured into the sea. It was a dark, moonless night with the light of the stars sparkling on the water. For the past hour, Corianum, Armora's father, had carried her.

A blazing fire, casting dancing images of light and shadow on the girls sitting around it, marked their meeting place. After a hurried conference, Corianum told Moroni that it was too late for him and his men to head for Moroni. They would camp the night and journey on the morrow.

A tantalizing smell rose from the fire and, after introductions to the other girls, everyone enjoyed a meal of steaming clams right from the fire. It had been a full day and soon most of the men and girls were asleep. Moroni lay watching the dying fire, wondering about the funny sensations he was feeling. In the past he had paid little attention to girls, but now . . . ?

He had heard his parents talking about love. Could this be love? Or was it just his feeling of compassion for this girl who had almost been raped

and killed? He was still struggling with that thought when he finally dropped
off to sleep.

He awakened to the smell of baking fish. Corianum had gone back
along the river, found some heavy clay, and had wrapped each fish in a
ball of the clay. Then he put the clay balls into the hot coals which cracked
open as they got hot letting delightful smells escape.

Moroni decided that he was suddenly very hungry. He stripped down
to his loincloth and waded into the river. It felt so good. He had bathed
often in the surf but had always had the sticky feeling on his skin. The river
water was very refreshing. He ducked his head below the surface rubbing
his hands rapidly through his matted hair and beard. Stepping ashore, he
dried his hair as best he could and combed it straight back with his fingers.

Back at the fire, Corianum was pulling the fish-mud balls from the
fire. Moroni took two sticks in each hand and, using them as a pitchfork,
lifted a mud ball from the sand, balanced it on the sticks, and walked back
into the shade of a large tree. Noticing that Armora was watching him
with interest, he motioned for her to join him. His heart skipped a beat
when she accepted and walked to where he was sitting.

She sat next to him on the ground, apparently unaware of just how
much her nearness was affecting him. He took a rock and broke open the
clay. Steam rose past their faces and the fish, baked to a flakey doneness,
smelled delicious. Moroni paused to give thanks for the food, then they dug
in with their fingers. He could not remember anything ever tasting so
delicious.

As they ate, licking their fingers, Moroni became increasingly more
aware of Armora, and he felt that she was becoming more aware of him.
They were awkward at first with their small talk, but as a feeling of being
more in tune with each other developed their talk became lively. They talked
first of yesterday's adventure, then of each other. Moroni breathed an
inward sigh of relief when he found that Armora was not bethrothed. She
smiled a little when he said that he had never been interested in girls.

Although they were not physically touching, Moroni could feel Armora's
nearness. He wondered whether she was having an effect on him because,
in changing positions in the sand, she let her shoulder brush his. It was
electric! He had never been affected this way by a girl. For half an hour a
veritable cocoon seemed to be drawn around the two of them.

Armora did not look at him as she said, "Fate sometimes arranges
things between people. Perhaps it was fate that caused you to be in just the
right place to rescue me."

Moroni reached over, cupped her chin in his big hand, and turned her
head so she was looking into his eyes. "No, Armora, it is not fate. There
is a God who directs men's lives. It was He who put us together at this
time."

Armora said, "I have never heard anyone talk with such conviction about God. Which god is it that you believe in? I believe in many gods and I faithfully attend temple ceremonies conducted by the priests."

Moroni paused a moment before answering. He had spent much of his youth in missionary work with his father and had answered similar questions of those they taught. This time he wanted his response to be especially right. Weighing carefully what he would say, he prayed silently that the Holy Ghost would help him and would bless Armora with His presence.

"In your city are many statues and images of Quetzalcoatl, the feathered serpent," he began. Armora, looking at him intently, nodded. "Your legends say that Quetzalcoatl will take a human body and come to earth to lead his people." Again she nodded. Looking into her eyes, he added, "The God I know is the God whose image you believe in. He is the bearded god." Moroni said this with such conviction and force and he felt a tingling response from Armora. "God is a God of miracles," Moroni continued. "It was He who created the heavens and the earth. He also created man."

He paused again, responsive to the keen attention that Armora was showing him. "But most importantly, God is a God of love. He loves me. He loves you. He loves all mankind. He is not desirous that anyone hurt or kill anyone else. In fact, one of his laws says, 'Thou shalt not kill.' He loves us because we are his children. He is our Father."

This was too much for Armora to comprehend. Because of the conviction in her heart she believed Moroni, but it was difficult for her to comprehend a god of love. All of the gods her father worshipped were gods of vengeance, gods of hate, gods of anger, blood gods! Gods that required human beings to be sacrificed to appease their anger. She shook her head in confusion. But she knew she would accept it if Moroni said it.

Moroni misinterpreted the shake of her head. He so wanted her to believe in and love Jesus Christ as he did. He picked up a handful of sand and let it sift slowly through his fingers.

"A little more than three hundred and fifty years ago, this God took a body and came to earth," he continued. "His name was Jesus Christ. I am a Christian." He said the last with quiet pride.

Armora looked at him with renewed interest. She had heard of the sect of the Christians—a generally despised group in Moroni. Feeling his sincerity, and wanting to be more a part of his life, she said, "I want to know more about this Jesus Christ."

Just at that moment Corianum called. "Come, it is time to go. The tide is out and we can cross the river."

Moroni reached over and squeezed Armora's small hand. "If you will permit me, I will tell you of his life and teachings. May I spend more time with you?"

Returning the pressure, Armora replied, "Please stay with us. You will be welcome. You can meet my mother and we will have plenty of time to talk. I desire to learn more about you, about your religion, and about your God."

Happily, Moroni stood up and pulled Armora to her feet. They walked side by side and joined the group at the water's edge. Casting glances at each other, his teammates exchanged nudges. He didn't care. For the first time in his life he was in love.

* * *

Moroni stretched, shifted on his cushion, and looked at Amonihah who was smiling at him through misty eyes. "A beautiful and touching story. Armora was converted and became your wife?"

"Yes, and it didn't take very long," responded Moroni. "We spent the next few days in her home in the city of Moroni. She proved herself to be the person I wanted to marry. By the third day there I asked for her hand in marriage. After less than a week she asked me to baptize her, which I did in the River Sidon. It was a beautiful experience . . . for both of us. I then went home to Desolation, received my parents' blessings, and in two months returned to Moroni with my father and married Armora." He sat in contemplation, remembering that choice experience.

As he looked up, there were tears in his eyes. "Mormon, acting both as my father and my priesthood leader performed the marriage ceremony. It was one of the most beautiful experiences of my life." Moroni again lapsed into silence, missing Armora. He wondered what she was doing now.

Interrupting his reverie, Amonihah asked, "And what of your children?"

"We had three sons. Our oldest, Gidgiddonah, became a rock sculptor following his warrior training. Our second son, Moronihah, is still in warrior training and hasn't made up his mind as to what occupation he will follow." He smiled as he thought of his fair-haired Moronihah. He looked more like his mother, having her fair complexion, blue eyes, and golden-blonde hair. "He has talked of being a professional warrior like his grandfather, but I guess that many of us have had such dreams."

A look of sadness crossed his face. "Our third son we named after my friend and fellow warrior, Bilnor, who stood as best man at our wedding." He paused reflectively. "Our son, Bilnor, was killed." It was difficult for him to talk about it.

Amonihah said, "It is difficult for you. You needn't continue."

Moroni shook his head. "No, it still hurts but I want to tell you." He paused, then continued. "Bilnor at twelve was a perfect example of youth. He was everything a father would desire in a son. His body was without flaw; he loved the Lord and kept the commandments. He was a choice son. It was his third year of warrior training and he was on a solo mission, isolated from the rest of the boys in a test of stamina and endurance.'' He paused again, licking his lips. ''When they went to round up the boys, Bilnor was not to be found. From signs in the area, there appeared to have been a scuffle. Bare footprints of many warriors had trampled the area . . . probably a Lamanite raiding party. We have searched and searched but no trace of him has been found.''

Amonihah realized that much had been left unsaid. It was a common practice of the Lamanites and robbers to capture boys and girls to use in their sacrificial rites. It was better not to speculate about the fate of young Bilnor.

PART II

A Spiritual Giant

The next day was the Sabbath. Amonihah had asked Moroni to speak in their synagogue. This was to be his last day in Bountiful and he was anxious to be on his way home. The synagogue was old and run down but inside it was pleasant and comfortable.

Several of the older men spoke, with teary eyes, of the "good old days" of their youth when the Church was stronger. One speaker addressed the topic of faith, saying that the "young people of today don't know what real faith is." Then he ended his remarks almost apologetically by stating, "I am not even sure that I now know what faith is. I have lost all hope."

It was Moroni's time to speak. "Brothers and sisters in Christ," he began. "Hope is not lost. We have always been in the world and not of the world. We need not be accepted of men in order to live our religion and enjoy our eternal reward. Life is to be lived. Nothing is impossible if we but believe. Any one of us, with God as our partner, can do anything we determine to do."

Using notes from his leather bag he continued: *"Whoso believeth in God might with surety hope for a better world, yea, even a place at the right hand of God, which hope cometh of faith . . . faith is things which are hoped for and not seen . . . [so] dispute not because ye see not, for ye receive no witness until after the trial of your faith. For it was by faith that Christ showed himself unto our fathers, after he had risen from the dead; and he showed not himself unto them until after they had faith in him, . . . "* [2]

He talked more about faith, quoting again from his papers: *"For if there be no faith among the children of men, God can do no miracle among them."* He pulled out another folded paper—tattered and worn from much use. It was a sermon that Mormon had given. He read: *"My beloved brethren, I would speak unto you concerning hope. How is it that ye can attain unto faith, save ye shall have hope? And what is it that ye shall hope for? Behold I say unto you that ye shall have hope through the atonement of Christ and the power of his resurrection, to be raised unto life eternal, and this because of your faith in him according to the promise."* [3]

Moroni paused. He could see that the spirit had touched their hearts. Tears were glistening in many eyes. Faces glowed with renewed determination. He continued, "It was here, in the land Bountiful, where the Savior showed himself after the resurrection. Here were the people who were most righteous, whom the Savior chose to visit. You are the descendants of those people. Don't let them down. Don't just give up because you are having a trial of your faith."

After the meeting was over the members thanked him, then went away seemingly with renewed faith, hope and determination because they had met and listened to a disciple of the Master.

Amonihah patted him on the back. "That was one of the finest sermons I have ever heard," he chortled. "Perhaps the only one better was that given by your father."

Moroni smiled, grateful for the sincere compliment. "The spirit deserves the credit."

The synagogue scribe came up and presented some bark papers to Moroni. "Here is a copy of your sermon," he said.

Moroni was grateful. For hundreds of years the Church scribes had kept a faithful record of everything the disciples said. The Lord had asked that such records be kept as a means of spreading the gospel and developing the scriptures. Moroni carefully placed the papers in his pouch, along with his other sermons and letters from Mormon.

Amonihah put his arm on Moroni's shoulder. "Moroni," he began, "you have done much to strengthen our faith."

Moroni nodded, "Thank you, my friend, but I am just doing what the Lord has called me to do. I have not attempted to teach your people anything new. What we need most of all is to have our people really converted to the principles they have already been taught. As leaders, we need to bear our testimonies often so our people feel our faith and commitment."

As they approached his home, Amonihah asked, "Moroni, you have told me of your youth, of your marriage, and of your family. May I ask you to tell me one more thing before you leave?"

Moroni shrugged his shoulders. "Just ask," he laughed. "My only concern is that I am boring you with details of my life. We haven't even talked of your life or family."

Amonihah waved his hand indifferently. "At this point my life is relatively unimportant. You are one of the few remaining disciples still on the earth. As you bear your testimony and speak of the spiritual experiences of your life, my testimony is strengthened. Tonight I would be excited to know more of how you gained your testimony. I know a testimony such as yours just doesn't happen. What were the circumstances? What obstacles had to be overcome?"

Moroni laughed easily. "You're right. It doesn't just happen. And, yes, there were obstacles to be overcome. I was speaking from personal experience today when I said that you receive no witness until after a trial of your faith."

That night, following a dinner of fresh fruit, baked fish, and honey-bread, the two friends sat once again in Amonihah's sitting room. Moroni began.

"You asked me this afternoon about my testimony and spiritual growth. I cannot remember a time when our home was not filled with the spirit of the Master. From my youth I have been taught to pray and to walk uprightly before the Lord. I have already told you of some great experiences when my prayers were answered. Of course, there were many other times, and many other experiences."

Amonihah waited as Moroni prepared to launch into his story. "I told you that I had a burning desire to see the new Temple City to the north. Well, I finally got a chance to do so, but in a very unexpected way."

Chapter 4

The Trial of Faith

Moroni sat hunched up on the veranda, his head in his hands. He paid no attention to the honey-sweet smell of the brilliant red flowers blooming over his head, or even the steady hum of the insect flitting among the blossoms. He needed to make some decisions and he didn't know which way to turn.

Rising from the porch, he quietly walked to the sleeping room. Here was his main concern. As a man with a wife and a child, his first obligation was to support them. A tender look crossed his face. Armora was curled supinely on the bed, with Gidgiddonah cradled in her arms. They looked so peaceful. Moroni wished that his own life could be.

He left carefully so as not to disturb Armora, walking the short distance to the home of his parents. Although it was still early, Merena was in the yard caring for her flowers. Moroni knew that she had always enjoyed the pretty flowers that she dug up in the forest and transplanted to her garden. This morning their heady aroma hung on the air.

Merena looked up at her son. Her deep pride was obvious and Moroni gave her a bear-like hug, then launched immediately into his concern.

"Mother," he said, "I am really confused as to what to do. I am a good goldsmith and can support my family doing that. But on the other hand, I feel an obligation to our people. The Lamanite invasions become closer each year. Perhaps I should be a warrior like father."

"Moroni, my son," she replied. "You have been taught the right principles from your youth. I think you know what it is you need to do." Then she asked, "Is that all that is bothering you?"

Moroni, touched by motherly insight, hesitated. "No. I guess that I am feeling more additional responsibilities since Gidgiddonah was born. He is over a year old now. I feel it is important to care for my family, but I really wonder when the Lord will have me fulfill the blessing he has given me to be a missionary."

Merena put her arms around her son. Looking into his eyes, she said, "My son, you have been a fortunate young man. The Lord has chosen you as a favored son and has answered your prayers on many occasions. Don't you think this is a matter for Him?"

"Mother, I've tried," he responded. "But this time there doesn't seem to be any answer. I have prayed, but the heavens seem closed to me. I don't know what the Lord wants of me."

A sound at the gate startled them. It was Mormon. He was still dressed in his warrior armor, but there was something different about him. After he gave Merena a kiss and hugged his wife and son, he said, "The Lord has spoken to me. For the first time since I was in my fifteenth year He has commanded me to preach repentance to this people!"

Moroni was elated. Could this be the answer he was seeking? Had the Lord chosen this way to answer his prayers? He asked, "What did the Lord say?"

Mormon carefully repeated the words which had been spoken to him: *"Cry unto this people—repent ye, and come unto me, and be ye baptized, and build up again my church, and ye shall be spared."* [4]

He put his large, calloused hand on his son's shoulder. "Moroni, I am calling you to be the first missionary to assist me in this work."

Merena used the back of her dirt-soiled hands to wipe the tears from both cheeks. Moroni offered a heartfelt silent prayer. "Thank you, Lord, once again you have answered my prayers."

Mormon continued, "I was given the feeling that your mission would be in the cities north of Desolation."

A disturbing thought hit Moroni. "But what of my family? I have a wife and son to be concerned about."

His father nodded. "I can understand your feelings, my son, but the time is short. The Lord has indicated to me that if the people do not repent they will be totally destroyed. This is our last chance to save our people." Putting his hand on Moroni's shoulder, he added, "You will be hated, ridiculed, and even physically abused in the cities in which you will teach. The people will revile you. Your family would be in constant danger if you took them with you. They will be safe here with your mother."

Moroni knew his father was right, but this would be the first time he had to leave his family. He stiffened his shoulders in resolve. The call had to come. He would obey it.

Saying a quick goodbye to his parents, he hurried home to tell Armora the news. As he walked into the house Armora could see that something exciting had happened to him. With the insight with which the Lord blesses wives, she said simply, "You have been called to the Lord's work."

Moroni was taken back. How could she know? He was continually amazed by this good woman and her love and gentleness with him. "Yes, it is true," he said. "The Lord has told father that we are to begin missionary work amongst the people."

She wiped her hands on her apron. "Where will you serve?"

He looked down. "Father told me that I should begin my work in the cities north of Desolation." He looked for her reaction, but she seemed very calm. Her stoic acceptance surprised Moroni. She was so small, but so strong!

He reached for her and held her close, his fingers lightly caressing the soft skin on the back of her neck. She stood on tiptoes and whispered in his ear, "I have some good news, also."

He held her at arms length. "What news?"

Her hands gave him a gentle squeeze. "I am expecting another baby."

It was too much. He sat down heavily on the cushion.

The next few weeks were hectic for Moroni. He gathered up his gold-smithing tools so he could earn a living for himself while he was gone. He packed several of his most recent creations so he could sell them as he journeyed. Daily he found more excuses to delay his departure. He reviewed the scriptures, conferenced with Mormon, made a few more gold trinkets, and prayed daily for strength and wisdom to understand the gospel well enough to teach it to others.

Mormon gave him good advice. "Keep your teaching simple, my son. The gospel is not complicated. Teach faith in the Lord, Jesus Christ, repentance, and baptism. These are the keys. The spirit will guide you concerning anything else. You will also need to find leaders to carry on after you are gone. Rely on the spirit for guidance."

Moroni was nervous to be on his way but torn inside. Duty to family or duty to God—which came first? Family won. He stayed until the new baby was delivered. Another boy! He christened him Moronihah, "Moroni's son." After staying around long enough to know that everything was all right, he knew he was free to go.

He said his goodbyes to his family. Holding Armora close, he told her of his great love for her and his appreciation for her devotion to him and their children. Almost reverently he took little Moronihah in his arms. The baby was too young to recognize his father, but he seemed to enjoy the strength of those large arms. Saying goodbye to Gidgiddonah was equally hard. He took him on his knee, jostled him a little, hugged him close, and then let him run off to play. Once again he pulled Armora into his arms, holding her tightly.

The next few months fused together in Moroni's memory. Every city he visited seemed to be the same: Boaz, Teancum, Jordan, and all of the little towns and villages. He found no active Christians. He would set up his shop in the square, preach from the street corners, knock on doors, but no one would listen.

People scoffed at him, children threw stones at him. He was reviled, spat upon, kicked, knocked down, and beaten. In Jordan, he was stoned and left for dead. Managing to drag himself out of the street, he prayed for strength. "Why?" he asked the Lord. "Why can't I get even one person to listen? Here I have been a missionary for months and have yet to find my first prospect . . . let alone my first baptism. What is wrong? What else can I do?"

From the heavens came no response. The Lord had left him on his own. He was sick at heart, dejected, and very weary. "I could be home enjoying my family," he said aloud. It was a real temptation to just go home. Then he realized what he was thinking. "No, I am not a quitter. I will continue to do the Lord's work until he tells me to stop." With that resolve, he struggled to his feet and left the city.

Joshua was no different. Even though he hadn't seen this city since he was twelve, there were no great changes. There was still the familiar hustle and bustle as warriors and workmen continued construction on the walls. The farmers and tradesmen still shouted with loud voices in the market place as they hawked their wares. But no one listened here, either.

Discouraged, he left the city, prepared to return home to his own city convinced that no one wanted to hear his important message. He found a quiet area in the forest and dropped heavily to his knees. Minutes went by which seemed to turn into hours as he knelt there, unable to utter a sound. A prayer just wouldn't come out. He felt as if all the evil of all the cities he had visited was now circling about him. He had little spirit left to go on. It seemed to him that the forces of evil had totally won the battle for the minds of the people.

He thought he must feel like Samuel the Lamanite felt as he attempted to preach to the people from the walls of Zarahemla. He thought with chagrin, At least he had the Lord's word with him. A pang of guilt hit him.

What am I thinking? I, too, have the word of the Lord. He has commissioned me to be his servant. Why am I feeling sorry for myself?

Finally he prayed. "Father, why am I not able to convert these people? Why do they mock and revile me? Am I doing something wrong? If so, tell me." On and on he prayed in the anguish of his heart, finally just telling the Lord that it was now in His hands.

He fell into a fitful sleep, tossing and turning on the hard ground as the questions kept revolving in his mind. In that state, a vivid dream came to him. He saw himself in a great city, a city filled with mighty palaces and temples: a city unlike any city he had ever seen. A voice came to him in his dream: Visit the new Temple City. Your mission is there. The dream faded and Moroni awakened. The dream and the words were still vivid to him. The Temple City? He knelt and thanked the Lord for answering his prayers. An audible voice came into his mind: *"You are a faithful servant, my son. Your mission will yet be rewarding."*

The next day Moroni entered Joshua for the last time. He plied his wares and asked directions to the Temple City. Several people he talked to had been there. They described to him the city. It was the city he had seen in his dream.

Moroni sold his few remaining gold ornaments and bought supplies for the ten-day journey. The next morning, shaking the dust of Joshua from his feet, he started off. Within a few days he was climbing laboriously upward. The mountain faces were steep, the trail sweeping back and forth across the slope. Deep canyons dropped sharply on either side. After what seemed like endless climbing, he arrived at the mountain pass. He gasped in surprise. Instead of a valley on the other side, a plateau stretched out as far as he could see. The humid heat of the coast was replaced with a cool mountain breeze making him pull his robe more tightly around him. As he looked across the great plateau, its vastness made him feel very small. Far in the distance the sun's rays reflected off the surface of lakes.

It was truly a land of sharp contrasts. Stretching out as far as he could see were mountain ranges—one on the east and one on the west. Many of the peaks were snow-capped even though it was summer. Moroni stood where the two ranges of mountains came together to form one mountain chain which continued on down to the land of Desolation. Instead of the lush rainforest he was used to, he was standing among pine trees. He reluctantly left the beautiful forest, descending easily to the plateau.

It took several days to get to the lakes he had seen from the mountain pass. He noted that there were actually three of them joined by narrow inlets. The first lake he came to was of fresh water, fed by a mountain stream. He stopped to drink and filled his water gourd. The center lake was yellow and briny, surrounded by salty deposits which oozed from the soil. The third lake was even more brackish, with a reddish cast to the water. There were small villages around all three lakes but Moroni gave them a wide berth. He had no desire to stop and preach now. His mission was to the Temple City. His stride lengthened as he recalled his dream. He was very anxious to get to the city.

At night, as he camped on the plain, he gathered brush and made a small fire to ward off the chill. As he lay on the ground each night, he thrilled at the nearness of the stars. It seemed that he could almost reach out and touch them. Never had he seen them so brilliant. Each star was a little hole in the sky. In the mornings, the stars were replaced by a bright blue sky, laced with flimsy strands of rolling cotton clouds that seemed to prance across the sky. He enjoyed camping by himself, especially the quiet time before he dropped off to sleep. It was a time for reflecting over the day's activities, a time to develop closer communication with the Lord; but it was also a time when he really missed his little family.

Tonight he had especially enjoyed the brilliant sunset. Never had he seen such glorious colors—from deep tones to soft rosy lights. The earth itself seemed to mirror the colors, magnifying them and sending them back to the heavens. It seemed to be God's benediction over the land.

The day he anticipated arriving in Temple City he arose at dawn. Some of the pilgrims he had passed had called it Tula—city of light. As he came over a slight swale there it was. The red walls of the city seemed to gleam and burn in the early morning sun. He was still some distance from the city, but in the clear mountain air it seemed to be almost upon him. There was a rosy haze above the city which Moroni knew was probably caused by the cooking and heating fires of the inhabitants, but it created the illusion of a city floating in the sky.

When he reached it, he saw that the city was even more magnificent than it had been described to him. There seemed to be a majesty about it. Walking down the Avenue of the Dead, among the masses of people, was unlike any experience he had ever had. Temples rose on all sides of him, towering majestically in the air, making the people seem like bustling ants surrounding giant anthills.

He was impressed. Most of the people he met seemed cultured and refined. As he learned more about them, he found that they were a people of deep religious faith. Their god was Quetzalcoatl, the bearded god. The more he studied their religious beliefs the more he was amazed at the closeness of those beliefs to Christianity.

It looked to Moroni as if the center of the city had been carefully planned. It was laid out as if in accordance to a great master plan. There was order and symmetry in the design of the streets, the location of the temples, and even in the way the city had grown outward from this central core. Great aqueducts brought water from nearby springs.

The colors which surrounded Moroni were dazzling. Murals were everywhere. Every wall had its own painting. Never had he seen anything in all of the Nephite lands to match the beauty and massiveness of this city.

He would have liked to spend more time sightseeing but he could not forget his purpose in being here. Moroni traded some of his completed wares for more gold and set up his shop. He found a place in the marketplace surrounded by hundreds of other craft workshops.

Business was slow and soon he became restless. He was a man of action but the spirit whispered to him to remain where he was. Moroni didn't understand, but he obeyed.

One day, while sitting in his shop tooling a fine bracelet, a large barrel-chested Lamanite stopped and browsed through his shop. The man had a weathered look as of one who had spent his life in the open. His face was handsome with high cheekbones and piercing black eyes. Several jagged scars lined his rugged cheeks. His body was lean and hard like that of an athlete although he looked to be almost forty. Moroni knew he was a man who would impress all who saw him and, after appraising him, he started back to his work when the spirit quickened within him. A small voice whispered, This is the man who will lead the church in this city.

Moroni scrambled to his feet and approached the stranger. "I am Moroni. Is there something you particularly like?"

The stranger smiled exposing straight white teeth. "I am Palorem, captain of the palace guard." He picked up a gold amulet. "You are very skillful. Where did you learn your trade?"

"My father was a goldsmith in Zarahemla and later in the city of Desolation. He was my teacher."

Palorem arched his black eyebrows. "Zarahemla? Desolation? Those cities are many days travel from here." There was an unspoken question of what Moroni was doing in the City of Light.

Searching for just the right words, Moroni responded. "I had heard much about your fabled city. But all I have heard can not come close to what I am now seeing. It is very impressive.

A look of pride lighted Palomer's rugged face. "We are proud of our city. Have you had opportunity to see its features?"

"No. I've only been here a few days. I am hoping that sometime I can make a real tour of the city."

Palorem smiled broadly. "You shall see it as my guest. Come. Put away your tools and join my family for dinner."

The home of Palorem was several blocks from the center of the city. From the outside it looked like many homes that Moroni had seen in his travels. The inside was beautiful! It was much more elegant than the fine home of Mormon in the city of Desolation. It was in a square shape with all the rooms opening onto a central patio. Though the evening was cool, the table in the patio was sagging with mouth-watering foods. Moroni glanced around, noting that the entrances to each of the rooms was draped to provide privacy.

A beautiful woman, dark, with high cheekbones and blue-black hair, stepped out to greet them. Palorem gave her a quick hug, then turned to Moroni. "Moroni, this is my wife, Tabor." He stood with his arm around his wife, the other hand on Moroni's shoulder. "My dear, my friend Moroni is a goldsmith from the marketplace. He's a stranger in our city and he is our guest."

Tabor smiled. "Welcome to our home. Dinner is prepared. We will eat as soon as the children arrive from their play."

Moroni pulled from his sleeve a gold medallion he had made. "Your kindness and hospitality are very much appreciated. May I give you this as a token of my appreciation?" Tabor graciously accepted the gift, her eyes lighting in appreciation.

Moroni felt the great warmth of these people. Now he knew why the Lord had chosen them for this important mission. "Tell me of your children."

With a mother's pride Tabor talked of their two children. As they talked, the children arrived. Zilar, a beautiful girl of ten, looked like her mother. She was bubbly and she was obviously excited about everything. Kishon, a boy of twelve, was more reserved. He was in warrior training.

Following the meal of corn, roast wild pig, and strawberries from a small garden in the patio the adults visited. Tabor asked Moroni about himself and his family. He told them of Armora and their two sons. Tabor asked, "How could you leave your family? Especially with a new baby?"

Moroni looked at these new-found friends. Many thoughts quickly went through his mind. Then, with the spirit burning within him, he bore his testimony. "My friends. Do not think ill of me, but if you want to know my reason for being in your city, I will tell you. You worship the plumed serpent, the god Quetzalcoatl. We know Quetzalcoatl by the name of Jesus Christ. He came to the earth almost four hundred years ago. He taught the people how to live and how to show love for each other. He was killed by wicked men but through His great power He raised Himself from the dead. After His resurrection, He came to this land showing Himself to the people. He ordained twelve disciples . . ." Moroni was puzzled by the look that passed between Palorem and Tabor, but he continued, ". . . who then became teachers for all the people. He healed the sick, raised the dead, organized His Church. After He left, the twelve disciples continued teaching the people. My father has been ordained and is the last disciple on the earth. Jesus Himself appeared to my father and He has taught him. My father has sent me here as a missionary to this people."

Palorem and Tabor sat quietly for a few minutes seeming to digest what Moroni had told them. Then Palorem stood. "Moroni, our hearts burn within us. We know what you say to us is true. Stay with us so we can talk more."

Moroni was thrilled but humbled. Other than his family, he had never met anyone he liked as much as he did Palorem and Tabor. The Lord had truly guided him to these people.

The next few days were precious ones. Palorem showed him the fabled city, taking him into palaces and temples. The city was dominated by the Pyramid of the Sun. It was the largest building Moroni had ever seen, by far. It stood over two hundred feet high and the pyramid was built of adobe bricks faced with volcanic stone and plaster. Palorem led the way as they climbed to the top of the pyramid. They rested for a few moments on each of the five terraces and Palorem pointed out other places of interest from these vantage points. When they reached the top, they stood next to a huge temple made of inlaid woods. Moroni could only shake his head at the wonder of it all.

After descending the pyramid, they walked to the temple of Quetzalcoatl. It was next to a huge stadium where Palorem indicated religious festivals were held. Surrounding the stadium were more temples—four on three sides and three on the other. Moroni was amazed. Could it be that these temples stood for the twelve disciples and the Godhead?

The temple itself was fascinatingly beautiful. Murals were on every wall. The front was covered with beautifully carved serpents' heads surrounded by quetzal feathers. All the serpents' heads had twelve teeth in their mouths. Again that magic number. As they climbed the stairs to the top of the temple, Moroni noted the six serpent heads on each side, again making twelve. It could not be coincidence. It astounded him that these people had the form of the gospel—without the substance.

The days melted together as Moroni taught his new-found friends and toured the city with Palorem. They visited the observatories, the Pyramid of the Moon, the huge altar in the center of the square for Quetzalcoatl which was faced on all four sides with stairways of thirteen steps which Palorem told Moroni symbolized the fifty-two years of the Nephite century.

It was a time of exquisite joy for Moroni as he taught Palorem's family the principles of the gospel. They were so teachable and so humble. As they became more sure in their knowledge of the Savior, they invited other loyal friends to be taught until their patio was filled with investigators although Palorem told Moroni that they had to be very careful, for if the ruling priests became aware of the growing sect they would all be killed.

Baptizing Palorem and his whole family was one of the great thrills of Moroni's life. As they came out of the water many spoke in tongues, or saw marvelous visions. Moroni laid his hands on their heads and conferred upon them the Gift of the Holy Ghost. He ordained Palorem to the priesthood and made him his assistant in the missionary work of the city.

A year had now passed since he had left his family and he was more and more lonesome for them. Now that he had a strong church established and leadership ordained, Moroni began to think of returning home to his family. But each time he approached the Lord about it the spirit whispered, Not yet.

More people came forth requesting baptism. Moroni and Palorem interviewed them and only accepted those who *"came forth with a broken heart and a contrite spirit, and witnessed unto the church that they truly repented of all their sins. . . . [and] took upon them the name of Christ, having a determination to serve him. . . ."* [5]

Moroni set apart elders, priests and teachers as leaders to handle the increased demands of time in the growing church. The Church met together often to fast and pray and strengthen each other. It was thrilling to the leaders to hear the testimonies of each new convert. There was great joy as they partook of the sacrament. They were led to teach and preach by the Holy Spirit, and never had Moroni had a congregation where there was such an outpouring of the spirit. Even with all this, there were still those who sometimes reverted to the old ways and had to be chastized. Those who committed sins were given opportunity to repent. Those who were unrepentant had their names blotted from the Church. It required the testimony of three witnesses to condemn any who had committed iniquity. Moroni carefully organized the Church so that it could function in his absence. Moroni knew he had chosen strong leaders, and that Palorem was the strongest of all.

One day, while he was busy in his booth, he received an urgent message from Palorem. Zilar was ill! He quickly put away his tools, gathered up his wares, and hurried through the busy streets to Palorem's home. As he neared the home, the spirit whispered to him that Zilar had died. It was therefore no surprise when he entered the patio and heard the keening wails of the mourning family. Tabor was broken-hearted, rocking back and forth beside the bed of her daughter. Palorem, pale and distraught, stood behind her, his hands on her shoulders, his head bowed in anguish.

He looked up at the approach of Moroni. Stepping forward he threw his arms around Moroni, burying his head in his shoulder. Tears ran down the cheeks of both men as they embraced.

Moroni stepped to the bed where the still form of Zilar lay. There was a smile upon the lips of her who had laughed so often. It was as if she had awakened to a joyous new life. Her lips and cheeks were paled, her limpid brown eyes, so full of laughter and life, were now closed. Her lashes lay upon her cheeks lending a starkness of color.

Moroni took one of the small limp hands in his own. Turning to Palorem, his eyes asked the question, "How?" Palorem mumbled, "She became tired last night. This morning she was hot to the touch and delirious. And suddenly . . . she was gone." He again dropped his head in anguish. This daughter had been his greatest pride and joy.

"I have told you that Jesus raised the dead," Moroni said quietly. "Do you believe that He did?"

"Yes, I truly believe," responded Palorem, looking at him.

"Do you believe that through His priesthood we can do the same thing?"

Palorem paused before answering. Moroni could guess his thoughts: to believe that a God who had come to the earth had the power of life and death was one thing; to believe that mere mortals could have the same power was something else. "I don't know," he replied. "But I want to believe that it is possible."

Moroni motioned the mourners to leave the room. With only Palorem and Tabor present, with the still form of Zilar before them, Moroni knelt. In his prayer he pled with the Lord to give him power over the adversary, to grant him the opportunity to prove His goodness and mercy. He stood.

There was power in his bearing, a new look in his eyes, a radiance in his demeanor.

Again he reached down, taking the small, pale, limp hands of Zilar in his large tanned ones. In a solemn voice of authority, he commanded, "Zilar, in the name of Jesus Christ and by the authority of His priesthood which I bear, I command you . . . AWAKE AND ARISE!"

The silence after this pronouncement was deafening. The veins stood out on Moroni's temples. He stood as a statue, waiting.

Then Palorem gasped. The color was returning to the pallid cheeks of Zilar. There was again warmth in her arms and hands. Her stiff jaws relaxed letting her mouth drop open, showing her white, even teeth. And then, wonder of wonders, her eyes slowly opened. She didn't move but her eyes gazed upon each of them.

Palorem fell on her, draping his body across hers, sobbing loudly. His joy was full! His daughter who was dead was now alive! Tabor stood nearby, seemingly not knowing what to do. It was too much of a shock for her. She had given up her daughter for the blackness of death and here she was—bathed in the light of life! She stepped close, lifting the still form of Zilar to her breast.

Now Moroni knew why the Lord had wanted him to stay. Never had he felt the Lord's power in such force within him.

Palorem, tears still streaming down his cheeks, turned to him. "Thank you. Thank you." His lips formed the words but no sound came out.

Word traveled fast. The membership of the Church continued to grow as people came to realize that within the Church was the true priesthood. Moroni knew that he could now go home. The Church in Tula was in good hands. Palorem was set apart as the leader of the Church and with him were twelve ordained priesthood leaders set apart as a council to manage the affairs of the Church. He said his goodbyes and started home.

He had organized a faithful branch of the Church, found able leaders, healed the sick, raised one person from the dead, and conducted the affairs of the Church for over a year.

The journey home was difficult but uneventful. As he approached Desolation, a feeling of great anticipation came over him. He was running by the time he neared his home. He felt his heart would burst as he entered his home on the run, picked up the surprised Armora in his arms, danced around the floor with her, and showered her face with kisses. Their faces were so wet with tears that their kisses were salt-flavored.

He picked up the boys and held them close to him. Gidgiddonah looked from one to the other, wondering what was happening. Moronihah was just content to be held—even by this large man whom he didn't know.

Later, as they walked arm in arm to the home of his parents, Armora caught him up on the news. The Lamanites had attacked the southern cities and were even threatening Desolation. Mormon had been gone most of that time, trying to strenthen his armies.

Merena was pleased to see her son. She sensed the changes that had taken place in him. It was obvious to her that he had known the pain of suffering as well as the joy of giving and loving.

Moroni noticed how his mother had aged in the time he had been gone. He knew that Mormon's continued absence and the Nephite defeats had put a real strain on her.

That night, as he held Amora close, he was thankful for a very successful mission. He was also thankful to be home. As he lay there with his arms around his sleeping wife, he wondered what the Lord would next have him do.

Chapter 5

Called To Be a Disciple

Amonihah sat entranced as Moroni described his experiences in the beautiful Temple City. Tears ran freely as he described the raising of Zilar from the dead. Now Amonihah sat stroking his beard. It had been normal bedtime several hours before, but sleep could wait, he was being taught by a disciple of the Lord!

Moroni was lost in thought—still reliving the scenes he had been so vividly describing. Amonihah waited, not disturbing Moroni's reverie. Moroni looked up, suddenly aware of the silence in the room.

He yawned and smiled. "It's been a long day. I'm sorry I get so carried away with my stories. I didn't realize it was so late."

"You owe me one more story," Amonihah responded. He placed a hand on Moroni's knee. "You've already shared much of your life with me, but there is one more thing I would have you tell me."

Moroni looked quizzically at Amonihah.

"You've brought me forward through your life to the most important point . . . now you're willing to leave me dangling."

Moroni laughed easily. "I can imagine what you are going to ask." His eyes twinkled as he looked at this older man whom he had come to love as a friend and brother.

"I am very interested in how you were called to be a disciple of the Master," Amonihah seriously persisted.

Moroni, a far-away look in his eyes, began.

*   *   *

Four years had passed since Moroni had returned to his home from the Temple City. It had been a time of great sorrow as well as great joy for Moroni and his family. There were wars and destruction, but there was also the peace of his little family. Now, once again, there was a semblance of peace in the land.

Moroni thought back over those four years—years that had virtually changed the lives and the very existence of the Nephite people. He and his father had changed roles during those years. Because of the wickedness and the aggression of the Nephite army, Mormon had resigned his command. At the time of his resignation he was fifty-one years of age and had led the Nephite armies since he was sixteen—thirty-five years of war and bloodshed.

On the other hand, Moroni and all other able-bodied men had been drafted into the army of the Nephites. He thought it paradoxical that just a few short years before he had actually wanted to become a warrior. Now for four years he had prayed daily that he could be released so he could return home to his family and his goldsmithing trade. He was anxious, also, to return to his missionary labors. The letters he received from Palorem kept him informed of the Church in that land, making him very happy. He desired to see his friends again.

Moroni's prayers for release were finally answered. The Nephites, angry at the Lamanite atrocities against their women and children, had fought savagely, driving the Lamanite armies from the land, recapturing Teancum and Desolation. After winning a decisive victory, an uneasy peace once again had come to the Nephite lands.

He had written to Mormon, attempting to describe the scenes of blood and carnage, but he couldn't find the words. The Nephites had hardened their hearts and actually seemed to delight in the shedding of blood.

Early in the fighting Mormon had been warned in a dream that Desolation would be captured and destroyed. He had moved his and Moroni's families to Boaz, a city several day's march north of Desolation. It had been just in time. The Lamanites had pushed back the retreating Nephite army, captured Desolation, and sacrificed thousands of prisoners to their gods. Moroni's warrior army had retreated from Desolation to Teancum. Again the Lamanite hordes had come upon them, pushing them even further back toward Boaz. But this time the army held its ground. For four long years it had been a back and forth battle between Desolation and Teancum. Now it was over.

Moroni thought of his aging parents. He was especially concerned over the frailness of his mother. Mormon seemed as hearty as ever, secure in his testimony of the Savior and working diligently on the records of his people which he had retrieved from the hill Shim.

The most joyous thing that had happened in those four years was the birth of another son to Moroni and Armora. They had named the boy Bilnor, after Moroni's boyhood friend. He was a sweet child, smaller and less robust than the other boys. Armora was pleased that he looked like his father. He was such a joy to them, a perfect baby. Mormon enjoyed this grandchild more than the first two boys. He now had time to spend playing with his grandchildren.

Furrows appeared on Moroni's brow as he thought of the saddest happening of those years. His little sister, Sophrista, frail because of a childhood disease, had not been able to take the strain of the fighting and the move from Desolation. In her weakened state, she had contracted some disease which seemed to drain away her very existence. She had never married, but her quick smile and radiant laughter had made her a real joy to the family.

On one of those dreary days, Moroni had approached Sophrista's bed. She had smiled up at him from the pillow. He took her small hand in both of his hard brown palms. He noticed how transparent her skin was, showing each blue vein tracing its way down the wrist and into the fingers. Her hand was hot. The fever was consuming this sweetest of sisters. The anguish of despair wrinkled his heart. He laid his hands on her head to bless her, but the words wouldn't come. He smoothed her long black hair and asked himself, Why can't I raise her from her illness? I raised Zilar who was dead. Have I lost the power? Then he caught himself. His only power had been the power that the Lord had given him. Was he to question the Lord? A voice whispered to him: *"Moroni, I am taking Sophrista unto myself."*

Moroni was saddened but he felt the peace of the gospel within him. He listened to the slow, tortured breaths drawing through her weakened lungs. He could see, by the flickering light of the lamps, the throbbing arteries in her thin throat. He lay his head on her breast wanting her to feel his strength and closeness. The pounding of her heart came to him, fast and frantic.

Sophrista put her small hand on Moroni's head. "You must not grieve, dear brother. The Lord has prepared a place for me in his kingdom." She was silent for a moment, reviving her strength. "God has a great destiny for you, Moroni. You will be a mighty instrument in His hands." Her voice softened as she weakened. "I go now to Him."

Sophrista slept. Moroni dared not move as he listened to her heart slow down, then stop. He raised his head and Sophrista's limp hand fell from it. There was a smile on her face—the same smile that had greeted him so often when he had come home from his journeys. Now Sophrista had completed her journey and had returned home. Her lips and cheeks paled to whiteness, freckles standing out sharply in contrast. "The Lord's will be done," Moroni murmured.

He decided it was important to move the family as quickly as possible back to their homes in Desolation. Carrying what they could with them, they left Boaz. Merena, in her frail condition, traveled with them but Mormon was still away visiting several distant villages. Moroni left word for him to catch up as quickly as he could.

It was good to be back in their own home. After cleaning it out, rebuilding broken furniture and repairing the damaged areas, the family settled down. They were somewhat crowded in their little home with Merena and her servants living with them, but they were happy. They expected Mormon back at any time and then things would ease up. Moroni set up his shop back in the marketplace, letting Gidgiddonah run it while he worked at home.

This day had started out to be an ordinary day. Moroni had helped Gidgiddonah load up the wares and together they walked to the marketplace. Moronihah was off somewhere with his friends, probably playing army. Bilnor was content to just follow Armora, or "Granny," around.

After setting out his wares in his stall, Moroni wandered around, visiting with friends and fellow artisans. It seemed good just to relax. He returned to his stall to find Armora, red-faced and breathless. "Where have you been?" she asked. Then without waiting for a response, "You are wanted at home. Come quickly."

Moroni caught up with his small wife, turned her around and asked, "What is the hurry? What is the matter?" He was fearful that something had happened to Merena or to one of his sons.

Armora turned again toward her home. "I'm not sure what it is, but some men want to see you."

After catching up with her, he reached down and took her hand. Walking together, they arrived at their home. Moroni was surprised to find three strange men standing in his front room. He had a strange sensation that he had met these men before, but he could not place them. They had a look about them that puzzled him, and yet he felt very calm in their presence.

Stepping forward and holding out his hand, he said, "I am Moroni."

One of the men stepped forward, grasped his arm, and said, "Yes, we know. We have come to see you on a matter of great importance."

Suddenly the door burst open. It was Mormon. Obviously he was no longer in the top physical condition which had distinguished his youth. His face was haggard and his breath came in huge gulps. "I don't know why I am here," he said hoarsely between breaths, "but the spirit whispered to me to return home as quickly as possible. So here I am."

He turned to the three strangers, apparently noticing them for the first time. An exclamation of joy escaped his lips. Moroni could tell that his father had immediately recognized the men which just added more mystery to the whole affair. Mormon stepped forward, embracing each of the men. He stepped back, a joyous expression on his face.

Turning to Moroni, he asked, "Do you know who these men are?" A broad smile played on his face.

Moroni shook his head.

"These are the three Disciples of the Master . . . those who elected to stay upon the earth to continue teaching the people. I haven't seen them since my youth when they ministered to me." Tears of joy were in his eyes.

Moroni, too, was overjoyed. He had listened many times as Mormon had told him of the visitations of the three Disciples. He had told of their ministrations and ordinations, of their concern for the people. With less confidence than before, Moroni stepped forward and grasped forearms with each of these choice servants of the Lord. The touch of them sent tingles through his arm and up his spine.

As the three visited with Mormon and Merena, Moroni recalled what he knew of them. They were part of the original twelve disciples that the Savior had ordained in Bountiful after his resurrection. At the time of the Savior's departure, they had expressed a desire to remain on the earth to continue their ministry. The Savior had said to them that they would never taste of death. The three had been persecuted, thrown into prisons and into pits dug into the earth, and into wild animals' dens. The prisons and pits could not hold them and they played with the savage animals. They had also been thrown into blazing furnaces and had received no harm. Now here they were in his very own house. Moroni was excited, but humbled. What was their purpose?

As though he sensed the family's anticipation, the leader of the three placed his hand on Moroni's shoulder. "Moroni, the Lord has observed your faithfulness. Your commitment to Him and to His work is beyond question. Therefore, we have been commanded by Him to ordain you as a disciple and a special witness."

Moroni was astounded. He heard his family members loudly suck in their breath. He, an ordained disciple of the Master! The thoughts of all the foolish little things he had done as a child passed through his head. Was he worthy? Could he handle the task of being a special witness? Mormon had been called early in his life as a disciple. Now he was to have the same honor. Armora stepped to him, taking his hand in hers. Mormon placed one of his big arms around his shoulder. He could feel the presence of his mother and children. Even little Bilnor was quiet in the presence of the Three Disciples.

Again the Disciple spoke. "Mormon has been faithful to his calling as a disciple of our Lord, Jesus Christ. Now you, as his son, will have the same opportunity. It will not be an easy task. Satan will use his power to destroy you, but if you are faithful to your trust you will perform a great mission for the Savior." He looked Moroni squarely in the eye. "Do you accept this holy calling?"

Moroni finally found his voice. "It is a great honor to be asked. I will do all in my power to be worthy of the Savior's love and trust in me. I am prepared to dedicate my entire life to his service, regardless of the consequences." He looked down at Armora, who had tears running freely down her cheeks. He squeezed her hand. His mind went back to the time he killed the jaguar. He had the same feeling of family loyalty and support as he had felt then. His heart was full.

He looked again at the Disciples. "I have only one request." The family looked expectantly at him. "I desire that my father stand in during the ordination."

The leader of the Disciples smiled gently. "Yes, that will be permitted." He motioned to the other Disciples. Moroni knelt on a cushion. A surge of power came into his body as he felt the hands of these chosen servants laid upon his head. Closing his eyes, he listened.

The Disciple began, "Moroni, we, your brethren, commissioned by Jesus Christ, lay our hands upon your head and ordain you as one of His chosen disciples, to administer in all of the affairs of His Church here upon the earth. . . ."

Many promises were given to Moroni in the blessing, including one that he would have great treasures of wisdom, the ability to teach by the spirit, the gift of healing, the gift of prophecy, the gift of tongues, and the gift of discernment. The words of the blessing were imprinted deeply on his mind.

The voice of the Disciple continued ". . . Moroni, you are called as the last disciple in this chosen land until the Gospel is restored in its fullness among the Gentiles who shall inhabit this land. You will be a special witness of the Savior to many people, imparting to them the knowledge you have of Him."

At the final "Amen," and as he felt the hands which were on his head lifted, Moroni opened his eyes. It seemed like a sweet dream. Here were his family members, their faces glowing and tear-streaked. He could still feel the imprint of the Disciple's hand on his head but they had vanished. Mormon helped him to his feet, and father and son embraced. Holding to each other tightly, Moroni felt the strength and love of his father. He then embraced each of the family members in turn, ending with Armora. As he held her, he could feel her heart beating through her skin, mingling with the beat of his own heart. Oh, what joy and ecstacy he felt!

* * *

"That was eight years ago," Moroni said. "Much has happened since that time. It has been a time of peace, a time of preparation." He smiled. "It has also been a time of joy for our family. Our first daughter, Greta, was born three years ago." He looked again at Amonihah. "And here we are."

Amonihah sighed. This has been a precious and enlightening time for him. He stood. "Thank you my friend for sharing your life with me. I am now a better man because of you."

Several days later Moroni was again united with his beloved Armora and their children. As Armora hugged him around the neck and Greta hugged him around the knees, he asked himself, Can anyone be happier than I?

PART III

The End Comes For the Nephite People

The rays of the searing sun scorched down upon the shimmering desert plain. A man, clothed only in a loincloth, staggered and fell to lie inert on the hot, burning sand. Dried blood, caked and rusty brown, had come from numerous criss-crossed scratches and cuts on his sun-scorched body. His lips were blackened and cracked. He lay there without moving. A vulture, ever watchful, wheeled and circled in the cloudless sky far above the fallen man.

A short distance to the north, at the edge of the desert, another man swung easily towards the south. Though his hair and beard were streaked with tell-tale patches of gray, he showed no signs of fatigue or exhaustion. This was unfamiliar ground to Moroni so, as he moved with easy strides across the desert, he noted the location of the vulture circling above something that he couldn't see. As he came nearer, he saw the body of a Lamanite lying in a little natural hollow in the ground.

As he approached, the man stirred. At least he wasn't dead. He raised his head, saw Moroni, struggled to rise, and then fell back. Moroni quickly moved to the man's side, put his gourd of water to the man's lips, allowing him to take only a small sip before pulling the gourd away. After another drink, Moroni stooped and lifted the man to his shoulder. "We will find food and water," he said, "and then you may tell me what you are doing alone in the middle of the desert."

The limp, dead weight of his burden told Moroni that the man was unconscious. Occasionally he would mumble incoherently, but for most of the journey he was as one dead.

When they finally came to water, Moroni carefully laid his burden down in the shade of a large, spiny cactus. He refilled his water gourd from a small seep, moved back to the man and forced a few drops of water between his cracked lips. When he saw that the man was going to be okay, he laid him back in the shade. "Rest now," he said. "I will get some food."

When he returned from the hunt the man was sleeping peacefully and night was falling. Moroni was glad for the company even though it might be dangerous. He scooped out a small depression in the warm sand, chuffed some bark between his palms, carefully laid it in the depression, and started a small fire. When it was burning brightly, he prepared a brace of quail and a hare that he had caught in a snare. He sharpened a stick and impaled the quail on it. After jointing the rabbit, each piece was skewered on a stick and grilled over the glowing coals.

He glanced up to see that the man's eyes were open, staring at him. The eyes were without fear, but the expression was one of puzzlement. Moroni, tanned and darkened by his long exposure to the burning suns of many years, could almost pass for a Lamanite, but his blue eyes gave him away.

"Who are you?" mumbled the man. "How did I get here?"

"I found you in the desert," explained Moroni.

"O-oh," exclaimed the other. "Now I remember. You gave me water and carried me here. I owe you my life." He glanced around. "Is there more water?"

Moroni gestured towards the small seep. "Are you strong enough to reach it?"

The man turned, saw the water, and crawled to it.

"Be careful not to drink too much at one time," Moroni cautioned.

After the man had drunk he turned again to Moroni, eyeing the food hungrily.

"Who are you, and what are you doing alone in this barren country?" Moroni asked. Noticing the look, he smiled. "Perhaps you had better eat first, and then we can talk." He reached down, picked up a stick holding a quail and handed it to the man. "Be careful, it is hot."

It was, but the famished stranger didn't seem to notice. He ate one quail and half the rabbit before anything else was said. "My name is Kilihu," he finally said as he sat back. "I am of the tribe of Kath, and came from the West Sea. We were a fishing party who departed from the Land of Zarahemla. A great storm drove us northward and out to sea. Our boat was wrecked and I was the only survivor. I planned to get back to our city by traveling eastward over the mountains without realizing that I would have to travel through the desert. Without knowing the waterholes, and without food. . . ." He paused in his story, looked gratefully at Moroni, and added simply, "Thank you for saving my life."

Moroni shrugged. "It is the least that one human being should do for another." He busied himself at the fire, noting that Kilihu was watching him closely, still with a look of curiosity in his expression.

Leaving the obvious question unspoken, Kilihu softly said, "I am surprised to find a Nephite still alive in the land."

Moroni, feeling the need of talking with someone, told Kilihu about the last battle, and of his wanderings for so many years. As he talked, he noted the look of understanding in the face of the younger man. That night, around that small campfire, a new and lasting friendship was born.

For the next twenty days, Moroni and Kilihu traveled south. Moroni set a slow pace, avoiding the harshest parts of the desert. Kilihu improved daily and by the end of the first week he was able to help hunt for food.

Each night they sat around the campfire and talked. Moroni learned that Kilihu had been born in the land of Nephi, but after the Nephite surrender of Zarahemla his tribe had migrated there, taking up residence in the abandoned homes of the departed Nephites. He had been too young to participate in any of the battles with the Nephites, but his scars attested to the fact that he had battled since. From afar, Moroni had observed some of the battles between the Lamanites. Curious, he asked Kilihu, "Why do your people fight amongst themselves?"

Kilihu paused before answering, then he said, "The gods need blood sacrifices. The only way to get them is by taking prisoners from other tribes. When enough prisoners were taken by both sides, then the battles would end." He stopped talking, apparently attempting to interpret Moroni's reaction.

Moroni stared into the fire, shaking his head almost imperceptibly. Finally he spoke, as if to himself. "The whole face of this land is one continual round of murder and bloodshed, and no one knows the end of the war. None of these people know the true God. Oh, my people! As my father said, 'How could you have departed from the ways of the Lord?' "

After speaking, he sat there, thinking of those great temples once dedicated to Jesus Christ, now being used as sacrificial altars. He felt sick inside. That night he had difficulty going to sleep. He lay there thinking of how the people had perverted the civilized ways of the Lord. His mind went back to his father's mourning for his people after the great battle at Cumorah: *"O ye fair sons and daughters, ye fathers and mothers, ye husbands and wives, ye fair ones, how is it that ye could have fallen!"* [6]

Mormon's words brought back painful memories. His thoughts went back to the events leading up to that final battle. He thought again of Armora, Greta and his sons. The pain in his heart was awful to bear. He moaned in anguish as his mind returned to those terrible times.

Chapter 6

The Beginning of the End

It was the middle of the rainy season. The Lamanites were ready to launch a main attack against Desolation. The warriors, standing on the walls of the city, peered out into the mist, their eyes straining, not knowing where or when the attack would come. The damp, clingy smell of the rain hung over everything. The water ran down the helmets and into the armor of the waiting warriors, making their weapons slick in their hands.

Four men wound their way back to the city, carefully avoiding the enemy patrols. The men moved slowly, burdened down with heavy packs. Mormon, warned in a dream that the plates were in danger, had taken Moroni and his sons to retrieve them from the hill Shim. After traveling all night they approached the city walls just as the morning sun climbed over the horizon, partially dispelling the clinging mist.

People were already lining the streets. Refugees were moving northward. Merena met them at the door, a look of anxiety on her face. She said to Mormon, "Generals Lamah and Gilgal are waiting for you. They have been here since daybreak." There was a pleading look in her eyes.

Leaving the plates in the outer room with the two younger men, Mormon and Moroni hurried to the sitting room. The two Nephite commanders rose from where they were sitting. Mormon strode forward to greet his two friends, grasped their arms, and gave each a bear hug. "It's good to see you," he said. "How have the battles been going?"

Lamah and Gilgal avoided his eyes. "Not well." replied Gilgal. "The Lamanites outnumber us greatly. They have taken Bountiful and their main army is within a day's march of Desolation. We must retreat again."

Mormon looked at them, a question in his expression. "Why are you telling me this?"

Lamah said, "Mormon, we need your help. Without your leadership we are doomed. The men respect you and will follow your commands. We may be able to save the city. We are asking you to resume command of the armies."

Mormon turned, looking at Moroni and Merena at the door. For years Merena had supported him in his calling as general over the Nephite armies, suffering loneliness and anxiety while he was away fighting the innumerable wars. Now all she wanted was that they spend their few remaining years together. Mormon stepped to her, put his arm around her, and held her close. He looked back to the warrior leaders. Torn between loyalty to his people and Merena's desires, he asked, "How much time do we have?"

"Our scouts report that the main Lamanite army could be here by this afternoon," responded Gilgal. "It is barely light now and we have been working all night reinforcing our defenses around the walls."

Mormon put a hand on the shoulder of each of his faithful comrades. "I am sixty-four years of age. Well past the age of retirement. It has been thirteen years since I lead the armies. Many of your warriors are so young they won't even remember me. How much do you think they will respect me?"

Lamah turned to Gilgal who replied, "You are a legend among the warriors. I am convinced you are the only one who *can* lead them."

Moroni knew the battle which was going on inside his aging father. "I must give it prayerful thought," Mormon said. "It is a decision I cannot make by myself. I know the pressure you are under, but give me an hour."

Lamah slapped him on the back, "Thank you, General. We look forward to your answer." They left the room, returning to their demoralized army.

Mormon sat heavily on the cushion, looking at the floor. Merena wiped a tear from her eye. Mormon said, "I must pray." Moroni started to leave the room but Mormon waved him back. "Moroni," he said, "sit here. Pray with me."

The three knelt shoulder to shoulder. Mormon hesitated for only a moment, then began, "Father, what is Thy will? Should I repent of the oath I have taken? Should I again take command of the armies?" For some time, he pled with the Lord.

After his prayer they remained silent, kneeling there, waiting for whatever answer the Lord would give them. Each had learned long before that it did no good to pray if you were unwilling to wait for an answer. Mormon finally rose to his feet then helped Merena up. Moroni looked up at him expectantly. Mormon shook his head. "I have received my answer. The Lord feels my first responsibility is to the plates."

Mormon put an arm around each of them, guiding them to where Gidgiddonah and Moronihah were standing over the records. "We must leave the city with the sacred records before the Lamanites attack. I have been told where to deposit them. After that, I will decide what to do about Lamah's and Gilgal's request."

He pulled Merena to him. He was obviously concerned about her. During these last few years her health had deteriorated greatly. While cradling her greyed-head against his chest, he gave orders to his family.

"We must depart Desolation. Gather up your bare necessities and be ready to leave within the hour."

Moroni and his sons hurried through the city to their home. He quickly informed Armora what had happened, and the whole family hurriedly packed and started back.

As they turned into the street where Mormon lived, they almost ran into Gilgal and Lamah. Gilgal, approaching Moroni, said, "We will miss you and your father in this battle. Take care of him. We will yet need him in defense of our nation."

In Mormon's home everyone was ready. Merena's few possessions were carried by two maid-servants. The men carried the plates and Armora and Greta each carried a small pack. The little group picked its way through the clamor of the city, joining many families who were exiting the city to the north—away from the imposing threat of the advancing Lamanite armies.

The plates were very heavy, forcing the family to stop often. Merena was thankful for the rests. Her tiredness was obvious to the men, and Mormon shifted his load so he could help her. Each step seemed to be more painful for Merena and the rests became more frequent. It was dark when they arrived at Teancum. They stayed there overnight in an inn where they could get food and rest.

The next morning, Mormon hired a servant to go with them to carry his pack. He devoted his full energy to his sweetheart. By the afternoon of the second day they had reached the outskirts of Boaz where Mormon felt the women would be safe. He arranged lodging for them and the men again continued on their way, promising to deposit the plates and return as quickly as possible.

It was a tearful goodbye. Each of the men was immersed in his own thoughts as they plodded on, burdened down with the heavy plates.

Mormon didn't call a halt until it was pitch black and they could no longer see where to step in the slippery mud of the trail.

Moroni marveled at the stamina of his warrior father. Age is truly a matter of the mind, he thought.

By first light, after a snack of dried fruit and a drink from a bubbling spring, they were once again on their way. All day they headed in a north-easterly direction, stopping only to drink from the streams they crossed. There was a sense of urgency which lent strength to Mormon's tired old legs. He was very uneasy about leaving Merena and Armora. Moroni was having similar misgivings. He, too, was anxious to be back to take care of his wife and daughter.

Finally, on the second day, they saw a large hill looming up before them. It was surrounded by an open valley devoid of people. Moroni turned to his father. "I have seen that mountain before. What is it called?"

Mormon replied, "It is the Hill Cumorah. It is here that the Lord desires us to hide the plates."

Moroni thought back to the first time he had seen this hill—at the age of twelve. Even then he had felt that somehow this mountain would have some great meaning in his life. He again felt that sensation and wondered whether it had something to do with the sacred plates.

Near the top, under the lip of a deep gully, they found a volcanic cave. It was as tall as a man but narrow and deep. Protected by nature from inquisitive eyes, and from the effects of wind and weather, it was a perfect place for the plates. Carefully depositing the plates inside the cave, the four men then covered the entrance, piling stones and brush together until it blended into the hillside. Mormon stepped back, admired their work, and said, "It is good. Let us return to Boaz. Our women need us."

A feeling of dread hung heavily within Moroni. Without the weight of the plates to slow them down, they made good time. Mormon hardly let them rest, even at night, but kept urging them onward. Moroni knew how close his father was to the spirit and was even more concerned. When they were still a half-day's march from Boaz, they began meeting streams of terror-stricken refugees who had fled the city. They quickened their pace.

A cry came from a passing group. "Father! Father!" Moroni was startled! It was Greta's voice. Looking quickly around him, he spotted her. It *was* his Greta. He ran to her, scooping her up in his arms. She was covered with dirt and grime. The feeling of dread in is stomach became a gnawing ache. His heart felt as if it would pound right through his chest. His breathing came quick and shallow.

Greta buried her head in his chest, sobbing with relief. When her little body finally stopped heaving, he tilted her tear-stained face up so he could look into her eyes. "Greta," he cried, "where are your mother and grandmother?"

He knew even before he asked what the answer would be. Greta lowered her head again, sobbing uncontrollably. Mormon stood nearby, his head hanging. They were too late. Armora and Merena were dead.

Moroni walked off by himself just desiring to be alone. Greta turned and ran to her grandfather. He picked her up, holding her close. Moroni slumped against the trunk of a tree, slowly sliding to the ground. He wept— wept as he hadn't wept since he was a child. Why? Why? Father, why did she have to die?

A voice spoke inside him: *"My son, Armora is now with me. She will never feel pain again. Peace be unto you, my son."*

From Greta and other refugees bits and pieces were put together to tell the story. Desolation had been attacked the day the family had left. The Nephites had put up a valiant defense but to no avail. After a sore battle, they retreated pell mell to the north with the Lamanites in close pursuit.

The brave commanders regrouped their forces at Teancum, but it did no good. At the first attack of the Lamanites, the Nephites again fell back. At Boaz, they regrouped again. When the Lamanites came against them, the Nephites, with renewed courage, stood firm. But again it did little good. The Lamanites fell back, regrouped, and then attacked again in even greater numbers. Wave after wave of the attackers battered against the city's walls. Breaching them, the Lamanite hordes poured into the city. As they moved through the streets they cut down everyone in their path—men, women and children.

Armora, when she had seen what was happening, pushed Greta out the door and urged her to flee for her life. Merena was too old and feeble to run and Armora chose to remain and die with her. Moroni could just visualize his darling wife giving comfort and solace to Merena, protecting her to the end. He hoped they had not suffered.

Mormon, always the soldier, refused to take time to grieve. He had loved and enjoyed Merena for over forty years. He knew that now she was well taken care of and that he would see her again. He straightened up, stiffened his back, and looked around with renewed determination. As the army of Nephites retreated with the mass of refugees, he sought out and found Lamah and Gilgal.

"I am ready," he said. "Pass the word to your troops to reorganize. We will march in an orderly manner to Jordan and Joshua."

The electrifying word passed quickly to the troops. There was yet hope. Mormon could deliver them once again. The slink of defeated men became the stride of confident warriors. Mormon placed proven commanders at the head of each small army group. Moroni, Gidgiddonah, and Moronihah each assumed a command. Gidgiddonah and Moronihah seemed excited about their new leadership role. Moroni was less than elated.

The retreat lasted all the way to Jordan and Joshua. Here were the army's last defensive positions. Behind these cities were only the small unprotected villages of the peasants. The refugees who had not kept up with the army were hewn down by the advancing Lamanites. The people could look back and see huge clouds of smoke as their towns and villages were burned by the Lamanite armies.

Mormon knew he only had a few days to consolidate his defenses. With a skill borne of many years of warfare, he carefully placed his men where they could do the most good. By midafternoon of the second day after they arrived in Jordan, the lookouts spotted the first line of Lamanites advancing on the city. Knowing their pattern of attack, Mormon had posted his archers along the top of the wall. As the enemy lines approached, volley after volley of arrows arched through the sky. The Lamanite lines broke, with warriors attempting to turn back to get out of range of the deadly arrows. But they couldn't turn back—the next line of warriors was right behind them. Panic was everywhere. Finally, the lines broke and the Lamanites retreated the way they had come. A cheer went up from the wall.

The next day the Lamanites attacked again, and again the defenders held the wall. Mormon and Moroni were heartened by the brave defenders' actions, but they both knew it could not last.

Moroni turned to Mormon. "Father," he said, "the only way we can be victorious is for the Nephites to turn to God."

"Yes," Mormon assented. "If they would just offer their prayers to Him for deliverance, we could win this battle." He shrugged. "The other alternative. . . ." He left the sentence unfinished. They both knew the consequences.

The Nephites did not turn to their God. For two years the city held out against the attacking forces, but finally the last defenders were beaten down and the city taken. Mormon now had to adopt a new strategy for his forces. He engaged the enemy in a running battle knowing it was just a matter of time. Mormon feared that, for the Nephites, time had almost run out.

Chapter 7

The Gathering

Moroni watched Mormon carefully. He had never seen him so discouraged. Mormon sat despondently in the corner of the tent, absent-mindedly chewing on his stylus, paying no attention to the conversations that were going on around him. Greta, his granddaughter, asked if she could sit on his lap. She was a bright spot in his old age but today even she could not cheer him up.

Rousing from his reverie, he called, "Gidgiddonah, I need brushes and bark paper. Moroni, summon the tribal commanders."

Moroni stepped out of the command tent where the old general and his family were presently located. It was in the center of his army, sitting on a slight rise so he could see the entire area. As Moroni stood there, observing the activity of the camp, he noticed his second son, Moronihah, striding towards him. Moroni called, "Son, Mormon is calling a council of the tribal commanders. Will you give them the message to assemble in the command tent as quickly as possible?"

"Father, before I do that," Moronihah said, "I wanted to tell you there is much discontent among the warriors. Our last battle was sore and many are wounded—both in body and spirit."

"I know," Moroni answered. "I think that is the reason why father is calling us together. I have never seen him so discouraged. He is ready to make a major decision concerning our future."

Moronihah hurried off in the direction of Shem's tent. Moroni stepped back inside. Mormon was busy painting a message on the bark paper. As Moroni approached, he raised his eyes with a pained look.

"Son, do you remember the prophecy of Samuel, the Lamanite, from the plates?"

Moroni was startled. "You mean where he prophesied that in the fourth generation there would be a total destruction?"

"Yes. I feel that now is the time that he prophesied. Our people have hardened their hearts, have lost all contact with the Holy Spirit, and are a vengeful and bloodthirsty people. I'm surprised that the Lord hasn't caused their destruction before now."

Moroni searched through his papers. Pulling out one that was dog-eared and well used, he said, "Here it is. Samuel quoted the Lord as saying: *"Four hundred years shall not pass away before I will cause that they shall be smitten; yea, I will visit them with the sword and with famine and with pestilence."* [7]

Sitting back with the tip of his brush in his mouth, Mormon said, "To the best of my calculations, it has been almost four hundred years since Samuel made that prophecy." He turned and picked up a piece of bark paper from the floor. "I am proposing a final battle. Our people will probably be totally destroyed in such a battle, but I see no alternative. We cannot continue to retreat from the Lamanites, being picked off a few at a time." He stopped talking as Limhah and Joneam came into the tent.

As the commanders assembled, Mormon moved around the tent, giving encouragement where needed; a word of praise to someone; a word concerning an injury or some advice to someone else. Moroni smiled with pride. Here was the Nephite general—the commander of all the armies. He was sixty-nine years of age, his hair was white, but he held himself as erect as a twenty-year-old.

Moroni listened intently as Mormon discussed the situation they were facing. He began by reminiscing through his fifty years of leading the Nephite armies, then reminded them of their present situation.

"The enemy pursues us daily with fresher and fresher armies while our armies become less able and willing to fight. I see at this time we must make a critical decision concerning our future. We have several alternatives—but none give much hope.

"One, we can continue as we are until our entire army is destroyed, our land devastated, our wives and children killed. Or, two, we may have a chance to gather our people, have some time to heal our injuries, to make new weapons, and to see if we can gain any advantage over the armies of the Lamanites." Mormon paused which gave emphasis to his words. "We are at a crossroads. I am recommending a truce and a final battle."

Mormon was through. He looked around the room, obviously waiting for his commanders to comment.

Gidgiddonah broke the silence. "I fear that my men cannot fight another battle. They are wounded and weary. I am in favor of a delay."

Others nodded in assent, causing a general buzz in the tent as each commander voiced his opinion. Holding up his hand for silence, Mormon pulled the group together.

"It seems to me that most of you are in favor of getting some breathing time." Heads nodded in assent. "I will write to Shoninum, the Lamanite king, requesting a gathering time as allowed under our formal agreements of war.

The commanders left the tent in groups of two or three, discussing their new strategy—wondering what its results would be. Gidgiddonah and Moronihah hung back and, as soon as the others were gone, stepped up to Mormon.

"We just want to let you know that we will support any decision you make," they said.

Moroni's heart was full as he looked at his two stalwart sons. After they left, Mormon and Moroni sat in silence in the tent. Finally Mormon spoke up. "My son, please write what I dictate." Moroni picked up his brushes and bark paper and wrote as Mormon spoke:

> Shoninum, I salute you. We are weary of fighting but know that battles must still be fought. We request a truce, according to our agreements of war. Your army would grant our army time to gather to a battlefield for a last battle. This will be a decisive battle which will determine for all time the occupancy of this land. We request that we be granted that no battle take place until four years from this day so that we may gather all of our people to the valley surrounding the hill named Cumorah. Signed, Mormon, General of the Nephites.

Moroni was puzzled. "Why do you choose Cumorah as the battleground? It is not central in our land."

"It is neutral ground, has plenty of water for our people, and has fertile valleys upon which we can grow much food to sustain us as we are gathering our people." Mormon paused in his answer, appearing to be deep in thought. "It is also close to the hiding place of the plates which will give me more time to complete my abridgment before I am killed." Moroni winced at the thought of his father's death. Mormon smiled. "Besides, the Lord has told me it is His choice for the final battle."

The message was taken by Ahitol, the courier, to the enemy camp. Mormon worked on the plates while he waited for an answer from Shoninum. He motioned to Moroni.

"Son, come here. I feel my time is very short. When I return home to my God someone will have to carry on the important work of abridging the records. My son, will you take that responsibility?"

"Father, you know I will. But I am not as skillful in writing as you are. I can write Hebrew but your Egyptian writing is still difficult for me."

"Moroni, my son, the Lord will provide. All we need is time together so that I can instruct you more completely."

The day wore on as father and son, undisturbed, painstakenly inscribed hieroglyphics on the malleable golden plates. At evening, just as the golden sun was dipping behind the western hills, someone shouted outside the tent, "Ahitol comes!" Mormon stepped out of the tent, and strode off to meet the returning courier.

Moroni lifted the flap of the tent and watched. Reaching the courier, Mormon took the bark paper from his hand, shook it open, and silently read it as he walked back through the gathering commanders. He looked up. "It is done. He has agreed to our truce."

A cheer went up from the assembled commanders. Mormon and Moroni did not cheer. Through their prophetic eyes they could see the future. Just four short years until all would be gone—men, women, children, everyone!

The army was temporarily disbanded. All of the warriors were instructed to return to their homes, to gather up their families and friends, and then to begin their migration to Cumorah. They were to bring their flocks and their herds, their seeds, their tools and weapons. Cumorah would be a gathering place—a place of brief respite before that last great battle.

No one was to be excluded from the gathering, so Mormon sent small troops of warriors in a giant swing through the land to enforce the edict and to gather up the stragglers.

Moroni noticed how Mormon was finally feeling his seventy-plus years, so he assumed as many responsibilities of placing the people as he could. It was an awesome task. He organized people into fifties, hundreds, thousands, and ten thousands. Over each group of ten thousand he assigned one of his battle-tested commanders. Families were kept together but the majority of each command were warriors. It was imperative that he develop a fighting force. Each commander was given the responsibility of training his army group and equipping them with their weapons of war. The task was almost overwhelming. How to develop an effective fighting force from women with babes in arms, the old and infirm, the young girls and boys, and even little children?

Often Moroni felt like just giving up. It was an impossible task! Then he reminded himself that nothing is impossible to him that believes.

Smiths and carvers were kept busy around the clock forging swords and other weapons. Laborers were sent to the nearby mountains to quarry obsidian for arrow and spear points as well as chips for the blades of the swords. Bows and arrows were made and tested. And all the time there was the continuous and pressing need to keep almost a million people fed, to handle camp cleanliness and sanitation, and to maintain morale. It was a big job just to keep the warriors from fighting with each other. People were cramped together for living, eating and sleeping. Tempers flared often. Moroni chuckled wryly as he thought of Moses attempting to lead a similar group out of Egypt to the promised land. It was no wonder that none of the original group made it!

During all of this time he spent as many hours as he could on Cumorah with Mormon learning to write the reformed Egyptian. At times, when he could get away, he would sit for hours and practice using the stylus. Practice, practice, and more practice. Many times he hurled the stylus to the ground in disgust. Then, knowing that the task of writing might soon be his, he would pick it up and continue to practice.

He became very discouraged—both with the gathering and directing of the people, and also with his writing. He felt very insecure in writing Egyptian, but he never gave up. He had learned persistence as a youth from his father.

Three years had passed since Mormon had sent his letter to Shoninum. The valleys around Cumorah had become a huge tent city, with still more arrivals. From the top of Cumorah Moroni could look in any direction and see what looked like an ocean of tents and crude shelters. A pall of smoke from the camp and cooking fires hung over the tent city. Almost a million people had migrated to this place: the remnant of the once mighty Nephite nation.

Moroni observed this makeshift army with feelings of deep sadness. He watched as children, playing their make-believe games, seemed unaware of the impending disaster. As the agreed-upon day grew closer, a pall of gloom settled over the valley—a pall of anticipation . . . and death.

As often as he could, Moroni sought out the solitude of Cumorah where he could enjoy some peace. His soul needed it. Besides, he had another motive. Mormon had been told by the spirit that he would live through the battle in order to complete the records. So, under Mormon's direction, he had prepared a secret cave as a hiding place. He covered the entrance with rocks and brush, stocked it with food and writing materials, and made of it a private retreat.

Moroni also needed a chance to commune with God. He felt that his prayers were the only things that helped him through the frustrations of each day. Many times he would retire to his favorite glen. There, surrounded by trees, he would kneel on the soft grass and pour out his heart to the Savior. The smell of the abundant wild flowers and the cries of the lively and colorful birds reminded him that life would go on.

Often he received the solace and comfort he needed from his Maker. Sometimes he took his daughter, Greta, along. As he watched her play so innocently in the forest, he mourned over what he knew would soon come to pass. He wished with all his heart that she could be spared—but knew that she couldn't. He did hope that the end, when it came, would come quickly for this beautiful and sensitive child.

Chapter 8

The Final Battle

The appointed day was now at hand. Tents were struck. Lines were formed. Weapons were readied. It was awesome to see the great army forming up on the plain west of Cumorah: it bristled with spears and sparkled with bright colors.

Mormon had prepared his commanders well. Everyone knew that this would be a fight to the death. There would be no quarter, no surrender, no retreat. Each group commander employed his army in a series of lines. In front were his archers followed closely by the lance soldiers. Behind these were lined up the balance of the motley army armed with a wide assortment of weapons.

The professional warriors were an impressive sight clothed in their quilted cotton armor of yellow and white, their leather helmets topped with colorful feather crests. Each carried a heavy shield inscribed with the tribal insignia. In front were the colorful feather banners decorated beautifully with the insignia of the army groups. The long hours of preparation had at least helped the men and women to keep up their morale.

The warriors kept to themselves, not liking to mingle with the old men, women, and children. There was a constant beating of drums and shrilling of flutes as they prepared themselves for war, their bronze and obsidian weapons flashing in the sun. Moroni shook his head sadly. He knew it was too late for such pageantry to do any good.

A great hush fell over the Nephites as they saw the armies of the Lamanites arriving and forming on the hillsides surrounding the valley, completely ringing the Nephites. Endless columns trailed in with their huge feather banners and multicolored cloth flags.

To Moroni the scene which spread through the valley was almost a scene of grandeur. But the ring of swords and spears kept him painfully aware of the seriousness of the situation they faced. The fear of death which fills the breasts of the wicked was real to many. Mormon and his commanders had all they could do to keep their armies from just bolting or sneaking away.

Few Nephites slept that night. Nerves were taut. Mouths dry. Tempers flared. For many, knowing what was coming in the morning, it was a time for a last caress, a thoughtful word to someone who had been neglected too long. Others were in a contemplative mood, thinking of what they had or hadn't accomplished in their lives. Some were boisterous and bragging of what they would do on the morrow. Some were praying earnestly to their gods.

Moroni, his family, and a few loyal church friends, met for one last time to partake of the Lord's supper. As they passed the cup of wine and partook of the bread, they spoke reverently of their love for the Savior. Moronihah walked over to his father, hugged him tightly, and with tears in his eyes said huskily, "Father, thank you for the example you have set. We are glad that you have given us the knowledge of the Savior and His teachings. We are now prepared to meet Him. We don't fear death."

Moroni blessed those assembled and then embraced each of them. After final goodbyes, the few members of the true Church returned to their places in the ranks to await the dawn. Moroni held on to Greta. Her childlike faith was complete, but for her sake he wished that morning would never come. Yet, he knew it must. As he held her close for the last time in mortality, he told her once again the story of Jesus and how He loved little children. He told her of the Savior taking the little children and blessing them and of how the heavens opened and angels came down and encircled them and ministered to them.

"Greta," he said, his voice husky with emotion, "tomorrow you will be with your mother in Paradise. If I am not there, will you give her a kiss for me?"

"Of course, father," she replied, strong in her childlike faith. "And will I see grandmother, also?"

"Yes, my girl," Moroni responded, his heart heavy. He held Greta tightly in his arms until she slept. Reluctantly he laid her on the ground. "Goodbye, my little one," he said quietly, and then he left to make his own preparations for the morning.

The dawn came gloriously, bathing the earth in radiant hues and tones. As the sun came over the eastern hills, a roaring thunder rolled from the drums of the Lamanites. They were on the move. Moroni gripped his sword tightly and called for his warriors to stand fast. The Lamanite warriors surged forward. The Nephites stayed in place, waiting for the onslaught.

When the Lamanites were within shouting distance a roar of voices beat upon the ears of the waiting Nephites. The din was indescribable as the Lamanites yelled and beat upon their shields with their weapons. The thundering drums added their own clamor to the already deafening tumult which echoed and re-echoed from the sides of the valley.

The Nephite ranks wavered, then held. A rain of arrows arched over the field between the two hostile forces. A rush of thousands of Lamanite warriors, running and leaping, beating on their shields, yelling loudly, bore down upon the waiting Nephites.

Moroni looked around, hungry for one last look at Greta. She was not to be seen. He looked to the sides seeing Gidgiddonah and Moronihah stand unwavering in front of their armies. He had no more time to look, but his heart ached as he thought of his beloved children.

The two armies met with a loud crash—body against body, sword against sword, shield against shield. The thuds of battle were punctuated with the cries of children and the screams of women. The warriors grunted and panted as they thrust, parried, hit, thrust, and parried again. The earth muffled the sounds as bodies fell, never to rise again.

Moroni was in front of his army, challenging, inspiring, daring. He moved back and forth, plugging holes in the line, urging his people to greater efforts. But it was to no avail. The Nephites could no longer be called an army. The people were dismayed and terrified. They had no impetus to fight or will to win, but scattered and milled about the field of battle. It was a slaughter. Blood ran in rivulets as the Lamanites struck and struck and struck again.

Moroni grew exceedingly weary. He lost all track of time, only remembering to hack and thrust at the sea of snarling screaming faces. He panted in short shallow breaths and his sword arm became so weary it was hard to lift if one more time.

Harrassed as he was, he did see Mormon fighting as he led a group to his right. Then Mormon was cut down. Courageous as he was, his old body hadn't been able to keep up with his desire. A Lamanite spear pierced his side and he fell, his white hair tinged red with blood. Other warriors fell dead on top of him as the battle continued to rage around him. As he fought, Moroni mentally marked the spot where his father had fallen. If he lived through this he had a desire to give his father a hero's burial. He yearned also to find his children. He shook his head in sorrow. All those he loved were lost to him and he didn't even know where their bodies lay. As he continued to fight, a constant prayer was in his heart and on his lips. I care not what happens to me, but let my children and my father have peace. Please accept them into Thy bosom, Father. Sweat and blood ran down his forehead into his eyes, almost blinding him, but he fought on.

Finally the blessing of darkness settled around the few who were still alive and fighting. Moroni and a small band of warriors had been pushed back until they were in the trees on the slopes of Cumorah. All around them was the smell of blood and death. Out in the flat the Lamanites slayed any wounded they found.

When it was too dark to see, the Lamanite drums sounded the call to regroup. They moved back to their encampments surrounding the valley. Wearily Moroni looked around, counting those who had survived with him. Only ten warriors! All of the women and children were dead, including his sons, his father, and his beloved Greta. Almost a million bodies lying dead in the valley. He needed to find his father's body before it was mutilated by the Lamanites. Leaving their swords and shields, armed only with their knives, he and a trusted lieutenant started across the dark valley. The two quietly threaded their way through the field of bodies, flinching as they stepped on those who just a few hours before had been alive.

As they made their way towards the area where Moroni had seen his father fall, he again felt an urgent need to search through the heaps of bodies for his children. Where were they? His heart ached with the desire to find them but he knew it was futile. He could do nothing. There was no way of finding them in the darkness. In fact he began to wonder if they could even find his father's body—even though he had seen him fall and knew his approximate location.

Nearing the spot he had marked in his mind, Moroni and his lieutenant were startled to hear a soft moaning. Moroni quickly moved to the pile of bodies from which it came. He roughly pulled bodies aside until he got to the bottom person. It was Mormon, and he was alive! Moroni was overjoyed. They bound his wound as best they could in the dark and carried him carefully back to the shelter of Cumorah.

Moroni was glad there was no moon. He didn't want the Lamanites to see that some Nephites had survived. As they neared the spot in the trees where he had left the others, he was met by Limhi. "We have found others who were not killed," he whispered. "There are now twenty-three of us."

"Not so," Moroni whispered, nodding towards Mormon. "There are twenty-four!"

During the rest of the night the survivors toiled towards the top of the hill carrying their wounded and covering their tracks as best they could. On the crest, they found a deep lava-rock depression. They camouflaged it with limbs and branches and then laid Mormon on a pallet of leaves and grass. Moroni dressed his wound once again wishing that he could build a small fire in order to cauterize the wound.

Dawn was breaking by the time the small band had put the finishing touches to the shelter. In the pre-dawn light they carefully obliterated all traces of their nighttime activity, climbed into the shelter, and waited for whatever the day would bring. Moroni appraised the situation. Twenty-four men, one badly wounded, several slightly wounded, against an army of several hundred thousand Lamanites. They had no food and could not build a fire. It looked pretty hopeless, but they were alive! And where there is life, there is hope.

He was nervous. From where they were it was impossible to see what was happening. By the time the sun had reached its high-point of the day, he decided to take a look. He carefully poked his head out through the covering branches, looked around, and seeing that the area was clear, pulled himself out. He found a rock outcropping from which he could observe the valley. The Lamanite armies were marching back to their camp. It was all clear.

They carried Mormon out to where he could see the valley. Moroni noticed how old his father looked. The weight of this final battle had sapped all his strength. He had no more resources to call upon. His desire to finish the abridgment was all that had kept him alive.

The old general looked over the valley. He saw where his ten thousand had fallen, and where the ten thousand of Moroni's army had fallen, and all of the other ten thousands. His head, bobbing slightly from side to side in his sorrow, slowly turned as he mentally marked the place where each commander and his ten thousand had died. He thought of his great leaders: Camenihah, Moronihah, Antionum, Gidgiddonah, Shiblom, Shem, Josh, and others—each of whom had led ten thousand into the battle. All dead— his whole family, with the exception of Moroni, wiped out. His whole people, with the exception of these twenty-three men, destroyed. He felt the comforting hand of Moroni on his shoulder but he would not be comforted. Tears of anguish ran down his wrinkled cheeks.

He cried out in great sorrow: *"O ye fair ones, how could ye have departed from the ways of the Lord! O ye fair ones, how could ye have rejected that Jesus, who stood with open arms to receive you! Behold, if ye had not done this, ye would not have fallen. But behold, ye are fallen, and I mourn your loss. O ye fair sons and daughters, ye fathers and mothers, ye husbands and wives, ye fair ones, how is it that ye could have fallen."* [8]

The remaining warriors looked at each other. They did not understand. Only Moroni knew what was going on in that great heart. Only he knew how his father had loved his people. He knew how often Mormon had prayed to have his people repent of their iniquities and return to their God. Mormon continued:

"Behold, ye are gone, and my sorrows cannot bring your return. And the day soon cometh that your mortal must put on immortality, and these bodies which are now moldering in corruption must soon become incorruptible bodies; and then ye must stand before the judgment-seat of Christ to be judged according to your works; and if it so be that ye are righteous, then are ye blessed with your fathers who have gone before you. O that ye had repented before this great destruction had come upon you." [8] Wearily he lay his head back upon the ground. Moroni reached down and cradled his father's head in his hands. Mormon's eyes were clenched shut in his great anguish. He murmured, *"But behold, ye are gone, and the Father, yea, the Eternal Father of Heaven, knoweth your state; and he doeth with you according to his justice and mercy."* [9]

* * *

The remaining warriors left by twos and threes during the next few nights, leaving Mormon and Moroni alone on Cumorah. Moroni moved his father to the limestone cave in which he had previously cached provisions and writing materials. A spring bubbled near the entrance to the cave giving a plentiful supply of fresh water. Moroni spent most of his time caring for Mormon, doctoring his wound, seeing that he was comfortable.

Even though he had lost much blood, Mormon improved rapidly. He spent his days recuperating in the cave or on a sheltered rock where he could work on the abridgments of the writings of his people. Moroni watched him carefully trying to keep him from tiring himself. His urgings did no good. Mormon had a sense of urgency to complete the records and nothing could keep him from that task.

It was still difficult for Moroni to sleep at night—the memories were too painful. For many nights, and often in the years ahead, he awoke sweating and shaking at the memory of those blood-filled hours. His feeling of loss at those times was overpowering but the spirit of the Lord would whisper to him: *"Peace be unto you, my son. Your family is happy with Me in Paradise."* Sometimes as he lay awake after one of his bad dreams of the battle, he would feel the presence of Armora's spirit, caressing him and giving peace to his soul.

Chapter 9

Death of Mormon

Moroni watched in silence as Mormon skillfully applied the stylus to the metal plates. The Egyptian characters were now at least readable to Moroni even though he still felt somewhat insecure in writing them.

Leaning back with a sigh of relief, Mormon exclaimed, "Well, son, that finishes up the book of Fourth Nephi. Only one more section to write—the story of my life from the time of Ammaron to the present. When that is done my work will be finished. Into your hands I commit any writing which is left to do." He meditated a moment. "After I am gone, please finish up the history of this people and then preserve the plates to the Lord. The Lord will bless you as to what you should write."

With Mormon approaching the end of his writing, Moroni was feeling restless. He was used to activity and he felt the need to do something. He asked Mormon, "Father, you have spent your entire life in abridging the records. Why is it so important?"

"Moroni, my son," smiled Mormon, "I have never questioned the Lord as to His purposes." Moroni looked chagrined. "Mormon continued, "My lifelong mission has been to keep the records of our people and to abridge the records of those who have gone before. Now," and he breathed a sigh of relief, "that work is all but finished."

He looked solemnly at Moroni. "I have my own theory about the necessity for abridging the records. I have been shown in vision that the person who will receive these records will be born in a land far from here. In order to transport the records to that place, they have to be lighter and smaller." They both remembered the effort it had been for four of them to carry the plates from the hill Shim to Cumorah. He added, "Besides, it has been a labor of love. I have learned so much by reading, studying, and pondering the writings of these great prophets and then putting their thoughts into my own words."

He leaned back, stylus in hand, and flexed his fingers. Moroni knew the stiffness and pain that his father must be feeling. He was now seventy-six years of age, white-haired and a little stooped, but still a man of might and spirit. Reflectively, he went on. "Ah, but it is almost finished. The account I have just written was inscribed by one of the disciples that the Savior ordained. He was the fourth Nephi to write in the plates since Lehi and his sons left Jerusalem. You can be very proud, my son, that you are a literal descendant of that first Nephi.''

Moroni stood at the entrance of the cave, looking off into the distance, drumming his fingers on a rock. The East Sea was less than a day's journey. He could go there, dig some clams and catch some fish, and be back in two days. He could almost smell the aroma of fresh fish roasting on the rocks by the fire. He turned back to Mormon.

"Father, wouldn't it taste good to have some fish and fresh clams? I believe that I could get all I could carry and be back very soon.''

Mormon, seeing that Moroni had already made up his mind, said, "Food to me at this time means nothing, but if you do go, be careful.''

"I will be.'' Excitedly, Moroni walked to the rear of the cavern and began packing a few necessities for the trip. As a man of action the past few months had been difficult for him. It would be good to just get out and walk. "Tonight will be a good night to go. There will be a full moon, and by sticking to the trail I can be at the seashore by morning. I am concerned about you, though. Will you be all right for a couple of days?''

Mormon smiled. "Who would want to disturb an old man? I believe that I can look after myself. I want to finish this writing and get the plates secure once again.'' He stood up and walked back to where Moroni stood. Putting a hand on his shoulder, he said, "My only concern is, if anything does happen to me, will you finish the record?''

Moroni's face broke into a full grin. "I will complete any writing that you don't do, but knowing your tenacity, I won't have to worry.''

Father and son clasped arms, then Mormon impulsively wrapped his arms around his son's shoulders and gave him a bear hug. Thus they stood for a few moments, savoring the closeness and love which they felt for one another. Finally Mormon wiped a tear from his eyes and returned to his stylus. Moroni busied himself around the cave, making sure that there was plenty for Mormon to eat while he was gone.

As darkness settled over the hillside, he said one last goodbye to his father and started out. Staying in the trees on top of the ridge he headed east. As the hill tapered off into a saddle he found a well-traveled trail to follow. It felt so good to stretch his legs—to walk without fear of detection. He hated to leave Mormon alone but he decided it would be good for both of them. Father needs some time alone, too, he thought to himself.

At last, descending a long sloping hill, just as the sky started to lighten with the dawn, Moroni saw his goal—the East Sea. In the early light of morning the beach seemed to stretch endlessly in each direction. The waves were calm, gently easing up on the white beaches. In the distance the water was deep blue but closer to shore it became almost a brilliant green with patches of brown. The green was flecked with small strands of white as the waves crested on their way to the beach. A few pink-edged clouds were in the brightening sky adding even more to the picturesque scene before him.

The area looked totally deserted but Moroni took no chances. He found a brush-choked ravine, settled in amongst the thick brush, and promptly fell asleep. He awakened about noon, hot and covered with sweat. He had forgotten how humid it was this close to the sea. He ate some fruit and lay back down, watching the movement of the clouds above him.

As the sun started sinking below the hills behind him, he decided it was time to get busy. He sharpened a large stick and dug clams until his bag was filled. Finding a small inlet where he knew fish would be feeding, he crawled on his stomach and peered over the bank. The evening light was fading fast and he had to wait a few moments until his eyes adjusted to looking into the water. A big silver-colored fish lazily swam right beneath him. He carefully maneuvered his spear into position, waited until just the right moment, then thrust with all his might. Disappointed, he pulled back. He had missed and it was too dark to try again.

He retreated back to the ravine, feeling safe enough to light a small fire. As the fire burned down, he placed several of the clams on the hot coals. After just a moment they began to steam and the shells opened. When they were fully cooked, he ate them, relishing every bite. He thought of his father and what he would be doing. Since it was now dark, he would have put away his stylus, eaten some dried fruit, possibly mixed himself a drink of warm cocoa, and gone to bed.

After his refreshing meal Moroni was very sleepy. He smothered the fire with sand, rolled on one side, and was soon asleep. He awakened in the middle of a dream, seeing himself in a unfamiliar land surrounded by strange people. He lay pondering the meaning until it was time again to venture forth.

In the late afternoon he dug a few more clams to refill his sack and again approached the small inlet. This time he was more successful, spearing two large fish. After carefully cleaning and washing them, he placed them in his sack. A strange premonition had been bothering him all afternoon and he immediately started for Cumorah.

As the first rays of sunlight sparkled on the leaves of the higher trees, he arrived back on Cumorah. He cautiously approached the cave and stepped inside. Mormon was not there! Perhaps he had just stepped out for a few minutes. Then he noticed that the stylus and the plates were hidden. That was not like Mormon if he were to be gone only for a few moments. Now he was really concerned. He followed Mormon's footprints outside the cave until they disappeared. It looked to him as if Mormon had deliberately covered his tracks to prevent someone from following them to the cave. The situation became stranger by the moment. He was tempted to call out but knew he shouldn't. He cautiously moved away from the cave, searching in ever-widening circles for footprints.

At last he found them. Moroni could tell by the way the toe was dug in that Mormon had been running. His heart missed a beat! After a few steps Mormon's sandal prints were covered by a mass of barefoot prints. Moroni cried out, "No, father. No. No!" Another hundred feet and the story in the dirt was plain to see. He could see where his father had stood, his back to a large tree. He had held off his attackers for some time according to the way the ground was beaten down. Blood stains on the ground indicated that several had been killed or wounded. As he looked at the signs of what had happened, he recalled that Mormon had said that he would not be taken alive. He had no desire to be sacrificed to the gods of the robbers and Lamanites. He would rather die fighting!

Moroni saw where his father had fallen. There was a large pool of blood. He followed a bloody trail where a body had been dragged. After a few feet he came upon the badly mutilated body of his father. He dropped to his knees, tenderly caressing the bloodied white hair. As he knelt there he offered a fervent prayer. Father in Heaven, forgive me for leaving my father at this time. It is my fault that he is lying here. Please forgive me for not fulfilling my responsibility to him. His voice broke and tears welled in his eyes as he pled with the Lord.

A peaceful feeling came over him. A quiet but penetrating voice entered his consciousness. *"Moroni, do not despair. Your father has completed his work and has come home to Me. Don't you see? If you had been here both of you would have been killed. You are the only one left to complete the history of your people. The rest of those who survived the battle have been slain by the Lamanites. You will not be slain, my son, for I have a greater mission for you. There are yet some things that you must do for Me."* The voice stopped. All was still. Moroni was on his knees in the sand but now he felt no anguish—only a feeling of loneliness. Thy will be done, he prayed.

Scooping out a shallow grave, Moroni carefully buried the father whom he had loved so very much. He scrounged stones from the hillside, carefully mounding them over the heap of dirt that covered the mortal remains of Mormon. Convinced that no wild animal could now disturb the body, he stood up. Then, standing with head bowed, he thought of all that this man had meant to him.

He knelt once more beside the grave. Scooping up a handful of dirt and letting it sift slowly through his fingers, he offered a prayer of dedication.

"Father in Heaven, in the name of Jesus Christ, and by the priesthood I hold as one of His disciples, I dedicate this spot as a final resting place for the remains of my father, Mormon. I ask Thy blessings upon this sacred portion of Thy earth and pray that it will not be disturbed until his body shall rise to join his spirit in the resurrection of the just." He then reminded the Lord of Mormon's many great accomplishments on the earth and how he had been such a faithful servant all of his life. He ended his prayer by saying, . . . And Father, please receive my father's spirit into Paradise and let him know of the great love which I have for him, and that I look forward with longing to be there with him.

He ended his prayer and returned to the cave. There he found a piece of bark paper that he had missed before. Mormon had written, "My son, there is a Lamanite patrol on the mountain. I am fearful that they will discover the cave and the precious plates. I will lead them away from the cave. You know where the plates are. I admonish you to finish the record. I will not see you again in the flesh, but I know that I will see you in the kingdom of our Father. Goodbye my son, I go now to my God, and to your God."

Moroni, his father's letter in his hand, sat down on the rock where his father had sat for so many hours abridging the plates. Silently weeping, he said, "Father, I will complete the work."

He didn't know how long he sat there. It was almost dusk when he got up and hurried to the rear of the cave. Moving aside a stone, he pulled the plates from their hiding place. He read the last words Mormon had written. He had written his history and then he had closed his record with a special message to the Lamanites.

As Moroni read, he could hardly see the inscriptions through his tears. His father, so recently murdered by the Lamanites, had spent his last hours on earth writing to them about their salvation:

"Know ye that ye are of the house of Israel. Know ye that ye must come unto repentance, or ye cannot be saved. . . . Therefore, repent, and be baptized in the name of Jesus, and lay hold upon the Gospel of Christ, which shall be set before you. . . ." [10]

Moroni sat for a long time with the plates on his lap. When he aroused himself it was dark. He was fearful about starting a fire, and, with all that had happened, he had no desire to eat. Soon sleep brought him more peace.

Morning found him up early. He had much to do. He must complete the record, put the plates in their hideaway, and leave this place with all its sad memories of blood and carnage. He could not help again feeling pangs of sorrow at losing his father, and the feeling of loneliness as he contemplated his existence as the sole survivor of the Nephite people was far beyond sorrow. He picked up the stylus, noticed that there was only one section of a plate that had not been written on, and began to write:

"Behold I, Moroni, do finish the record of my father, Mormon. Behold, I have but few things to write, which things I have been commanded by my father. . . . after the great and tremendous battle at Cumorah, behold, the Nephites who had escaped into the country southward were hunted by the Lamanites, until they were all destroyed. And my father also was killed by them, and I even remain alone to write the sad tale of the

destruction of my people. But behold, they are gone, and I fulfill the commandment of my father. And whether they will slay me, I know not." [11]

He paused in his writing, flexed his cramping hands, and laboriously continued:

"Therefore I will write and hide up the records in the earth; and whither I go it mattereth not. Behold, my father hath made this record, and he hath written the intent thereof. And behold, I would write it also if I had room upon the plates, but I have not; and ore I have none, for I am alone. My father hath been slain in battle, and all my kinsfolk, and I have not friends nor whither to go; and how long the Lord will suffer that I may live I know not." [12]

Once again Moroni put down his stylus. He was finished. He had no more room on the plates and he had said what needed to be said. It was now important to leave Cumorah before he, too, was discovered by the Lamanites. He had only one more task to do—protect the plates.

That evening he carefully gathered up his father's abridgments and the remaining plates of Nephi. Using great caution, he returned the plates to the hiding place where he and his sons had helped Mormon cache them so many years before. So many memories in this place! The plates would be safe in their hiding place until the Lord would have them brought forth. Erasing his tracks as he went, he returned to the cave where he and Mormon had spent those choice past two years.

He gathered up what possessions he would need, waiting until darkness settled upon the land, and stepped out of the cave not knowing if he would ever return.

* * *

"That was fifteen years ago," he said as he looked at Kilihu, "and now I am returning to write some more. I have lived to teach many peoples and to fulfill the mission that my Savior commissioned me to fulfill."

It was a moment before Kilihu spoke. Tears brimmed in his eyes and his voice shook with emotion. "Moroni, my friend, you have saved me from a physical death on the desert, and now through your words I have gained a strong belief in Jesus Christ. Would you teach me more of Him and thus save me from a spiritual death also?"

Moroni was thrilled at Kilihu's simple faith. He reached out and laid a hand on his arm. "Kilihu," he began, "nothing would thrill me more than to bring you to a complete knowledge of the Lord. I love to teach his message."

A few days later, as they walked along a meandering stream, Kilihu looked up at his teacher. "Moroni, I desire to be baptized."

Moroni stopped in midstride and turned to Kilihu. "My friend," he replied. "Do you feel that you are ready for a life of total commitment to the Savior?"

"I am ready," was the firm reply.

They found a deep place in the stream where an eddy swirled around a large, smooth rock. They took off their sandals and stepped into the cool water. Feeling his way among the small rocks on the bottom, Mormon led Kilihu to deep water. He offered a silent prayer of faith, requesting the presence of the Holy Spirit. Then, taking Kilihu by the hand, he raised his right arm. "Kilihu, I baptize you in the name of the Father, and of the Son, and of the Holy Ghost, Amen."

Kilihu came out of the water sputtering, a new glow in his demeanor. Without leaving the water Moroni laid his hands on Kilihu's head, blessing him and conferring upon him the gift of the Holy Ghost. What radiance shone from Kilihu's face! What joy he felt! The Holy Ghost was with him! His mind was filled with the Spirit. He seemed to be floating in the air, free from the burdens of his past life. He was clean once again.

PART IV

Fugitive and Wanderer

The day following his baptism, Kilihu was still radiant with the Spirit. Moroni chuckled at his friend's new found exuberance. As they sat around the fire that night, Kilihu sat close to Moroni. After their scant meal he asked, "Moroni, tell me of your missionary journeys. Where did you go? What peoples did you teach? How many did you convert? How . . . ?"

"Wait a minute," responded Moroni. "One question at a time." Moroni thought back over those fifteen years. They had been good years. Years of joy and compassion. Years of service to God.

* * *

After being restricted to the cave for so long, Moroni was anxious to be on his way. He packed what few possessions he had kept, his writing stylus, his personal care items, his roll of bark paper and writing brushes, the leather pouch with letters and sermons which he had saved from his and Mormon's ministry, the white robe that Armora had made for him, his blanket and extra pair of sandals.

The moon was full, bathing the land with quiet beauty, as he left the cave for the last time. Moroni glanced around the now familiar terrain. It was beautiful, but he was glad to say goodbye to this place with its memories of death and destruction. He walked quickly away without even a backward glance. All night he walked, and as early morning light crept across the land he saw that he was once again nearing the East Sea.

Finding a shelter in a brushy ravine, he settled down for the day. There was a small spring and overhanging tree branches which gave shade and protection. There Moroni stayed until the protective darkness of night came once again to cover his movements. He had a choice of going north or south along the beach. Which way? The prompting of the Spirit told him to go north. The north country had become a refuge for remnants of the Nephite and Lamanite nations for years. Surely he could find a place where he would not be hunted like an animal.

During the next week Moroni traveled at night. When he came to the waters of Ripliancum, he was forced to detour inland. Ripliancum was made up of lagoons and swamps. The lagoon was wide and flat and its clear blue waters contrasted sharply with the brown mud of the swamps. The swamps were filled with stumps of dead trees, naked and gray, with fungus growing where the bark had peeled off.

The detour inland was not too bad except for the innumerable insects. Flies gathered in huge clusters near the fetid water and wherever he stepped they swarmed around him by the thousands. Twilight was especially bad when the air actually seemed sooty with flies. He was thankful for the bats which came out at sundown and whistled by in a frenetic hunt for their supper. Even in his discomfort he enjoyed the beauty of the clouds of white butterflies which darted to and fro just above the water. Or the blue ones, big as birds, which fluttered like brightly dyed pieces of linen cast into the wind.

Moroni soon gave up traveling at night. Without a moon the nights were black as a deep cave—a black sometimes so dense it felt like a wet sponge on his face. He was also afraid of falling into one of the innumerable sink holes. The smells at night were terrible, swamp gas rising all around him, casting off its putrid smell. And the nights were furious with the ringing cries of insects and the bird grunts that often rose to screams.

Even though the days were miserably hot, Moroni made much better time. By evening, cool breezes from the sea brushed across the lowlands. This was low coastal country, salty; hot, and full of skinny flies. The only animals he saw were the vari-colored lizards sunning on the tree roots and the agile monkeys leaping to and fro in the trees. His diet consisted primarily of berries, clams, and fresh fish. Occasionally he travled inland and was able to supplement his diet with bananas and fruit.

He bathed often and even though the salt stuck to his skin and grated under his clothing, he enjoyed feeling clean. He found several small streams flowing into the sea which gave a chance for a real freshwater bath. After one such plunge in a small sluggish stream, Moroni settled back in the shade of a large rock outcrop. It was very hot and very still. The black flies buzzed about singing a droning lullaby. He lay in the shade, watching the few fleecy-white clouds as they drifted northward through the azure-blue sky. He closed his eyes, listening to the sounds of the leaves as they brushed together; enjoying the steamy smell of the sun on the grass and the trickling sound the water made as it flowed in the nearby stream.

The sounds of children laughing and splashing in the surf awakened him. He slid further under the rock, looked around, and saw the naked brown bodies of children as they frolicked on the beach and in the waves. Looking further up the narrow strand of beach, he saw the children's mothers, motioning and gesturing as they talked. They were too close for him to just get up and run, and if they continued in the direction they were sauntering, they would be upon him in moments. Knowing that surprise was the only advantage he had in his situation. He rolled on his side, pulled his white robe from his pack, and slipped it on.

The village women shrunk in fear as the tall bearded white man, clad in a shining robe, seemed to materialize out of thin air. Moroni, hand raised in a gesture of friendship and peace, strode quickly towards the women. They appeared ready to break and run but Moroni called, "Peace, my friends. I will not harm you. I seek friendship in your village." He hoped they understood his language.

Shyly the women waited his approach, gesturing and whispering among themselves. Finally one who was obviously the spokesman said, "We welcome you to our village, pale one. What name do they call you?"

The language was strange to Moroni, yet he understood it perfectly. "My name is not important," he said in their tongue.

The women again whispered among themselves. "We will call you Waikano: 'He who drops out of the sky.' "

Moroni was surprised and somewhat chagrined when he found how close the village was to where he had been resting. He was overwhelmed by the warmth of the welcome the villagers gave him. They treated him almost as if they had been expecting him. That night, as he sat in council with the elders and chiefs of the village, he found out why.

Chapter 10

The Pale One

The musky odor of sweaty bodies filled the council house. The building was windowless and a heavy rug covered the entry. Moroni had not had a chance to speak, but he listened politely as the debate concerning him continued.

The tribal chiefton questioned him. "Pale one who dropped to us from the sky, our legends tell us that someday a white god will come to our people. He will be a healer and a teacher. He will teach us concerning our gods. I ask you, are you he of whom it is spoken?"

Moroni paused before answering the question. His very life could depend upon the answer. Thoughts went rapidly through his mind concerning his mission as a special witness for his Savior, Jesus Christ. He was thrilled that legends still persisted among the tribes concerning His coming. He stood, raising his hands with the palms towards his audience in the traditional manner of him who has authority to speak.

"I bring you a message from the god of wind and water," he began. "He is a god who loves His people. He dwells beyond the rainbow. He has made all things, from ant to tiger. I am not He, but I am His follower. He has given me power to bless, to heal the sick, and to teach you His ways. I desire to dwell with you and teach you about Him." He sank back to the rug.

His message was received by murmers from around the room. After a long silence the chieftain again spoke. "Tomorrow we will test your power against our priests. Your god of wind and water will have his chance against the god of the tiger." He turned to the lesser chiefs. "Have your people bring the sick and the lame. We will give this god a chance to show his power." He motioned to a black-robed priest who sat in a dark corner of the council hut. As the priest of the tiger rose the chief said, "Prepare a sacrifice for tomorrow."

Nodding his approval the priest swirled his robe around him, gave Moroni a look of intense hatred, and stalked from the room. The chief clapped his hands, ending the meeting.

Moroni was led to a white-washed hut and shown a clean straw bed upon which he was to sleep. He noticed that even though he had not been mistreated in any way, a warror guarded the single door of his dwelling.

When he was sure the guard was asleep he knelt upon the straw and poured out his heart to the Lord. Father, here is the work for which thou hast prepared me. I thank Thee for leading me to these people. I praise Thee for the opportunity of teaching Thy word. Bless me with the power to bless this people.

Throughout the night he continued to pray. His knees tingled and became stiff, but he continued. He fought off the weariness of his long journey as he talked with the Lord. As the room began to lighten in the early dawning of the morning, Moroni felt an overwhelming peace enter his heart. His body radiated a new power. His prayers were answered once again. He whispered, Thank you, Lord, and then lay down for a few minutes of peaceful slumber before his day's ordeal.

The guard brought warm chocolate, sweetened with honey, and fresh fruit. Moroni left it on the floor, preferring to use the power of fasting to aid him this day. He was now a man sure of himself. He knew that the Lord was on his side. With the Lord as his partner, he knew he could overcome any problems or obstacles.

Along the highway, that morning, came Moroni. He was flanked on both sides by chiefs who had sat with him in the council hut the night before. The sides of the highway were thronged with people, chattering and pointing at him. Mothers and fathers held up their little ones to see this pale one. Moroni glanced about, noting that the lame and the ill were in abundance in the crowd.

He looked with compassion upon the noisy people but his escorts permitted no opportunity for him to slow down or to mingle with them. They set a fast pace for him as they strode past small houses towards the great temple.

When they reached the temple pyramid Moroni glanced up, a look of fierce determination on his face. He pushed his way through his escorts and quietly started up the dreaded stairway. About halfway up he realized what poor shape he was in. His breath was rasping in his lungs, his legs hurt, he even felt a little light-headed. He shook his head to clear it and continued climbing. As he approached the temple at the top of the pyramid, he was met by the blood-smeared and black-robed Priest of the Tiger.

"No mere man dares climb these steps of the Blood God. Come you as a god?" he loudly intoned.

"I come to you in the name of my Father—the one and only God of mankind. I am here to tell you to stop these sacrifices."

"Then you must come as a god. Therefore, we welcome you as one. We bring unto you now a sacrifice to show you our respect."

Moroni knew, through the power of inspiration, that the priests had met earlier to decide their strategy. He knew their very words: "We will offer him a captive. If he takes the sacrifice then he is silenced, for he goes against his own teachings. If he does not, we will declare him but a man and will kill him, offering his heart to the blood god."

Now the high priest's spoken words were a signal for the priests to drag a bound captive forward, bidding him kneel before the bloodstained rock image of a great tiger. Before the priest could raise his long-bladed obsidian knife to strike the sacrificial victim, Moroni leaped forward, freeing the captive. "Arise, friend! You are free!"

There was a gasp from the assembled villagers. They seemed to be horrified at the daring of the pale one. The intended victim cowered where he was. The high priest, red-faced and angry, stepped forward.

"You are not a god!" he screamed. "You are only a man." He raised the knife to strike Moroni. "Die as men die—for the tiger." [13]

Though much older than the priest, Moroni had the agility earned from many years of warrior training. He grabbed the priest's arm, wrested the knife from his hand, and turned to the people.

"My friends," he shouted, "I bring you a message from the God of wind and water. He is the God who created this earth. He is the God who has created each of us." He turned to the stone image of the tiger where the prisoner was still quaking. "Think you that there is power in this rock? It has only the power that *you* give it." He took the long knife he was holding— the knife of sacrificing—and smashed it upon the face of the idol. The priest stepped back. Arm across his eyes, he stopped in an attitude of terror.

Leaning down Moroni grasped the young man's arm and helped him to his feet. They walked down the pyramid and onto the street where the prisoner scampered off through the crowd—obviously grateful to be alive. Moroni made his way through the crowd to a platform across the street from the temple pyramid. He sat upon the platform and motioned the people to bring their sick and infirm.

One by one he blessed them. Withered arms became whole. Blind eyes saw. Useless limbs gained new strength. All was done in the name of the Savior and through the power of the priesthood. Moroni didn't even take time to eat. All day the stream of humanity pressed upon him. By nightfall he was physically drained—but exultant. "Thank you, Father, for letting me use Thy power. No longer will the evil priests have power over this people."

Moroni's prayer of thanksgiving was on his lips all evening. He ate with the members of the chieftain's family then sat, afterward, in a hot steam bath relaxing his tired muscles before making his way to his straw pallet. Sleep came quickly.

For several months Moroni continued to bless the people of the village. He taught them of baptism and then spent time baptizing those who were ready in the nearby stream. He was pleased at the teachability of these gentle people. Now he realized what the Savior had meant when he said: *"Moroni, there is much yet for you to do on the earth."* His tired body was no longer tired. He set new goals, one of which was to visit and teach many more peoples, sharing with all the message of salvation.

The children of the village often gathered around his feet to be taught. They were so lovely, so pure. He would hold them and teach them of Him who had loved all people—but especially little children. Loving them and teaching them was a choice experience. It brought back memories of his own children, especially of Bilnor and Greta whom he had lost while they were still in their youth.

Pulling from his satchel the tattered bark paper of his father's letters, Moroni read once again the words his father had written to him concerning little children: *"And their little children need no repentance, neither baptism. Behold, baptism is unto repentance to the fulfilling the commandments unto the remission of sins. But little children are alive in Christ, even from the foundation of the world; . . ."* [14]

Moroni's eyes became misty as he once again read the words of Mormon: *"Farewell, my son, until I shall write unto you, or shall meet you again."* [15] He put the letter down, sitting in deep thought.

After months of teaching and baptizing, Moroni decided it was time to continue his journey. He wondered how many more little villages and towns he would be able to visit. The people here could now take care of themselves. He had ordained twelve to be a council to administer the affairs of the Church.

He bade a tearful goodbye to these people whom he had grown to love, and again headed north. In each village he came to the people welcomed him with open arms. Word of his coming always preceded him. The people called him the Pale One. To them he was a god. He taught them in their own language, healed the sick, raised the dead, and worked many miracles among the people. Moroni considered his labor to be truly a labor of love.

A voice within him kept urging him to travel to the Land Northward. Leaving one village, he was told of traders who traveled across the great sea to the Land Northward. He determined to join them on their voyage. He was directed to a large river and prompted to follow it to the sea.

He set a leisurely pace, enjoying his travel on the river. Every bend opened a new panorama of beauty and contrasts—banks choked with water lilies and hyacinths, green ruffled leaves hanging in bunches almost to the water, and then a bend of clear, sparkling, open water flowing to the sea. Grass spikes grew out of the water, looking like clumps of turnips bobbing in the river. Lianas hung from the trees overhead, reminding Moroni of the long strands of rope he had seen the craftsmen weave in the market-places of Desolation.

Often the river became a virtual tunnel as trees on both sides joined their branches together in a mighty curved arch overhead. Always there was the incessant buzzing of insects and the putrid smell of decaying matter; but there was also the lilting cries of colorful birds and the refreshing smell of new life after each rain storm. As he drew nearer to the sea the river became wider and more sluggish. The water seemed to hardly flow at all.

Stopping to breathe in his surroundings, Moroni sat down with his back against a tree and looked upward. The tall trees rose to great heights with ferns filling in the niches between them—like pillars and fans with hanging flowers. The sky was visible in places, letting in vertical shafts of white light. Gnats and flies spiraled in the column of light and speckled it with their tiny bodies. The jungle was noisy with the cries of birds, but it was motionless. There was not even a slight breeze to stir the tender leaves of the giant ferns. The forest seemed patient and protective of Moroni, enclosing and embracing him.

After spiritually and emotionally replenishing himself in the forest, Moroni moved on. Once again he arrived at the seashore. As he broke from the protective cover of the trees, he stopped in astonishment. Near him on the shore were four hollow-log boats. Surrounding the boats were several score of handsome Lamanites dressed in linen robes, with gold amulets and bracelets.

The group spotted Moroni at the same time he saw them. The leader of the group stepped toward him, his hand raised in a gesture of friendship.

"Ho, Pale One," he said, "we have heard of your power to calm the waters and heal the sick. We are humble traders on a journey to the Land Northward. We would be honored if you would join us."

Once again Moroni saw the hand of the Lord guiding him. He returned the salute, raising his hand in greeting. "I am pleased to be asked." Here was the opportunity Moroni needed. Now he would be able to travel to the Land Northward and see what mission the Lord had for him there.

It surprised him that these people knew of his missionary work. Several of them had been baptized, and they seemed to be excited about seeing the Pale One in person. The traders told Moroni that they had stopped in this little cove to obtain fresh water before traveling across the East Sea. He had barely caught them.

They told him of the journeys they had made to the Land Northward, of the great cities and villages they had seen, of the mighty rivers and great forests. Moroni was enthralled. Again he knew in his heart that the Lord was guiding him on to fields where he could harvest many souls.

Chapter 11

The Land Northward

After a pleasant supper, much talk, and a refreshing night's sleep on the beach—lulled by waves breaking gently on the sand—the trading party was ready to go. Moroni was directed to the lead canoe where Kanuik, the chief trader, was seated.

Moroni thought how different this sea journey was than when he had accompanied Mormon so many years before. On this journey, the traders did not stay near the beach but headed straight into the surf. Moroni was concerned at how the canoes dipped down into the troughs and were hurled to the crest of the next wave. But after watching the skillfulness of the oarsmen, he relaxed and enjoyed the serenity of the sea. The canoes passed a few small islands, overgrown with vegetation, which came right down to the water. He saw giant turtles swimming near them with just their beaked heads sticking out of the water. Several times sharks swam near them, their fins sticking out of the water, following the flimsy dugouts.

At night, the men took turns sleeping with enough oarsmen awake to keep the forward momentum. The night was actually better for travel because they avoided the burning orb of the sun and the canoes kept a straighter course with the stars to give guidance. Moroni dozed, his arms folded on his knees, his head cradled in his arms.

The rising of the sun was beautiful, glistening and glimmering on the sea, making each droplet of water a precious jewel. By mid-morning the heat was devastating. There was no shade and the sea reflected the sun, doubling its penetration through the skin and eyes of the half-naked men. Moroni glanced at the sky hoping for clouds to provide relief. Huge banks of clouds lay to the south but it seemed that they were too far away to do the trading party much good. By afternoon, the clouds seemed much closer and Moroni noticed the worried glances of the oarsmen.

The gale blew up quickly. One minute the clouds seemed far away on the horizon. The next they had obliterated the sun and a strong wind pushed the traders to the north of their course. Rain came in torrents providing some relief from the sun, but causing a greater anxiety as the canoes seemed in danger of swamping. The sea grew mountainous with huge waves looming over them and breaking over the bows of the puny craft. They were flung high on the crest of a wave followed by a sickening plunge as they fell to the bottom of a trough. Everyone, including Moroni, wielded his paddles, rowing and braking, rowing and braking, rowing and braking. Moroni's arms felt like lead weights.

The obviously frightened Kanuik sat in the stern of the dugout, his hands gripping the rough sides. His eyes were large, his body trembling. Moroni remembered the teachings of his father: "When you fear something, you become less effective. You are unable to handle emergencies when they arise. Overcome fear by seeing yourself succeeding. The best way to overcome fear is by doing the thing you fear." Moroni looked again at the frightened Kanuik.

Then he did a daring thing! He stood up in the wildly tossing boat. The others looked at him with great surprise. Bracing himself as best he could, his legs bowed and far apart, he raised his face to the heavens. Arms outstretched, he commanded the storm to cease, the wind to stop, the sea to be calm once again. Within moments his plea was dramatically answered. Miraculously, the clouds faded, revealing the sun as a purple hoop in the gray sea haze. The wild, unruly wind became a gentle breeze. The tumultous waves of a few moments before became once again the gentle swells, capped occasionally with breaking whitecaps.

The oarsmen looked in amazement at Moroni. He slowly sank down in the canoe feeling drained of energy, but elated. How close he felt to the Lord. How appreciative he was of the Lord's power which was once again manifest through him. He closed his eyes, offering a prayer of thanksgiving.

Land was sighted to their north. The trading party, needing a respite from the sea, turned towards it. They beached their awkward craft on the shore—a shore cleft with bays and harbors and bayous. Moroni stepped to the shore and stretched to his full height, working out the kinks of sitting in a canoe for several days. The men, under Kanuik's direction, unloaded the precious cargo so it could dry out.

Moroni noticed with amusement how the oarsmen avoided him. They seemed to view him as a god fearful of close contact. He was somewhat embarrassed by their esteem of him but he could not convince them that he was merely a man such as they—but a man with the priesthood of the true God!

With a good night's sleep behind them and their water jugs full, the trading party was once again on its way. This time, instead of moving straight towards their destination, they stayed close to the shore, putting ashore each night for sleep and meals. After six more days of journeying, Moroni noticed a change in the color of the water. No longer was it blue or emerald green. The water was muddy—filled with mud and silt. They were at the mouth of a huge river. Rowing became more difficult as they faced into the sluggish current.

For hours they paddled, but the banks of the river seemed just as far apart. Moroni was astonished at the size of this river. It was the biggest river he had ever seen.

News of the trading party and its miracle-working passenger had once again preceded them. Signals were flashed with obsidian mirrors. Smoke puffs could be seen from afar signalling their passage. There was a great stir amongst the villagers. The "Pale One" was coming.

The destination of the traders was the Capitol City of the Puant nation. The city lay at the confluence of two mighty rivers. As they approached the city, Kanuik and his men donned feather headdresses and shirts of colored cotton embroidered with gold. Moroni thought that they were very impressive. He wore his white robe and rope sandals.

Moroni had never seen such a city or had such a welcome. He had witnessed the grandeur of Tula, the temple city. But this! The shining Capitol City was huge. Its boulevards radiated outward like the spokes of a giant wheel. The civic buildings stood on mounded crests. They were built of great logs and painted with beautiful designs. On the sides of the crests, and surrounding the buildings, were virtual carpets of flowering strawberries, mosaiced and bordered with garlands of flowers.

The streets leading from the river were lined with the city's inhabitants. They were curious to see this fabled "Pale One." As he and the trading party made their way to the council house in the center of the city, their way was paved with flowers thrown by the people. In the council house they met with the city elders. From them Moroni learned of the history of this great city.

They spoke of the great migration from the land of their fathers which had occurred about four hundred and fifty years before. Moroni recalled that the plates spoke of the departure of five thousand and four hundred men, with their wives and children, who had departed from the land of Zarahemla soon after the death of Helaman. The Elders of the Puant nation told Moroni of their teachings that a "Pale God" would come. They asked, "Are you He of whom it is spoken?"

Again, Moroni taught the people concerning his mission as a messenger for the Savior. They were humble and teachable. He lived for several years in the Capitol City, watching many trading parties come and go. The Capitol City was the trading capital of the Land Northward, trading hides, baskets, beadwork, and ore for the pottery, jewelry, obsidian, and weapons from the lands to the south. As the people became more faithful in their worship of Jesus Christ, Moroni appointed elders to teach so that he could continue his journeys.

Using the city as his headquarters, he taught the people for many miles around. He would be gone for weeks at a time, returning to refresh himself, to see how the Church was doing, and then he would return to the field.

Hearing of the five warring tribes of the Seneca near the East Sea, Moroni joined a trading party which was going that direction. They floated down the river for two days, steering their bark canoes into the fastest current. On the evening of the second day, they pulled their canoes to the left bank, camping where a large river flowed into the father of waters. This river would provide them with a water highway to the lands of the east.

Leaving the traders at the headwaters of the river, Moroni hiked alone over the mountains. The verdant lush forests always gave him a sense of peace. As he topped a mountain pass, he was awed by the tremendous majesty of this unmarred forest. The treetops continued as far as he could see, clear to the horizon.

He was greeted in the Seneca villages by the chieftains who made him feel very welcome. They had heard of his great powers and were expecting him. He spoke in their tongue, telling them of the One God. He talked to them of peace, asking them why they were continually fighting. They could think of no valid reason. Preaching, teaching, negotiating, he helped the five chieftains to form an alliance—an alliance of tribes which Moroni fervently prayed would last for centuries.

After forming the alliance, Moroni spent his time visiting the various villages teaching his message of peace. On one particular morning, he had been teaching in a small village near the foot of a large dome-shaped hill. Always in tune with the Spirit, he felt an urge to leave the village and climb the hill. Near the top, surrounded by the tall, stately trees of the forest, he knelt in the soft, lush grass. He had been praying for but a few moments when he was caught up in the spirit. Instead of the small villages of the Lamanites which presently surrounded the hillside, he saw villages and large cities built of stone and plaster. White people like himself, dressed in strange clothing, were everywhere. The vision faded and a quiet voice permeated his consciousness: *"Moroni, behold, I am Jesus Christ. You have done well, my faithful servant. Yet, there is still much to do. Look."* Again the vision opened before him. He beheld a youth, tousel-haired, climbing the hillside. The youth seemed to know right where to go. Stopping before what looked like a large stone, he took a branch and pried away the top. It was a stone box, inside of which Moroni could see the gold plates that Mormon had worked on so diligently to abridge. He involuntarily took a sharp breath. It was he, Moroni, handing the plates to the youth! The vision faded. Again came the voice of the Lord:

"Your mission will continue among the Lamanite people. However, the most important part of your mission is yet to come. Your life will be preserved until you are able to bring the plates to this hillside where you will deposit them. Then you may return to Me and your family." The voice was silent. Moroni returned to full consciousness of his surroundings. He felt weak and spent.

Excitement welled up within him. Tears streamed down his cheeks. His mission was to continue. The Lord still had plans for him. He stayed for a time where he was, on the hill which he, somehow, knew now would someday also be called Cumorah. He needed time to think, to ponder. Besides, it was hard to leave this spot which had now become sacred to him.

Ten years had passed since the bloody last battle of the Nephite people. It was eight years since Mormon's death. Most of those eight years Moroni had spent in teaching the Lamanite people of the Savior and His mission. He was now ready to return to the Cumorah of the South.

Chapter 12

Return To Cumorah

Kilihu had listened without comment as Moroni described his missionary journeys among the people of the Land Northward, ending on Cumorah. Now he interrupted, "I do not understand the importance of the plates."

Moroni looked into the embers of the dying fire. He poked the coals with a stick, sending spires of twinkling sparks into the black sky. "The plates give a history of your people. Someday a person will be given the plates and will write that history so your people will know their heritage. It is very important that I succeed with this mission."

Kilihu smiled, pleased that the Lord cared about the Lamanites. "That is good. Now perhaps you will tell me the story of the rest of your journey until you met me in th desert."

Moroni watched the sparks rising into the heavens, and began.

* * *

It had been a miserable winter. Moroni was cold all of the time. He had aches and pains he had never known before. He grumbled to himself that his body was just getting old. After all, he had lived through fifty-eight winters.

He had left the Cumorah of the north, traveling westward under the great lakes, heading back to the Capitol City. It had been impossible to move very quickly. Each village he came to was a teaching opportunity and he couldn't pass through without telling the people of the Savior. No village was too small to feel of his influence. He was now back in the lodge which was provided for him in the Capitol City.

The hills surrounding the lodges of the city rose up like mounded graves, crusted with snow and silent as death. The nearby river tossed and heaved its jagged ice throes in every direction until it looked like a set of sharks teeth, jagged and broken. Snow blew in the faces of the people, the pathways between the lodges were tramped hard and slick forcing Moroni to a slowness of pace he was not used to. Smoke rose from the smoke holes in the lodges, spiraling to the sky.

Inside the lodges people huddled close to the fires, pulling from them every particle of heat. The wintery winds, malevolent at times, seemed to descend upon the city in god-like wrath. Even the brave warriors stayed inside, leaving their lodges only for things of necessity. Moroni used the winter months to speak often to the people, strengthening their faith, encouraging their belief.

Moroni was glad when an early spring came to banish the snows and dreariness of winter. Never had the season seemed to last so long. The warm sun made the once barren trees bring forth new leaves, the verdant grass adding vivid beauty to the plains and forests. Strawberry vines, long dormant through the winter, turned their leaves of red and green toward the sun, sending out new tendrils to find a blank spot of earth. The ice in the river started breaking up to begin its long journey to the sea.

Moroni stood outside his lodge, running his hand gently along the branch of a tender sapling. He felt the nodules of the new buds and thought of life. Spring was so like the resurrection when that which appeared dead received new life. He thought of his family, all in the spirit world awaiting the resurrection.

His thoughts were interrupted by the honking of geese. He looked up, seeing the long vee-shaped flocks flying northward. He, too, needed to be moving on. A trading party was heading west toward the mountains. He had a feeling that he should accompany them so he invited himself along. They said they were delighted to have him.

They traveled westward up the river. The great plains were verdant now under the blue sky and warm sun. The wide-flung panorama of lush grass and leafy trees stretched out as far as the eye could see. Game was abundant; buffalo, deer, wild turkeys, and bustling flocks of sharp-tailed grouse. Four days of travel brought them to a fork in the river. They made their camp on a high bluff on the right side of the river.

The next morning as they prepared to leave, a strange feeling came over Moroni. The spirit whispered to him: *"Stay."* As he rolled his blanket, again came the message: *"Stay."* He looked around. There were no Lamanite villages near here. What purpose would there be in staying? Again the voice came to him: *"Stay."* He could no longer ignore it.

Striding to where the leader was squatting by the campfire, Moroni said, "I will stay here. You will have to go on without me." The men argued with him, but Moroni was adamant. Finally they bid him goodbye and left.

Moroni added a few sticks to the almost-dead fire. In a few minutes it was again blazing brightly, giving almost as much companionship as it did heat. He was puzzled. He had received the word to stay here but he didn't know what for. He had learned long before to obey the promptings of the Spirit so all day he stayed there on the bluff, praying and waiting for instructions. Night came, and still no message.

Morning found him more weary than when he had retired to his bed the night before. He wondered if he would have to walk back to the Capitol City. He started having doubts that he had really heard the voice saying to stay. He didn't relish the thought. He smiled at his wonderings. Why am I concerned? The Lord will provide, he thought.

Maintaining his lonely vigil by the small campfire, Moroni waited. He had confidence that the Lord would tell him what he was to do. He watched a herd of buffalo cavorting on the west bank of the river. He listened to the birds sing, enjoying their melodious song. Prairie dogs stuck their heads from their holes and, like little frozen statues, watched him. He made himself as still as they, hoping to entice them from their burrows. They were too cautious. There was still a chill in the air, especially in the evening and early morning, so he spent much time gathering wood.

Returning from such a wood-gathering expedition on the third day, Moroni started. He was no longer alone. Warming their hands at his fire were three men, dressed as he was, in long white robes. Recognizing them instantly, Moroni dropped his sticks and ran to them. Tears streamed down his cheeks as once again he embraced each of the Three Nephite Disciples. It had been many years since they had last visited him.

One of the Nephites spoke. "Moroni, you are standing on sacred ground. The Lord has directed you to this place for a purpose. It is here where the New Jerusalem will be built. Here will be the new temple, the House of the Lord. Here the Lord will direct the affairs of His Church following His second coming."

Moroni fell to his knees in wonderment. "Here? The New Jerusalem?" He picked up a handful of the dark soil in his large, calloused hands, squeezing it and pressing his hands to his forehead. "What am I to do?"

"It is your responsibility to dedicate this site as the gathering place, and to dedicate the spot where the temple will be built."

The leader of the Three said, "Come, we have much to do."

The next few days were enchanting to Moroni. To have the company of the Three Disciples, to be on the site of the New Jerusalem, to have had the opportunity of dedicating the site for the millenial temple! Moroni was so excited. More excitement was to come. The Three Disciples led Moroni northeast of the river to a beautiful glen surrounded by forest. Several deer grazed in the meadow, the sky was opague blue overhead, and Moroni heard the meadowlarks singing. It was a perfect day.

When the Three stopped in the meadow near a pile of scattered stones, Moroni looked at them inquisitively. The leader turned to Moroni. "This is Adam-ondi-Ahman," he said in a reverent voice. "Here it was that Adam, the father of the race, worshipped."

One of the others added, "These rocks are the remains of the altar where Adam called upon the Lord three years prior to his death when he gathered his posterity into this valley to give them his last blessing.''

Moroni picked up a chip from one of the stones, carefully placing it in his leather pouch. What a feeling it gave him to stand where Adam had stood and worshipped. He knelt down, the Three kneeling with him, praying in silence.

That night they made camp on the edge of the meadow. They visited long into the night. Moroni felt blessed to hear the marvelous stories of their missionary travels. Each of the Three bore his testimony of the divinity of the Savior. It was a humbling and spiritual experience.

Even after retiring for the night Moroni had difficulty sleeping. He lay on his back, looking at the magnificence of the heavens, carefully reviewing what the Disciples had taught him. Dawn found him still meditating on what had transpired. He rolled over to see if his three companions were awake. They were gone! Moroni was once again alone. No, he thought. That's not true. I am never alone. No one is alone who has the Spirit of the Lord as a companion.

Before heading back to the river, Moroni built a tower on a hill overlooking the meadow. It was a symbol to him of what had transpired here— a monument he dedicated to Adam, the father of the race.

He returned to the river, found a canoe hid in the bushes along the bank, and floated back downstream. He said his last goodbyes in the Capitol City and headed north. His first stop was at the city called Sacred, located in the center of the cross of waters from whence rivers ran to the four oceans. A light fog rested over the mighty river, giving an ethereal quality to his coming. The morning sun, shining on his greying hair, seemed to form a halo around his head. Word of his coming preceded him and rows of worshippers lined the streets. After teaching the people he again headed to the northwest.[16]

Through the summer Moroni traveled across the great plains. The wide-flung panorama of lush grass and green hills stretched endlessly ahead. He traveled from the villages of the tribes with their circular, dome-shaped houses with turf roofs to the villages of the tribe with their buffalo-skin teepees.

Moroni taught the people, staying a few weeks to a few months, then moved on to find more people to teach. He crossed a large range of mountains, walking through forests of pine and fir, finally coming to a broad river flowing to the west sea. After teaching the people in villages by the river, he rode with some fishermen to the sea. A large village nestled on a beautiful harbor. He stayed in the village for a long time, teaching the Yakima people.

As much as he enjoyed teaching, Moroni knew he must soon be returning for the plates. Finally, the whispering of the Spirit came to him: *"Turn south, it is time."*

Moroni said his goodbyes to the Yakima people and traveled southeast over the mountains. As he topped a ridge east of the valley, he stopped to catch his breath. Turning back the way he had come he observed a glorious sunset glowing above the trees of the mountain on which he was standing. He took a quick breath of pleasure. Never had he seen such a sunset, so full of golden light and subtle hues. The boughs of the trees picked up the brilliance from the sky and seemed to have a radiance of their own. The lake and harbor near the Yakima village was a mirror of light reflecting each tone and shade of the colorful sky. He felt a gentleness and majesty as he looked. It was as if a heavenly voice had bestowed a soft prayer over all the world. The tired face of Moroni softened, became almost childlike.

After leaving the mountains Moroni traveled through arid, desert valleys, skirting mounds of black volcanic rock, until finally he came to the shores of a huge, salty sea. He thought he was back to the ocean, and he skirted the water to the left. Something drew him to a small stream on the north end of a large valley and there he prepared to camp for the night. An early spring had banished the snows and the warm sun made the once barren trees bring forth new leaves. Along the stream banks the grass was high, adding vivid beauty to the scene.

Moroni knelt in prayer before lying down on his blanket. As he prayed once again a mighty vision spread out before him. The empty valley was now filled with buildings of many sizes. Directly in front of him rose a stately, multi-spired building in a park-like setting. Moroni didn't know what to make of it. Then a voice spoke to him: *"This is My holy house. Dedicate this spot for My people to build a temple unto me."* The vision left him and he was once more alone with his thoughts. It had happened so fast, he wasn't sure he had heard right.

Early the next morning, after a quick wash in the icy stream, Moroni walked to where he had perceived the temple to be. He planted his staff in the ground and dropped to his knees. For several moments he knelt there, searching for words. Then the words came: *"In the name of Jesus Christ, and by my holy calling as one of His disciples, I dedicate this spot of ground as the place where the House of the Lord will be built in the last days. . . ."* Adding other significant blessings, he ended his prayer. Kneeling there, Moroni once again beheld in vision the beautiful edifice that would be reared.

Two days journey south found him at the shore of a large freshwater lake. It was a delightful setting with the lake surrounded on three sides by mighty, snow-capped peaks. A rushing stream cascaded into the lake, adding its melodic music to the evening. Moroni rested by the lake the next day, taking the opportunity to bathe and to wash his white toga in the clear, fresh water. It was such a place of beauty that he hated to leave but the next morning he set out again.

He had hiked toward the south for almost half a day when the voice came to him: *"Turn east, through the canyon."* He looked at the easy valley lying to the south and at the rugged-looking canyon to the east. He took a few more steps to the south and again the impression came: *"Go east through the canyon."*

He turned east. He camped that night alongside a mountain stream with the canyon rising steeply above him on both sides. In the morning he came to a fork with one branch heading uphill to the left and the other ambling down a broader valley to the right. The impression was there: *"Go right."* He hiked down the canyon between red juniper-covered hills until it opened into a wide, lush green valley. The valley ran almost due north and south between high mountains.

After a good night's sleep in a grassy meadow, Moroni washed up in a stream, gathered up his supplies and started south through the valley. The grass was to his knees and wildlife of all kinds was plentiful. By midafternoon the warm sun had drained him of energy. He had been following a narrow winding stream and, on an impulse, he stripped down and jumped in. The cold water shocked his body, taking his breath away, but, oh, it felt good. After splashing around and rinsing the sand and dirt from his body, he clambered up on the bank, slipped on his loincloth, and lay there in the grass, enjoying the warmth of the sun on his body.

He shut his eyes, listening to the hum of insects around him, and was soon asleep. Startled, he came awake. Who had spoken to him? He looked around. He listened and the voice came again: *"Moroni, look!"* He looked around once more. There was still no one or anything of note near him. *"On the hill."* He raised his eyes. On a rolling hill near the southeast end of the valley stood a great building. It was pinkish-yellow in color with domes and spires on each end. It was surrounded by green carpeted areas and beautiful flowers. Stately trees framed it against the mountain backdrop. The voice came again: *"This will be another of My temples. In this hallowed building thousands of faithful people will serve Me. My son, dedicate this site for building My holy house."*

Moroni slipped on his robe, picked up his pouch and turned again to the hill. It was now bare. Where the temple had stood was a small, sagebrush-covered hillside with rocky cliffs on the north side. Walking quickly, he headed for the hill. The valley was longer than he thought and he didn't arrive at the hill until the sun was sinking over the west mountains.

There was no stream near the hill so Moroni made a dry camp right on top. He was so thankful that the Lord was using him to fulfill His purposes. This was the third temple site to be dedicated by him. Moroni pondered the significance of it. When would all of this come to pass? When would these beautiful buildings which he had seen in vision actually be built? He knew it would be after the Lord restored His church to the earth, but he did wonder how significant would be the role he would play in that restoration.

Morning came late this close to the mountains. By the time the sun's rays hit him, he had cleaned up his camp, had gone to a nearby stream for a morning bath, and was back on the hillside. Again Moroni knelt, staff in hand, and offered a dedicatory prayer—praying that this site would be a haven for the oppressed, a spiritual retreat, a place of repose.[17]

He stayed in the valley where he had dedicated the temple site for a week picking berries and currants, fishing in the streams, and just enjoying the beauty of the spot. Now he had to quickly move south. The leaves were starting to turn and a chill was again in the air. Each morning frost covered his blankets, laying a silvery mantle over the valley. The trees high up on the mountainsides took on varied shades of red, gold, orange and yellow. Winter was definitely on its way. Moroni longed for the mild climate of the tropics.

He traveled south through the broad valley, passing springs and small streams which just disappeared into the ground. Soon he came to a winding river which snaked its way to the west. It was the crookedest river he had ever seen, twisting and turning and almost meeting itself before turning again. For five days he followed the course of the river, ever heading southward.

As he approached its headwaters, the river became smaller and smaller. It had its origins in a long, gently-rising valley which finally topped out among long-leafed pine trees. Moroni crossed the saddle, leaving the river drainage of the winding river and immediately entering another drainage. It was interesting to him to have passed the beginnings of two rivers—one flowing north and one south.

He now followed the south river as it began its growth on the long journey to the sea. Moroni drew an analogy between the small beginnings of a river and the beginnings of his missionary work. Who knew the end results—how much the gospel would grow and spread because of his efforts?

This river was much different from the winding river to the north. The land, sloping down swiftly, caused the river to fall through rapids and waterfalls. As it reached a flat valley, the river turned sharply to the west. Another crossroads. Should he follow the river or cut overland? Seeking the Spirit, Moroni had an urging to follow the river. Several times in the next few days he almost wished he hadn't followed that urging.

Cutting through cliffs of pink and white, the river soon raged through huge boulders in a narrow defile. The walls were so high they shut out the sunlight, keeping the canyon perpetually dim. The river plunged and roared, drowning out all other sounds. There was only one path to follow—down the river. The water was from wall to wall. Tree roots and branches, deposited in cracks high in the walls, were mute evidence of what happened during floods. Moroni shuddered. He would not want to be here when that happened.

That night he slept as best he could on top of a boulder with the river lapping around his legs. The next morning he was stuck! The river flowed over a wild waterfall, plunging a hundred feet to the canyon floor below.

Moroni had several choices. He could retrace his steps, working upstream through the fast-flowing river, or he could find a way around the falls. The canyon walls were not so steep here, with rock slides and huge boulders lining the sides. He had no desire to retrace his steps so he carefully left the water, eased himself onto a large boulder, and surveyed the area with care. The scene before him was breathtakingly beautiful even though it hindered his travel. A heavy mist rose from the waterfall with a rainbow extending from one red and black canyon wall to the other. Overhead, the sky was a deep blue.

He found where high waters had etched a small ledge around the canyon wall. He said a silent prayer and started out. By standing and easing his feet carefully a step at a time, he was able to creep along the wall. He had no desire to look down but concentrated on each handhold and each place to put his sandals. Pulling and straining, he worked his way around the falls. Here the canyon opened up, revealing a tree-lined defile. He slid down a rock-strewn dirt slope, finding himself at the base of the falls. It had been perilous but now he was through it.

That night he camped in a grove of trees. The roar of the nearby falls gave him a sense of accomplishment—quite a contrast from his feelings of anxiety when he had listened to the roar from above. Like other aspects of life, he reasoned, once an obstacle is conquered it pales quickly into insignificance.

The rest of the journey down the river was pleasant. Moroni walked on gravel bars. Wild grapes and watercress were abundant. The high cliffs, in their shades of white and vermillion, were beautiful. Trees grew right out of the rock cliffs. Natural arches were forming along several canyon walls. By afternoon the river was joined by another flowing through giant rock walls from the north. He wished he had time to stay in the area long enough to explore the canyons but again felt the urgency to keep moving.

On the third day after Moroni left the falls, the river flowed into a large sagebrush valley protected on the east and west by large, black mesas. The valley ended on the north against a red hill.

Moroni set up camp along a small stream which flowed into the river. The water was bitter to the taste, discouraging any drinking. Searching for better water, he finally located a small spring on a rise of ground about half-way between the river and the red hill.

Again he set up camp. The valley was warm, the air pleasant, and Moroni was very weary. He sat with his back against a large clump of black willows. Over the red hill and far to the north a large, blue mountain rose majestically into the sky. Puffs of white clouds hovered among its rocky peaks.

What an artist the Lord is, Moroni thought, to have created such beauty. Everything seemed to be in balance—the black of the mesas, the red hills, the bluish-purple mountain, white clouds, and a light blue sky. The view to the south was a sharp contrast. The river meandered through the bottom of the valley hemmed in by thick brush and willows. Behind the river, a series of bare brown hills rolled to the horizon.

As he sat there, a still small voice pierced his consciousness. *"Moroni, you are a faithful servant. You have done well."* He stood, listening intently. *"You are on hallowed ground. Where you are standing another of My holy houses shall be built. This valley, from hill to hill, shall be a gathering place and a place of refuge for my people. Dedicate this spot for Me."* By the time the message ended Moroni was kneeling, head bowed on the reddish-brown dirt.

The Lord had guided his every step. He had wanted him here, in this very place. Moroni had supposed that he had walked the river and traversed the falls alone, but now he knew that was not so. The Lord had been with him all the way. He had brought him here to dedicate another temple site. So be it. Without rising he faced to the north, again gazing at the beautiful scene before him. He bowed his head, offering another prayer of dedication, prophesying that the temple built upon this spot would be the means of saving many souls. He was inspired by the Spirit to prophesy many things concerning this holy temple.

The sun had long since set behind the black mesa to the west when he finally rose to his feet. He completed preparations for his camp. Moving into a small gully to the east of the site he had dedicated, he ate his meager supper and soon was asleep.

Keeping the red cliffs to his left, the next day Moroni journeyed to the southeast. It was a land of cliffs and crevices. He would climb one hill and then after descending to the bottom start right back up another. He made slow progress, but each night he was able to locate a stream or small spring to replenish his water supply.

For six days he traveled through this veritable wasteland, seeing very little life except for the lizards and ground squirrels. On the seventh day he entered a magnificent forest—huge evergreen trees provided shade for the mottled forest floor. Wildlife abounded here. Moroni was pleased to once again see deer grazing in the meadows. Birds flew through the trees, providing a sweet litany of sound. Squirrels raced up and down the trees in their frenetic search for winter goodies.

Moroni sat on a log to rest, amused by the shrill chatter of a squirrel high overhead whose work he was interrupting. He sat very still. Soon he saw the head of the squirrel playing hide-and-seek with him as it moved up and down the tree. With a quick leap it scampered to a pile of residue honeycombed with holes, dropped in a nut cone, and was back in the safety of the tree in a flash. Moroni smiled, stood, stretched, and continued on his way.

By evening, Moroni stood at the edge of the forest overlooking one of the most awesome sights he had ever seen. A canyon stretched before him so deep he could not see the river he knew was at the bottom. The far bank of the canyon was bathed in soft shadow, giving a purplish depth to it. He camped near the abyss that night. It was cold with a gusty wind blowing from the south. Moroni lit a fire and curled up in his blanket.

The morning light made the canyon even more awesome. Moroni could now see the glint where the sun struck the water far below. Aside from the beauty, the thought struck him, How am I going to cross? He started along the rim to the east, skirting fallen timbers and large cracks which zigzagged back from the canyon rim.

After traveling less than an hour, he found a well-trampled trail which headed into the canyon. After a long and harrowing descent to the bottom, he found a village of Lamanites who called themselves the Havasu. He blessed their babies, healed the sick, and taught them of God.

Moroni did not stay long with the Havasu. He still had a long way to go before reaching Cumorah and the plates would not wait. He climbed out of the canyon still heading to the southeast. It was a wild and untamed land—a land of many contrasts. He trudged through sand dunes, over rocky escarpments, through narrow defiles, along pine-covered hills. It was a land of sagebrush and juniper, of cactus and stunted pine. In this wild and desolate land Moroni found another Lamanite tribe—a wandering tribe which was temporarily settled in the land where he found them.

He taught them of the One God, demonstrating to them the power of the Father, teaching them of love and consideration for each other. At evening, after watching a beautiful sunset, he sat with the people to eat a simple meal of corn cakes and honey. He was still wrapped in awe from his day of exploring the tall pinnacles which seemed to turn in the wind, following his progress as he walked through the valley. Two of the massive silhouettes looked like giant hands standing together, but when he came closer he found that they were an hour's walk apart—lifting their fingers high above the desert floor. The wind, dipping through the rocky defiles, played a lonely flute tune. Now, as the stars stared down at him from the dome of the sky, he sensed again the slow and mighty rhythms of this beautiful land.

* * *

Turning from the fire into which he had been gazing as he unfolded the story, Moroni glanced up at the night sky. "It was a night just like this," he said to Kilihu. "After leaving the land of canyons and rock statues I traveled south. There were many deserts and rocky canyons, many beautiful sunrises and sunsets, many days of struggling across dry wasteland with the hot sun burning down upon me." He paused and smiled at Kilihu. "And then I met you."

The two friends sat in silence, thinking of the friendship and love that had developed since that chance and providential meeting.

Chapter 13

Moroni's Capture

Climbing higher and higher onto the forested mountain slopes, Moroni and Kilihu penetrated deeper into Lamanite country each day. It was important that they get to Cumorah as quickly as possible, retrieve the plates, and journey back to the Land Northward where the people revered Moroni and would give him protection. He knew that many old enemies would delight in capturing or killing him, and he was concerned about traveling during daylight. He felt that if he avoided the populated lowlands he would be safe from those who sought his death.

As they climbed higher, he thought he recognized some landmarks. "Within a month," he told Kilihu, "we will be in the cave on Cumorah." Late one afternoon Moroni paused upon a lofty ridge and surveyed the country around him. "We are almost abreast of Tula, the Temple City," he said. Far below raged a turbulent mountain stream. He shaded his eyes from the glaring sun and followed the course of the stream with his eyes as it meandered towards the southeast. An east wind blew gently up the slope toward them, bringing the muted scents of wet greenery from the valley far below. The river tumbled and roared as it pursued its path over boulders and through rocky defiles on its way to the valley floor.

* * *

Immersed in the beauty of the scene before them, Moroni and Kilihu were unaware of the eyes that watched them from behind the summit of the ridge far above. There were a dozen pair. Their owners were tall, bronzed warriors dressed only in sandals and loincloths. One, who appeared to be the leader although almost as bronzed as the others, was different. His red hair, so tinged with grey that it appeared to be a soft pink, set him apart from the black-haired warriors with him. He was as well-built as the warriors, but one could see that he had weathered many more years. His sun-tanned skin contrasted sharply with the white skin under his loincloth. The most peculiar thing about him was the eagle mask which covered his entire face, giving him a fierce and sinister look. The men, armed with bows and arrows and short heavy spears, watched every move that Moroni and Kilihu made.

Moroni was exhausted. For a week they had scaled cliffs and climbed interminable hills as they made their way slowly toward Cumorah. The previous night his rest had been broken by the calls and wailing crys of several jaguars in the vicinity. Being unable to make a fire for fear of discovery, Moroni had felt the necessity of remaining awake. Now his lack of sleep was catching up with him. He rubbed his eyes, adding more to their soreness.

"I guess I'm getting old," he said to Kilihu. "I have had the privilege of living for sixty-two years. That's an age when many men would be lying around in their homes waiting to die." He smilingly added an afterthought. "Or, are already dead!"

The sun was still more than an hour away from setting when he picked out a place behind brush cover where they could lie down and catch some much-needed sleep. Part of the remaining journey to Cumorah would have to be through the valley at night. He drifted off into a deep, untroubled sleep.

When he awakened it was still daylight. Some noise had penetrated his subconsciousness. He opened his eyes and looked right into a black obsidian spear point. It was held by a silent bronzed warrior. Glancing quickly around he noted that a dozen warriors surrounded him and Kilihu, the points of their spears almost touching them. There was no necessity to speak or move. The warriors could have easily killed them at any time they chose, but apparently desired to take them as prisoners. In those circumstances, Moroni felt it pointless to say anything. He lay there calmly, wondering what would happen next. His eyes lingered on the masked man with the reddish hair, a flicker of recognition struggling in his subconscious. The mask puzzled him, but somewhere in the dim reaches of the past he had seen this man.

His silence and lack of fear surprised his captors. They had expected a show of fear and surprise. There was none. Moroni just lay there and appraised his captors with his calm blue eyes. For many years he had placed his life in the care of the Lord. Why would he be deserted now? Moroni thought. Besides, the Lord had promised him that he would not allow him to be killed until he had transferred the plates to the hill by the Seneca village in the Land Northward.

"Well, Moroni," commented the masked one, licking his lips as if he relished every word, "we finally got you."

The statement startled Moroni. He couldn't believe that anyone would know his name. His gaze didn't waver, however, to betray his surprise.

"Get up," directed Eagle Mask. He motioned to one of the Lamanite warriors who grasped Moroni's arm and pulled him to his feet. Moroni stood there, brushed the sand from his legs, and looked almost indifferently at his captors.

"Search him," snapped Eagle Mask. "See if he is armed." Several warriors stepped forward, stripped his leather pouch from him and roughly pulled his knife from his belt.

Moroni said flatly, "Other than my knife, I am unarmed." His curiosity was aroused by this man who knew his name and who spoke like a Nephite. He asked, "Who are you? And how do you know my name?"

The red-haired warrior reached up with his left hand and lifted the eagle mask. The face that smiled evilly at Moroni was twisted and scarred. One ear was almost gone and the side of his face had been so badly burned that the mouth showed a perpetual lop-sided grimace. One eye was half-shut, with a droopy eyelid.

Words came from that cruelly twisted mouth. "You do not remember me? I am Mishnor who you banished as a youth from your Christian church. For these many years I have desired the blood of the man who shamed me before my friends. When your body was not found on the battlefield I made a vow to search for you until I found you." He turned to his companions. "Tie their hands behind their backs."

Moroni and Kilihu were led, stumbling and falling, across the ridge and down the other side of the divide. It was dark and Moroni saw nothing of the country they were dragged through. His thoughts were of Mishnor. Reaching deeply into his memory he finally remembered.

* * *

There had been dissension in the growing church in the temple city. Many of the members were intimidated by the persecutions which they daily faced. Each day brought some new crisis as Moroni struggled to lead the young church. Persecution and antagonism from outside were bad enough, but the quarrels and petty disagreements among the members of the Church really bothered him. Daily, in his prayers, he asked the Father, How can I help them become strong? How can I teach them to persevere?

In the midst of this deteriorating spirit, with persecution from without and backsliding from within, Moroni had been faced with another challenge. A sixteen-year old boy, red-haired and angry, had been brought to him under charges of fornication. It had required two large men to hold his arms. The youth, Mishnor by name, was accused of taking the daughter of Ammah to a lonely place and there forcing himself upon her.

Moroni looked at the angry young man. "Is this story true?"

Mishnor had angrily replied, "No, it is not true. Pelta, the daughter of Ammah, and I are in love and intend to be married. Ammah does not like me so we were going to run away to be married. He caught us and has accused me of this great sin in order to stop me from marrying Pelta."

Moroni looked quizzically at the two men holding the boy. One of them shrugged his shoulders. The other spoke up. "Ammah would not lie.

His daughter, Pelta, has been violated by this man. He deserves to be punished.''

At that moment, the father of the girl in question strode angrily into the room followed by several of his relatives. Pointing menacingly at the boy, he said, ''I hereby condemn you before God and these elders for that which you have done.'' Much more was said, with angry words and accusations from both sides.

Raising a hand for silence, Moroni had finally stopped the shouting. ''Do you formally charge this youth with a moral sin against your daughter?'' he asked.

''Yes,'' shouted the father.

''Are there any other witnesses?'' Moroni asked.

Three men stepped forward. ''We are witnesses against this youth that he did in fact violate the girl, Pelta.''

There was not much more Moroni could do. The laws of the Church clearly stated that *''whoso was found to commit iniquity, and three witnesses of the Church did condemn them before the elders, and if they repented not, and confessed not, their names were blotted out, and they were not numbered among the people of Christ.''* [18]

Mishnor had been excommunicated from the Church. In a vengeful mood, he had attempted to burn down the synagogue. The pitch which he had been using splashed on his face and he had suffered severe burns.

*   *   *

But that had been almost thirty years ago. Moroni strained to see Mishnor but it was too dark. He sighed. Leading the struggling church had not been an easy task. Many judgments had to be made and perhaps some of them had not been correct. He hoped in his heart that Mishnor had not been wronged.

At length they left the canyon through which they had been descending and came out into open, level country. A dim, flickering light showed far ahead. As they got closer, Moroni saw that it was a hugh bonfire burning at the city's entrance. He realized that once again he was in Tula, the City of Light. Only this time the circumstances were much different.

As they approached the fire, Mishnor yelled. People appeared as if by magic from the houses near the entrance. Moroni was shoved along the street, suffering the abuse of the populace.

''Ho, Nephite,'' some yelled. ''You will soon be a dead man.'' Through a barrage of derogatory comments and ridicule, Mishnor led his prisoners to a large building in the city square.

Moroni was concerned about Kilihu. They had been separated on the mountain and he hadn't seen him since. Inside the building a heavy door was opened and Moroni was pushed to the floor of a dank, smelly room.

Rough hands grabbed him, trussing up his legs, pulling them cruelly backward until they touched his hands, and then tying them tightly together.

Mishnor gazed down at Moroni, an evil smile on his twisted face, then he said acidly between tight lips. "Get a good night's sleep, Christian. You'll need it tomorrow." He and the warriors departed, leaving Moroni to his thoughts.

His nose wrinkled at the overpowering stench of human waste. The air was stale and close. It was totally dark in the windowless room and even though he could not see them, he soon heard and felt the presence of rats as they scurried across the floor. He felt a whiskered nose touch his bare arm and he thrashed around. Finally realizing it was futile to struggle, he resigned himself to whatever would happen to him, knowing that the Lord had promised to protect him.

Lying there, trussed up like a wild pig at a barbecue, he turned once again to prayer. Well, Father, here I am. I don't know what you have in store for me, but whatever it is, I am in Thy hands. After his prayer, he fell into a fitful sleep with the ropes cutting into his body. Each time he moved he awoke in agony.

In his troubled sleep he had a dream. He dreamed he was once again with his father. His two sons were also there, plus a host of other friends and relatives. He could feel the love and support of each of them. A feeling of peace came over him and a quiet voice whispered to him: *"Moroni, I will see you through. Trust me."*

He then slept peacefully, no longer troubled by ropes or rats. The rattling of the door awakened him. Mishnor and two guards pushed their way into the room, a torch held high lighting their way into the dark cell. The two guards undid the ropes, cursing Moroni continually, pulling him roughly to his feet. He said nothing, but quietly stretched his cramped and stiff body.

Mishnor stepped in front of him, looked at him for a moment with baleful eyes, then spat in his face. Moroni didn't react. Instead, he recalled words the Savior had spoken for the assembled Nephites at Bountiful: *"Love your enemies, bless them that curse you, pray for them that despitefully use you."* He smiled to himself and worded a silent prayer of forgiveness for Mishnor.

The bright sun blinded him as he was dragged outside. The two guards stepped in front of Mishnor and his prisoner. As they walked, Moroni turned and asked Mishnor the question which had been bothering him. "I am curious, Mishnor. Were you wrongly accused when Ammah testified against you?"

Moroni couldn't see the man's eyes because of the mask, but a smirk appeared on his lips. "Oh, I did what they accused me of all right. But that gave you no right to humiliate me."

"But what of Pelta? What happened to her? queried Moroni.

Mishnor shrugged indifferently. "How should I know. We had our fun. Whatever else she did was her business."

Moroni tried one more question. "What of the Lamanite who was with me?" He did not receive an answer. By this time they were in front of the palace. The two guards again grabbed Moroni and dragged him into the palace, passing between two sentries at the outside door. They entered a large room with a huge throne on a dais at one end of the hall. Those standing around wore elegant clothing; beautiful embroidered robes and feathered plumes. Their sandals had flecks of gold and jewels worked into the braids. Several priests in black robes contrasted greatly with the rest of the people.

Sitting on the throne were two of the most beautifully clothed people Moroni had ever seen. Their robes were covered with sequins and beads, embroidery and sewn-in feathers. On their heads were golden crowns topped with colored feathers of the Quetzal bird. Moroni's attention was drawn to a man he presumed to be the king. He was a large man, much larger than either of the guards who were dragging Moroni. He had a barrel chest and massive shoulders. His unruly hair and tangled black beard were flecked with gray, but he appeared to have the muscle-tone of a young man. He was formidable-looking at best. Then Moroni saw his eyes—the eyes of a snake, beady and cold.

The guards threw Moroni down directly in front of the throne. He lay there without moving until the king said coldly, "Get up."

Moroni pushed himself to his feet and stood before the throne.

Again the voice. "Your name is Moroni." It was not a question. Moroni nodded. "You are accused of being a follower of Christ—a Christian!" The ruler spat out the last word like an epithet. He allowed time for this to sink in, then asked, "Do you deny this?"

Moroni responded with conviction. "I do not. I cannot deny that I am a Christian. Yes, I am a follower of Jesus Christ." One of the priests stepped forward, lifted his arm, and slapped Moroni hard across the face. A trickle of blood started from one nostril, dripping onto his bare chest.

The priest turned to the seemingly outraged monarch and bowed. "Let us sacrifice him to Quetzalcoatl. His heart at least would then serve the only god."

The king, apparently in deep thought, held up his bejewelled hand for silence. "No," he mused. "There is a better way." He chewed thoughtfully on his knuckle, all the time looking at Moroni. A twisted grin appeared on his swarthy face. "This so-called Christian worships one who was crucified. Let the same death come to him." He rose from the throne, extended a hand to his queen, and with her left the room.

For a moment no one moved, then Mishnor barked a command. The two guards stepped forward, grabbed Moroni, and turned him around. Once outside, Moroni looked at the sky. The sun was half way up its morning flight. He stumbled on a stone and had a difficult time regaining his footing. The guards dragged him through the streets and out the gate as if he were a sack of maize. They stopped at a huge, gnarled tree. The courtesans who had been following along howled with glee.

Moroni was hoisted up the tree trunk until his toes barely touched the ground. His arms were raised high above his head. Mishnor, carrying a short, obsidian spear, stepped forward. He measured his target with a practiced eye, reared back, and drove the point of the sharp spear through Moroni's palm and deep into the wood of the tree. He cried out in surprise and pain. Mishnor, a look of satisfaction on his evil face, reached for a spear held by another warrior. Again he balanced it in his hand, reared back and drove the point through Moroni's other hand. The two guards released their hold, letting him sag, causing the spear points to dig deeper into the flesh of his hands. He gritted his teeth, raised a fraction of an inch on his toes, and held himself there. Mishnor chuckled. The others also laughed, obviously in enjoyment at seeing Moroni writhing in pain. Through pain-clouded eyes he watched them—as they watched him. They seemed to anticipate his every move. his every effort to avoid the sharp cutting stabs of pain as the obsidian tips continued to tear his flesh.

Moroni hung there as the sun climbed to its high point then started sinking toward the horizon. He struggled between consciousness and unconsciousness with his thoughts sometimes clear, sometimes garbled. During one of his lucid moments he thought, I wonder if this is how the Savior felt when he was on the cross? And then he prayed, Dear God, let me be like the Savior. With that, his head dropped and blessed unconsciousness came. There he hung, blood dripping from his mangled hands, his head bowed, his back arched, his body apparently lifeless. Most of the crowd soon left, assuming that the entertainment was over.

Consciousness came and went. Each time Moroni awoke it was to the knowledge of pain. It was difficult to focus his eyes—to see through the red film which separated him from the rest of the world. All his senses seemed to gather together and cry out in a great chorus of pain. Wakefulness came in waves. He would be recalling a childhood experience—a hike with his father, or helping his mother in the garden—and then he would realize that he was not a child, but a man speared to a tree.

Again he stretched his toes to the ground, barely relieving the terrible pulling on his hands. When he was conscious enough to think, he wondered how the Savior suffered through such terrible pain. He not only had spikes through His hands but through His feet also. Oh, thought Moroni, if I could only cut off the feeling from my arms. The nerves in his arms were like hot coals to him with blood pumping down each arm and back to the hump of his shoulders. His chest felt as if it were caught in a vise, with air squeezed out of him and his breath coming in gasps. His stomach was a huge knot of furious pain.

Once he cried out, a terrible cry of pain and agony. Most of the time he suffered in silence, his strength and life slowly ebbing from him.

Time no longer was relevent. He couldn't tell whether any time had passed since he had been speared to the tree. A moment was eternity, and he felt that he had suffered in this place forever. As he slipped further from the living, his mind turned to hallucinations. He once again was watching the jaguar in the tree, measuring with fear the metronome of its tail. Once more he was with his father traveling between cities, watching a grotesque priest sacrifice a prisoner, holding a bloody heart high for all to see. Again he was fighting in the last battle, cutting arms off enemy soldiers which seemed to grow right back on again.

At times in his suffering, full consciousness returned and he looked compassionately upon the few people who were there. Once he thought he recognized a face, then decided he must be imagining things once more. Sometimes he remembered things with great clarity and detail. Other times the past became a nightmare of figures and men, fighting and dying.

Finally, the relief of total unconsciousness came. He was as one who was dead. The few hangers-on departed leaving Moroni alone with the two soldiers who had been assigned as guards. Moroni was now in the hands of that God whom he loved and trusted.

Chapter 14

The Journey Completed

Time and space seemed suspended for Moroni. His fitful sleep was filled with wierd and wild dreams. In his dreams he was being cared for by an angel who placed cool pads on his fevered brow, or spooned hot broth between his parched lips. There seemed to always be someone at his side, but his injured mind could make no distinction between what was real and what was dreamed. He remembered gentle hands changing bandages on his shattered hands, but the pain and fever kept him in an unconscious state most of the time.

Full consciousness came. He opened his eyes, and for the first time since the day of his crucifixion he could clearly see his surroundings. He was in a bedroom. Heavy curtains over the single window kept out the bright sunlight. A rug covered the door, permitting passage but maintaining privacy for the injured man within. A beautiful Lamanite girl of about eighteen years sat by his side. She was watching him carefully, and smiled with delight when he opened his eyes and looked at her. Before, his eyes had been dulled and without recognition—now they looked at her inquisitively.

Moroni croaked dully, "Where am I?"

"You are in the home of my father, Abalom," the girl responded. She stepped to the door. "Mother, he awakens."

The rug parted, letting in a Lamanite woman of about fifty. She had a youthful beauty with grey streaks illuminating and highlighting her jet-black hair. She smiled warmly at Moroni and a feeling of recognition surged through him.

"I have known you in the past," he stated. "Who are you?"

The woman smiled again. "I am Zilar, daughter of Palorem."

A flood of memories assailed Moroni. Zilar, whom he had raised from the dead with the Lord's help. He recalled once more the scene in Zilar's bedroom, especially remembering his feelings as the Lord worked through him in overcoming the coldness of death. Zilar had been devoted to the Church and Moroni had loved her as a daughter. Now here she was, almost thirty-five years later, serving him. The words of the Savior passed through his mind: *"Give, and it shall be given to you."* It was the law of the harvest. You could not give to others without a many-fold return.

He came back to the present. Zilar was still standing by the bed, a beautiful smile on her clear, unblemished face. Her dark eyes were moist, shining with a deep radiance that lent beauty to her face.

"What of your father and mother?" he asked.

She placed a hand on his forehead, caressing him with her long, supple fingers. "They are both dead. Father died in a battle north of the Temple City." She paused. "I think mother died of a broken heart. They were so close."

Moroni raised his hand to take hers and a lightning bolt of pain shot up his arm. For the first time he noticed the thick bandages encasing his hands. The throbbing of the wounds was intense and he sank back on the pillow, sweat standing on his forehead. He hadn't realized how weak he was. He lapsed again into unconsciousness. But this time his sleep was filled with pleasant memories—memories of Palorem and Tabor and their sweet friendship.

When he awakened again he was more refreshed. He looked around with interest, hoping to see Zilar. She was not there, but the young girl was sitting beside the bed dozing. Her eyes were closed and her head was gently nodding. She opened her eyes and, with Moroni's eyes upon her, she smiled prettily.

She placed a cool hand on his forehead. "Your fever is gone," she said softly. Her voice had a soothing quality.

Moroni's curiosity was aroused. "Who are you, my child?"

Leaning over him, she responded, "I am Namah, daughter of Abalom and Zilar."

He should have known. She had the same dark, beautiful eyes as her mother and her oval face was framed by her striking blue-black hair. He smiled. "You are a very lovely girl. You remind me very much of your mother when she was younger."

"Thank you," she said, blushing a little.

"How long have I been here?"

"You have lain her for many days and nights," she said. "We were not sure you would live."

"But how. . . .?" He looked at his still bandaged hands, a mute question in his eyes.

Namah smiled gently. "I will let Kilihu answer your questions."

"Kilihu?" his heart leaped. "Kilihu here? Where is he? I thought he was killed."

"He will be here any time," Namah said. "Father went to get him when it looked as if you would awaken."

Moroni stared at the ceiling, "Zilar, Namah, her daughter, Kilihu." He said, "My friends are with me. The Lord has blessed me once again."

The rug parted, letting in a shaft of bright sunlight. Three people stood in the doorway; Zilar, Kilihu, and a slight dark-haired man whom Moroni presumed was Abalom. Kilihu moved quickly to the side of Moroni's bed. He sobbed, reaching down to cradle Moroni's head in his hands, burying his head in the pillow. "You are well!" he exclaimed, tears running down his cheeks.

Moroni motioned toward Namah. "Yes, thanks to this little nurse." Then he looked at Kilihu and Zilar. "Thanks to both of you. You have saved my life."

Kilihu motioned to Abalom. "Abalom gave you a blessing, promising that you would recover."

Moroni turned his head to look at Abalom, a question in his eyes. Abalom stepped to the bed. "Yes, Moroni, we still hold and magnify the priesthood which you left with Palorem."

Inhaling sharply, Moroni asked excitedly, "There are still members of the church here?"

Abalom shook his head, "Just Zilar, Namah and myself. I was introduced to the gospel when I met Zilar and desired her hand in marriage." He chuckled. "She wouldn't take a second look at me until I joined the Church. Before Palorem died he set me apart and bestowed the priesthood on me."

"So you are the last remaining members of the Church?" Abalom nodded. Moroni turned to Kilihu. "How did I get here? How did I get free? How did you find Zilar and her family?"

Kilihu smiled and held up his hand. "One at a time. After bringing me to the city, the guards questioned me, beat me, and then let me go," he began. "I didn't know where you were, but supposed you to be locked up somewhere. Knowing no one I did not know what to do. I offered a prayer and the Spirit reminded me that you had established a branch of the Church here, under the leadership of Palorem.

"But that didn't help because I had no idea where to begin looking for him. I continued my prayers and started through town. I hadn't gone far when . . ." His face had a puzzled look. ". . . when I was met by three men. They motioned to me and as I joined them they said, 'You look for Palorem. He is dead.' Then they gave directions to find Abalom and Zilar."

Moroni smiled. Helped again.

I found Zilar," he continued. "We found where they had crucified you and went to retrieve the body. What a surprise it was to see the same three men standing among the crowd. You were unconscious and looked dead. We didn't know how to get you away from the guards but then the Lord interceded. A great thunderstorm, with blinding rain, moved through, sending the guards back to the city so seek shelter. With the help of your three friends we pulled you from the tree, then brought you here and the rain obliterated all signs of our journey. Mishnor was terribly angry. He executed the guards and had his men search the entire city. Luckily, they did not think to come here to search.''

Moroni appreciated the straightforwardness of Kilihu's story, but something still puzzled him. "How did you get my pouch? Mishnor was carrying it when I last saw it.''

Kilihu smiled broadly. "I knew the value of your letters and sermons. I bribed one of the guards.''

Moroni reached up with his bandaged hand, even though it pained, and put it on Kilihu's arm. "Thank you again—both for saving my life and for retrieving my papers.''

"We are friends,'' Kilihu said simply. "It is enough.''

Each day brought new strength to Moroni until he felt he was strong enough to get out of bed. Soon he was able to sit in the enclosed courtyard where he could once again enjoy the beauties of nature. His hands were stiff but he still had the use of all his fingers. In the center of each palm was a large, jagged, purple scar.

Often he caught Kilihu stealing glances at Namah. She was a beautiful girl, and very compassionate. Therefore, it came as no surprise to Moroni when Kilihu told him that they desired to be married.

Kilihu asked, "Will you perform the ceremony?''

Moroni was reluctant to delay his important journey, but he knew how important this would be for Kilihu and Namah. "Yes,'' he said. "How soon?''

"Just before the new moon!'' Kilihu said excitedly.

Moroni was excited for Kilihu. The light of love in his friends eyes reminded him of his own courtship of Armora. How he missed his sweet Armora. He had lived without her for over thirty years—thirty years of loneliness and longing. Many times he had prayed that he might soon join her and the rest of his family. The answer had always come: *"Not yet.''*

While he waited for the wedding to take place, Moroni gathered together dried fruit, nuts, and other provisions for his journey to Cumorah. He had Abalom purchase gold from a stall in the Temple City, and he had carefully beaten it into fine sheets which would hold the balance of his writings.

The day of the wedding finally arrived. Namah was a radiant bride. In the quiet of Abalom's courtyard, Moroni pronounced the ceremony. Using his priesthood power, he married them and pronounced a blessing upon them. He blessed them with posterity and happiness; he blessed them with a continued testimony of the Gospel and he blessed them that they would have the opportunity, during the millennium, to have their marriage sealed by the Holy Spirit so that their marriage could be eternal.

Soon after the ceremony, he said his goodbyes. Tears streamed down Zilar's face. He grasped forearms with Abalom and embraced Kilihu once again. This man had become as a son to him and it was difficult to leave, but he knew he must.

He slipped out of the village at dark and began the last leg of his journey to Cumorah. He had though earlier that Kilihu would be accompanying him, but he knew that his marriage was now more important. Moroni traveled at night, being careful to let no one see him. Two weeks later, on a clear moonlit night similar to the one when he had left almost fifteen years before, he stood at the base of Cumorah. He stood, looking up at the hillside that had played such an important role in his life.

Chapter 15

The Chronicle of Moroni

Moroni stirred uncomfortably, brushed a bothersome fly from his cheek, changed sides once again, and then woke with a start. His eyes drifted around the sparsely furnished cave, coming to rest on the gold plates and the engraving tools lying where he had left them at dusk the night before.

Yesterday he had been involved in recovering the plates from the dark cave where he had placed them thirteen years before, after the death of Mormon. With the supply of gold he had received from Abalom, he would be able to complete the work that the Lord desired of him and return "home."

He got up, washed himself in the gourd at the entrance of the cave. He munched some of the corn, fish and berries that Zilar had sent with him. He moved the plates out of the cave onto a flat rock in the warm morning sun. Picking up the stylus, he wrote:

"Behold, four hundred years have passed away since the coming of our Lord and Savior." [19]

He stretched himself, enjoying the feeling of the warm sun on his body. I am almost sixty-three years of age, he thought to himself. He contemplated what he should write, and then thought of the words of his father: "Complete the record. Tell what has happened to our people."

Moroni again picked up the stylus and wrote:

"Behold, the Lamanites have hunted my people, the Nephites, down from city to city and from place to place, even until they are no more; and great has been their fall; yea, great and marvelous is the destruction of my people, the Nephites. And behold, it is the hand of the Lord which hath done it." [20]

He wrote of the fighting he had seen as he stealthily worked his way back to Cumorah, and of what Kilihu had told him: *"And behold . . . the Lamanites are at war one with another; and the whole face of this land is one continual round of murder and bloodshed."* [21]

A sweet peace filled his heart as he thought of the many times the three Disciples had visited him. He wrote of them:

"There are none that do know the true God save it be the disciples of Jesus, who did tarry in the land until the wickedness of the people was so great that the Lord would not suffer them to remain with the people; and whether they be upon the face of the land no man knoweth. But behold, my father and I have seen them, and they have ministered unto us." [22]

He was so grateful that the Lord had permitted the Disciples to remain on the earth. They were always around when he had need of them, seemingly appearing out of nowhere. He wondered if he would see them again on the earth.

After flexing his fingers, he again picked up the stylus. Almost apologetically, he wrote:

"And whoso receiveth this record, and shall not condemn it because of the imperfections which are in it, the same shall know of greater things than these." Thinking to end his personal writing there, he continued; *"Behold, I am Moroni and were it possible, I would make all things known unto you. Behold, I would make all things known unto you. Behold, I make an end of speaking concerning this people. I am the son of Mormon, and my father was a descendant of Nephi."* [23]

He put the stylus down and looked over what he had written. "It is sufficient," he said aloud. By this time the sun was bearing down upon him. He picked up the plates and moved them back into the cool shelter of the cave. Returning for his stylus and stool, a thought hit him as he recalled the vision he had received on the northern hill which would become known as Cumorah:

But what of him to whom the Lord will give the responsibility of translating this writing. What message should I write for him? In his mind he saw again the young man who would translate the plates. Once again he picked up the stylus:

"I am the same who hideth up this record unto the Lord; the plates thereof are of no worth, because of the commandment of the Lord . . . but the record thereof is of great worth; and whoso shall bring it to light, him will the Lord bless." [24]

He wrote for several hours of the many judgments which would come against the people in the last days.

He set the sylus down and massaged his hands together. They cramped very quickly and he found that he couldn't write too much at a time. He read back through what he had written, and added:

"For the eternal purposes of the Lord shall roll on, until all his promises shall be fulfilled. . . . behold I say unto you, that those saints who have gone before me, who have possessed this land, shall cry, yea, even from the dust will they cry unto the Lord. . . . in his name could they remove mountains; and in his name could they cause the earth to shake; and by the power of his word did they cause prisons to tumble to the earth; yea, even the fiery

furnace could not harm them, neither wild beasts nor poisonous serpents, because of the power of his word." [25]

Moroni glanced at the sun. He had spent all day in writing, not even noticing the passing of time. Now he felt the hunger pains in his stomach. He hadn't eaten anything since his meagre breakfast of dried corn and fish. Laying down the plates he pulled out his pack and ate a cold supper of nuts, berries, and fruit. There was a little cocoa left from the previous night and he washed down his meal with that. He was thankful for the abundant spring which was so close to the cave.

As dusk came, Moroni stepped outside the cave. He had always enjoyed evenings and nighttime. His walks had mostly been of necessity, but he had found them to be special times to meditate and to commune with himself and God. As the evening star became bold in the night sky, Moroni left the shelter of the cave to explore once again the mountain he had known so well. He stayed close to the ridge, not wanting to meet any late-returning farmers. The base of Cumorah was now ringed with small villages. A large community was on the west side with many lights showing as the evening progressed.

Coming to the end of the main ridge of the hill, he looked down the gentle ridge to a smaller peak directly in front of him. Fifteen years ago the slope had been dotted with trees. They had all been cut down to be used in constructing the houses in the village below, and rows of crops now filled the slope. Looking carefully to make sure that no one was around, he slipped down the slope. He was surrounded by clumps of corn and had to walk carefully to avoid the vines filled with squash and beans. He approached the small peak carefully, picking his way up the rock-strewn slope. An outcropping of lava dominated the top of the peak. He moved through the smaller stones and found one upon which to sit.

The plain extended as far as he could see, dotted here and there by the lights of fires and weak candlelight. He pictured to himself the people of these villages, like thousands of villagers he had known, sitting near their cooking fires, enjoying each other's companionship. A wave of loneliness passed over him. He wondered what Zilar and Abalon, or Kilihu and Namah, were doing. They were the only family he had still living. Shrugging, he returned his thoughts to the special mission which the Lord had given him.

His reverie was interrupted by the barking of dogs in the village below. He reluctantly stood and carefully moved back through the farmer's fields. He tested a few squash, finding one that was ripe, and carefully picked it from the vine. He picked several ears of corn and silently thanked the farmer for tomorrow's dinner.

As he neared the hillside where the cave was located, his feet led him down to a small clearing several hundred paces from the cave. He approached the clearing almost reverently. Much underbrush had grown here during the time he had been gone, but he had no trouble recognizing the place where he had buried his father. There was the pile of stones he had placed on the shallow grave. He knelt down close to Mormon's grave. His heart was full. Tears welled up in his eyes. He squeezed his eyelids shut and the tears slowly coursed down his tanned cheeks.

Silently he knelt there for several moments, then opened his mouth and spoke to the Lord. He praised the Lord and thanked Him for his blessings, for his noble heritage, and for his father, Mormon, whose body lay so close to him at this time. After much supplication, he asked the Lord the questions which had been disturbing him while he inscribed on the plates. Father, will those who read the words I am writing, and the words which my father devoted his life to writing, laugh at our feeble efforts of writing? Will they understand what we are saying to them? How much more shall I write? Of what shall I speak? Once started, the torrent of questions flowed from his lips.

A quiet voice entered Moroni's consciousness: *"Peace be unto you, my son."*

Moroni looked up. Standing before him was the Savior. Jesus stretched forth his hand to Moroni. Moroni grasped his hand, electrified by its touch. Once again he was amazed that One so great and noble would speak to him—and show Himself in person! He stood, and looked up into the eyes of Him whom he loved above all else. The Savior spoke again in that beautiful quiet voice.

"Moroni, you have been faithful to all that I have asked you to do. Why is it that you are now feeling concerned?"

When Moroni unchoked his voice, the words poured out in a veritable torrent:

"Lord, the gentiles will mock at these things, because of our weakness in writing; for Lord thou hast made us mighty in word by faith, but thou has not made us mighty in writing; for thou has made all this people that they could speak much, because of the Holy Ghost which thou hast given them; and thou hast made us that we could write but little, because of the awkwardness of our hands. . . . Thou hast also made our words powerful and great, even that we cannot write them; wherefore, when we write we behold our weakness, and stumble because of the placing of our words; and I fear lest the Gentiles shall mock at our words." [26]

The Savior looked at Moroni with compassion, then responded in a kindly voice:

"Fools mock, but they shall mourn; and my grace is sufficient for the meek, that they shall take no advantage of your weakness; . . . I give unto men weakness that they may be humble; and my grace is sufficient for all men that humble themselves before me; for if they humble themselves

before me, and have faith in me, then will I make weak things become
strong unto them. Behold, I will show unto the Gentiles their weakness and
I will show unto them that faith, hope and charity bringeth unto me. . . .
the fountain of all righteousness.'' [27]

As Moroni thought of the Gentiles who would come, a great swelling
of love filled his heart. He wanted so much for them to accept what he had
written. He offered a silent prayer that they would receive grace from the
Lord and would have charity.

The Lord, hearing the prayer, and knowing the feelings which were
going on in his heart, said:

"[Moroni,] *if they have not charity it mattereth not unto thee, thou*
hast been faithful; wherefore, thy garments shall be made clean. And be-
cause thou hast seen thy weakness thou shalt be made strong, even unto the
sitting down in the place which I have prepared in the mansions of my
Father.'' [28]

Then he added, *"Moroni, your work is not yet through. There is much*
yet to do before that time comes when you will join me.''

Moroni quickly knelt again before his Master. "What would thou have
me do? My life is thine to do as Thou wilt."

Again the Savior gently lifted Moroni to his feet. *"Moroni, look.''*

A vision opened before his eyes. He saw far into the future. Once again
he saw himself handing the plates to the same young man he had seen in the
previous visions, instructing him in their uses and purposes. He saw men
fighting and dying. He saw towns and cities scattered through the land, with
churches defiled by the people. He saw earthquakes and volcanoes erupting,
hailstorms and fierce hurricanes, tornadoes which ravished and destroyed
huge villages and cities.

All through the vision the gentiles were laughing and doing evil. He
observed their fine clothing and their evil ways. Many things he saw [and
would later remember]. Finally the vision was closed. He found himself
alone, lying near Mormon's grave, his smock drenched. He lay there, trying
to remember all he had seen and heard, until his head throbbed with the
effort.

He stood, weaved a little in his weakened state, and determinedly
walked to the cave. Now he knew a purpose in writing! He could hardly
wait until morning. He recalled the words the Savior had spoken in response
to his questions: *"Fools mock!''* That statement repeated itself over and
over in his mind. Sleep wouldn't come, there were too many thoughts running through his mind. He rehearsed what he would write as soon as it
was light.

At the first light of dawn he was up and doing. He quickly took care of
his morning duties, and was ready to write. He laid out his materials on the
rock, sat down at his stool, picked up the stylus and began. All day he

wrote, not even taking time to eat. As the long evening shadows made seeing almost impossible in the cave, he took the plate he had been writing on and moved outside. He read back through what he had written that day. As he read, he pictured the Gentile of later days reading it and changing their lives. It gave him a very satisfying feeling:

"Behold, the Lord hath shown unto me great and marvelous things concerning that which must shortly come, at that day when these things shall come forth among you. Behold, I speak unto you as if ye were present, and yet ye are not. But behold, Jesus Christ hath shown you unto me, and I know your doing. And I know that ye do walk in the pride of your hearts; . . . ye do love money, and your substance, and your fine apparel, and the adorning of your churches, more than ye love the poor and the needy, the sick and the afflicted. . . . Behold, the sword of vengeance hangeth over you; and the time soon cometh that he avengeth the blood of the saints upon you, for he will not suffer their cries any longer." [29]

His hands were stiff and cramped from tightly holding and manipulating the stylus all day. He suddenly felt hungry. Looking around for the squash and corn he had got the previous night he suddenly realized that he had been so overcome by the appearance of the Savior that he must have left them at Mormon's grave. Even though it was still light outside, he left the cave and went carefully to the clearing. There were the vegetables, just where he had dropped them. He picked them up and had just started back when an urging stopped him in his tracks. What of the other records? What of the plates of Jared which Mormon had desired to abridge but had not got to? He walked carefully to the record cave, trying to avoid making any sign which could be followed.

Once again he carefully pulled away the stones until there was enough room for him to crawl through. There they were! Stacks of gold plates, brass plates; the bow with the interpreters, the sword of Laban, and the other relics of the Nephite people. Moroni restacked the plates, being very careful to place them so they would not be damaged. He found the twenty-four plates of the Jaredite people. These were the plates found by the people of Limhi during King Mosiah's reign. He blew off the thick layer of dust, lifted out the twenty-four plates, restacked the rest, and crawled back to the cave's entrance. With great care he replaced the rocks over the entrance and, exercising great caution, he started back for his cave.

Back in the cave he started reading the Jaredite record. He read of wickedness even greater than the Nephites had demonstrated. He read of greater faith than any had seen. He read of cruelties, wars, murder, and mayhem. He read of prophets and kings. He was thrilled by the story of the brother of Jared. He was terribly saddened by the stories of Shiz and Coriantumr.

In order to finish the story, Moroni had to light an oil lamp. He sat far to the rear of the cave so as to show no light. When he finished he gently put the plates down. What a history, and what lessons for future generations. He built a small fire, knowing that the darkness outside would hide the tell-tale smoke. He let the fire die down to a red-glowing bed of coals. Scooping out a depression in the coals, he put in the squash. Soaking the ears of corn in the spring, he wrapped the husks tightly around them, and then also placed them in the coals.

While his food was cooking, Moroni put together the balance of his precious gold plates. He hoped that there would be enough, especially now that he had so much more to write. He also had some lump gold which could be used in making more plates if he needed them. He laughed to himself. His feeling of anxiousness to write was quite a contrast to his previous reluctance. That's just like me, he thought out loud. All my life I have accomplished things only as I felt the burning desire within me.

From his tunic he pulled a small pouch of salt which Zilar had given him. He opened one of the steaming ears of corn, gently sprinkled on a few grains of salt, and after thanking his Heavenly Father, hungrily ate it. Never had food tasted so good. With a stick he pulled out the squash. With his knife he cracked the hard blackened shell. It fell away, exposing the soft interior, cooked to perfection.

He scraped the seeds into the coals and ate the squash. In the last few years eating had become somewhat a matter of survival for Moroni, but tonight he really savored the food. After his meal he again took a walk. This time he stayed on the ridge, moving in a southeasterly direction. In the starlight he could make out the outline of the volcanic peaks stretching in a row as far as he could see. It was in that direction where lay the city of Desolation, also the narrow pass leading to the land of Zarahemla. This night he did not stay out late. He wanted to be fresh on the morrow, because he was excited to start his own abridgment. He wondered if Mormon had had the same excitement when he started his first abridgment so many years before.

After a peaceful sleep, he arose refreshed and eager. He ate a quick meal and read over what he had written the previous day. Then he offered a prayer for his work—that it would be correct and acceptable before the Lord. He then began writing:

"And now I speak also concerning those who do not believe in Christ. . . . when ye shall be brought to see your nakedness before God, and also the glory of God, and the holiness of Jesus Christ, it will kindle a flame of unquenchable fire upon you." [30]

He continued to write, outlining what the unbelieving could do to become spotless and cleansed.

He talked of revelation and why continuing revelation is necessary for the Lord's Church. He wrote:

"I will show unto you a God of Miracles, even the God of Abraham, and the God of Isaac, and the God of Jacob; and it is the same God who created the heavens and the earth and all things that in them are. . . ." [31]

He wrote of the plan of salvation, from the fall of Adam to the atonement of the Savior. Then speaking of the resurrection, he wrote:

". . . and all shall stand before his bar, being redeemed and loosed from this eternal band of death, which death is a temporal death. And then cometh the judgment of the Holy One upon them; and then cometh the time that he that is filthy shall be filthy still; and he that is righteous shall be righteous still; he that is happy shall be happy still; and he that is unhappy shall be unhappy still." [32]

He then wrote to all who believed that God could do no miracles. He told them that "God has not ceased to be a God of Miracles." He wrote of the miracles of Jesus Christ and also those performed by the apostles. Bearing his testimony, he said:

"I say unto you he changeth not; if so he would cease to be God; and he ceaseth not to be God, and is a God of miracles." [33]

He looked over what he had written and wondered if there were a better way of saying that. He wrote:

"And the reason why he ceaseth to do miracles among the children of men is because that they dwindle in unbelief, and depart from the right way, and know not the God in whom they should trust." To emphasize this point, Moroni paraphrased the statement he had heard his father make so many times:

"Behold, I say unto you that whoso believeth in Christ, doubting nothing, whatsoever he shall ask the Father in the name of Christ it shall be granted him; and this promise is unto all, even unto the ends of the earth." Moroni smiled to himself as he wrote this. It had surely been proven many times in his own life.

He leaned back and chewed unconsciously on the end of the stylus. He thought with wonderment of all the things that had happened to him since he had taken upon himself the name of Christ. In the last fifteen years he had truly fulfilled the commandment to "go to all the world" and had experienced so many of the gifts the Savior had promised to those that believed. He continued to write, speaking the words of Christ:

"And these signs shall follow them that believe—in my name shall they cast out devils; they shall speak with new tongues; . . . they shall lay hands on the sick and they shall recover; and whosoever shall believe in my name, doubting nothing, unto him will I confirm all my words, even unto the ends of the earth." [34]

Continuing, he wrote of those who would deny the things he was writing, then told people to:

"Be wise in the days of your probation; . . . see that you do all things in worthiness, and do it in the name of Jesus Christ, the son of the living God; and if ye do this, and endure to the end, ye will in nowise be cast out." [35]

He paused in writing, rereading that which he had written. He asked himself, Did I write that? The words had seemed to flow from above, and he knew the sweet peacefulness of mind that told him that Jesus' spirit was with him, helping him to do that in which he felt weak. He was the best example of what he was writing that he could think of; he truly did believe in Christ, had asked for help in His name, did not doubt, and the blessings had been granted to him. He sank to his knees and offered a prayer of thanksgiving. Strengthened, he got back on the rock ready to continue. He remembered the vision he had received just two nights before, and wrote:

"Behold, I speak unto you as though I spake from the dead; for I know that ye shall hear my words. . . . these things are written that we may rid our garments of the blood of our brethren, who have dwindled in unbelief. . . . May the Lord Jesus Christ grant that their prayers may be answered according to their faith; and may God the Father remember the covenant which he hath made with the house of Israel; and may He bless them forever, through faith on the name of Jesus Christ, Amen." [36]

Even though very tired, Moroni felt a deep satisfaction as he put down the stylus. He punched holes in the ends of the plates he had just finished and added them to the stack of punched plates he had previously written. By the time he had finished the task it was getting dark outside the cave. He was so weary and emotionally drained from his writing that he decided against cooking supper. He ate some dried corn, chewed down a portion of dried meat, said a prayer of thanksgiving and praise, and crawled into his bed. He fell asleep almost instantly, sleeping the sleep of the righteous.

Chapter 16

The Book of Ether

It was a glorious morning. The rays of the sun quickly dispelled the slight mist lying over the valleys below Cumorah. Moroni stepped outside the cave to watch the sunrise, excited to be alive. He had always enjoyed the beauties that the Lord had created. He stretched, working out the stiffness of his aging body. It had rained during the night and he could smell the newness of the earth. He mused that all things smelled and looked better after washing, even the earth. With that in mind, he went to the spring and had his morning bath. Now, refreshed and eager, he picked up the first of the twenty-four plates of the Jaredites, a fresh plate of gold, and his stylus. He began his abridgment:

"I, Moroni, proceed to give an account of these ancient inhabitants who were destroyed by the hand of the Lord upon the face of this north country. And I take mine account from the twenty and four plates which were found by the people of Limhi, which is called the book of Ether. . . . And on this wise do I give the account." [37]

He used the same procedure that he had seen his father, Mormon, use for so many years. He would read a sentence or a paragraph, sometimes several paragraphs, and then with prayerful thought condense the material he had read down to a single thought. He quickly found that abridging was not an easy task. He strained with each sentence, attempting to get the same meaning as the author had intended, with as few words as possible.

Soon, he was fully immersed in his work. He lived each story, the words becoming real to him as he developed a sense of their meaning and intent. Occasionally he editorialized to those who would be reading what he had written. After describing the journey of the brother of Jared through the wilderness, he wrote:

"We can behold the decrees of God concerning this land, that it is a land of promise; and whatsoever nation shall possess it shall serve God, or they shall be swept off when the fulness of his wrath shall come upon them. . . . For behold, this is a land which is choice above all other lands." [38]

He wrote to the gentiles, warning them to repent or bring down the judgment of God upon them. He stated his feelings about the land—a land which he had traversed from sea to sea, and from north to south:

"Behold, this is a choice land, and whatsoever nation shall possess it shall be free from bondage, and from captivity, and from all other nations under heaven, if they will but serve the God of the land, who is Jesus Christ." [39]

All day he wrote, taking time only to relax his sore and cramped hands. He carefully read all he had written, seeking confirmation from the Lord. Now he knew the great joy Mormon must have felt as he read, pondered, and abridged the records. The account of the brother of Jared thrilled him, especially his great joy at seeing the Lord. It brought back joyful memories of his personal visit by the Savior.

He attempted to write on the plates the visions that the Brother of Jared had witnessed but the voice of the Lord came again to him: *"Write these visions on separate plates. They will be sealed up until the people have faith sufficient to understand them."* Moroni put aside the plate he had been writing upon, and wrote the manifestations of the brother of Jared on a fresh plate which he would later seal up. Tears welled in his eyes as he read. He wanted so badly for the Gentiles to have these great words, but he did the will of the Lord. He wrote: *"Behold, I have written upon these plates the very things which the brother of Jared saw; and there never were greater things made manifest than those which were made manifest unto the brother of Jared. . . . in that day that they [the gentiles] shall exercise faith in me, saith the Lord, even as the brother of Jared did, . . . then will I manifest unto them the things which the brother of Jared saw, . . ."* [40]

As the words of the Lord came into Moroni's mind, he wrote them down. It was important to him that he not leave out any precious truths:

"He that believeth these things which I have spoken, him will I visit with the manifestations of my Spirit, and he shall know and bear record. . . . Therefore when ye shall receive this record ye may know that the work of the father has commenced upon all the face of the land. . . . And blessed is he that is found faithful into my name at the last day, for he shall be lifted up to dwell in the kingdom prepared for him from the foundation of the world. . . ." [41]

The sun dipped below the horizon and Moroni laid down the stylus. He had written all day and was exhausted. He was still full of the whisperings of the Spirit, but was now having a difficult time sorting out his own thoughts. Before eating, he decided to lie down for a few minutes. When he awakened it was pitch black. He rubbed his eyes and stumbled to the entrance of the cave. It was a starless night with heavy, threatening clouds. He sat at the cave's entrance, watching the distant flashes of lightning, pondering the words of the Lord.

The vision of the translator of the plates came into his mind once again. He watched for the third time as he handed over the plates; he watched as the youth translated the plates with the interpreters; he saw himself showing the plates to three others. He realized that he was beginning to feel very close to this young man who hadn't yet been born. As the vision once again closed, he pondered its meaning. Absent-mindedly he ate some leftovers, found his way to his bed and after his daily prayer of thanksgiving, drifted off into a peaceful sleep.

After a skimpy breakfast, he again sat down to write. Thinking of his vision, he wrote directly to the young man—he who would be the translator of the plates. As he wrote, he pictured again the young man poring over the plates:

"I have told you the things which I have sealed up; therefore touch them not in order that ye may translate; for that thing is forbidden you, except by and by it shall be wisdom in God. . . . And in the mouth of three witnesses shall these things be established; [Feeling the closeness which he would have with this translator, Moroni finished by saying] . . . *and we shall stand before God at the last day."* [42]

He continued his abridgment, telling of the journey of the Jaredites to the promised land, the appointment of a king over the people, and the deaths of Jared and his brother. He wrote of wars and contentions, the wickedness of the people, and the prophets who attempted to preach to them. He sorrowed as the plates told of the secret combinations which came into being; recalling how those same secret combinations had ultimately led to the destruction of the Nephites as well as the Jaredites. Impassioned at what he was reading, he wrote:

"Whatsoever nation shall uphold such secret combinations to get power and gain, until they shall spread over the nation, behold, they shall be destroyed; for the Lord will not suffer that the blood of his saints, which shall be shed by them, shall always cry unto him from the ground for vengeance upon them and yet he avenge them not." [43]

He continued:

"For it cometh to pass that whoso buildeth it up seeketh to overthrow the freedom of all lands, nations, and countries; and it bringeth to pass the destruction of all people, for it is built up by the devil, who is the father of all lies. [He concluded his statement about the evils of secret combinations] . . . *I, Moroni, am commanded to write these things that evil may be done away, and that the time may come that Satan may have no power upon the hearts of the children of men, but that they may be persuaded to do good continually, that they may come unto the fountain of all righteousness and be saved."* [44]

Mormon wrote of the Jaredite kingdoms, their sins, their wars, their pestilences. He recounted the stories of the prophets who rose up to cry repentance unto the people. A pang of sorrow came as he read the prophecies which foretold the destruction of the Jaredite people. The Jaredites had rejected the words of the prophets just like the Nephites had rejected his and his father's words. Would people never learn to follow the commandments of the Lord? How many more nations would be totally destroyed because the people wouldn't live righteously?

When he came to the writings of the prophet, Ether, he was reminded of his own father, Mormon. What a great servant of the Lord! Ether had written many great prophecies, which Moroni abridged and included in the sealed plates. After writing all day from these prophecies, his heart was full. He editorialized on the concept of faith:

"And now, I, Moroni, would speak somewhat concerning these things; I would show unto the world that faith is things which are hoped for and not seen; wherefore, dispute not because you see not, for ye receive no witness until after the trial of your faith.'' [45] He read the statement again. Yes, that was right. It had been exemplified many times in his own life, and now he was reading the same thing in the words of Ether: *"Ye receive no witness until after the trial of your faith.''*

He continued with his own thoughts:

"For it was by faith that Christ showed himself unto our fathers, after he had risen from the dead; and he showed not himself unto them until after they had faith in him; . . . because of the faith of men he has shown himself unto the world, and glorified the name of the Father, and prepared a way that thereby others might be partakers of the heavenly gift, that they might hope for those things which they have not seen.'' [46]

With great love in his heart for those who would be reading his words, he wrote:

"Wherefore, ye may also have hope, and be partakers of the gift, if ye will but have faith.'' [47]

He recounted to his readers the marvels and wonders done by those ancient prophets such as Moses, Alma, Almulek, Nephi, Lehi and others. He solemnly told of the Savior's visit to him and the sweet peace which it had brought to his heart. The Savior's eloquent words came to him again:

"My grace is sufficient for all men that humble themselves before me; for if they humble themselves before me, and have faith in me, then will I make weak things become strong unto them. [47]

As he read what he had just written, he nodded his head in agreement. It was so true! His own life had been a great example of that very thing. He had been weak but the Lord had made him strong. The Lord had concluded by saying:

"Behold, I will show unto the Gentiles their weakness and I will show unto them that faith, hope and charity bringeth unto me—the fountain of all righteousness.'' [48]

This reminded him of something that his father had said. He walked over and picked up his leather pouch—the pouch which had accompanied him on all his travels. From it he pulled a tattered paper which contained one of Mormon's sermons. He scanned through it until he found the words he sought. Mormon had said, speaking of faith, hope, and charity that:

"Wherefore, if a man have faith he must needs have hope; for without faith there cannot be any hope. And again, . . . I say unto you that he cannot have faith and hope, save he shall be meek, and lowly of heart. . . . and if a man be meek and lowly in heart, and confesses by the power of the Holy Ghost that Jesus is the Christ, he must needs have charity; for if he have not charity he is nothing; . . . for charity never faileth. Wherefore, cleave unto charity, which is the greatest of all, for all things must fail— But charity is the pure love of Christ, and it endureth forever; . . ." [49]

A chill went up his spine as he read and contemplated Mormon's words. What a powerful and wonderful man his father was. What a great example he had been. As he thought about the concept of charity, he uttered a prayer to the Lord, thanking Him for his great love for mankind:

"I remember that thou hast said that thou hast loved the world, even unto the laying down of thy life for the world, that thou mightest take it again to prepare a place for the children of men . . . I know that this love which thou hast had for the children of men is charity; wherefore, except men shall have charity they cannot inherit that place which thou hast prepared in the mansions of thy Father." [50]

He ended his writings to the gentiles by testifying to them of the Savior. As he spoke of meeting them at the judgment seat of Christ, he said:

"And then shall ye know that I have seen Jesus, and that he hath talked with me face to face, and that he told me in plain humility, . . . concerning these things; . . . And now, I would commend you to seek this Jesus of whom the prophets and apostles have written, that the Grace of God the Father, and also the Lord Jesus Christ, and the Holy Ghost, which beareth record of them, may be and abide in you forever. Amen." [51]

One day flowed into the next as he continued writing from the plates of Ether. Many times he sat, pondering over what he was reading, shaking his head at the slowness of men to learn and come unto their God. As he came near the end of the plates, and read and wrote of the blood and carnage which covered the land, his thoughts reverted to his own generation and the final battle of the Nephite people. He sadly recounted the battle in which two million Jaredites were killed and their nation destroyed, including the story of the two antagonists, Shiz and Coriantumr, fighting their last bloody battle. How similar it was, he thought, that only two people survived the entire nation: Ether and Coriantumr—just like him and Mormon.

He finished his abridgment with the final words of Ether. *"Whether the Lord will that I be translated, or that I suffer the will of the Lord in the flesh, it mattereth not, if it so be that I am saved in the Kingdom of God. Amen."* [52]

He sat back exhausted. Days had become weeks as he had pored over the plates, prayed for inspiration, and written the words of the abridgment. He knew that he had completed a formidable task in abridging the record of seventeen hundred years into just fifteen chapters. The work was finished that he had promised to do.

He put away the stylus, punched the plates and put some into the stack of Mormon's abridgment and his own writings. He punched a second stack which he would seal. Hefting the stacks of plates in his hands he was surprised at how heavy they were. Moving even the abridgment to the Land Northward would not be easy. Once again he saw evidence of the Lord's greater knowledge and judgment. It would have been impossible for one man to have moved the unabridged plates. They would now remain safe in the cave and he would carry those of his own writing.

At dusk he returned the plates of Ether to the cave, placing them with the large and the small plates of Nephi. He was tempted to take the sword of Laban with him but he saw that it would just be extra weight. He had not needed the sword before, why would he need it now? As he was leaving the cave, though, a whisper came to his mind: *"The Urim and Thummin— the interpreters!"* Yes! It was important that he take the interpreters with him. He picked up the breastplate with the interpreters fastened to it, crawled back out of the cave, and sealed the entrance. As he carefully picked his way back to his own cave, he wondered whom the Lord would choose to unseal the cave and bring all of the records forth.

Chapter 17

The "New" Cumorah

One last day was spent on Cumorah in cleaning out the cave, packing supplies, and reminiscing. Moroni obliterated all signs of his occupancy, rearranged the rocks, brushed out his tracks, and buried the ashes from his fire. In the afternoon he made a pack from a deerskin to carry the plates. He adjusted the straps to fit his large shoulders and put the plates carefully inside. The rations he needed for the journey he placed in his leather pouch, then he filled his water gourd from the spring.

He hefted the breastplate which had the Urim and Thummin attached to it. It was heavy and awkward. How would he carry it? He examined the breastplate carefully, noting the fine workmanship. It was rounded to fit the chest of a large man and was made of a bronze-like material. Holding it to him, it extended from his neck to the center of his stomach. Four straps were attached to it, two to fasten it to the shoulders, and two to fasten it around his hips. The breastplate was a perfect fit. He wondered what ancient warrior had worn it. Could it have belonged to Nephi himself?

Fastened to the top of the breastplate was a thin silver bow which held two transparent stones. The Urim and Thummin: ancient tools of the seers, personifying truth and revelation. Moroni handled them reverently.

He looked from the breastplate to his pack in a real quandary. In desperation, he finally unfastened the bow holding the Urim and Thummin to the breatplate, wrapped it and placed it inside the pack. He closed the pack and with some thongs from the deerhide lashed the breastplate to the outside. It would be awkward but it would have to do.

Once more he sat at the cave's entrance, thinking of all that had transpired on this mountain. He could visualize Mormon, hunched over the flat rock, inscribing the plates. He heard again the beautiful words of counsel from his father's lips. From where he sat he could almost see the clearing where Mormon was buried, and where the Savior had appeared to him. When he looked out over the valley, he could almost see the mighty legions of the Lamanites and Nephites as they met in bloody battle. It was so real to him that the hairs on the back of his neck prickled. He could taste again the sweat in his mouth and smell the awful stench of battle.

143

He stood up slowly, glanced once more around the cave, and as night gently provided covering darkness, started on his journey. Traveling by land, he retraced the path he had followed from Abalom's house to the cave. He would need Kilihu's help to carry the plates. He was glad he hadn't turned down Kilihu's offer to accompany him to the Land Northward. Thoughts of his friend made him realize how much he had missed him.

Three weeks of slow tedious travel faced him. The rainy season was beginning and Moroni halted several times to wait out torrential rainstorms. Every stream and every river was overflowing its banks. Progress was painfully slow. No moon broke through the heavy overcast and he had difficulty picking his way through the dark trackless jungles and forested hillsides. As slow and laborious as it was, he still felt he could not take the chance of traveling during the daytime.

Upon arriving at the foot of the mountain range, he traveled up the bottom of a rocky gully. Even though there was the constant danger of thunderstorms which could create a raging torrent in minutes, Moroni felt that it was still a better choice than working his way through thick cactus and brambles which covered the hill sides would be. In the dark he stumbled over large rocks, bruising his knees and scraping his shins. Grimly he traveled on, tiring under the constant dead weight on his back.

He reached the mountain pass one morning just before daylight. It had been a long night of slipping and sliding as he struggled uphill over patches of loose shale. As he watched the glorious sunrise, all the discomforts were forgotten. It was just so great to be alive. Each day he gained more love and respect for the Savior, the creator of the earth. What an eye for beauty He had. Scenes of the various places he had traveled flowed in quick sequence through Moroni's mind: sunrises and sunsets, vistas of great and endless forests, blue seas flecked with white foam, deserts and mountains, lakes and rushing streams, wind-swept rocks and curiously carved spires and minarets. Dropping to his knees, he offered a heartfelt prayer of thanksgiving, praising the Lord once again for allowing him the precious privilege of living on the earth.

The next stage of Moroni's journey was easy traveling. He dropped several thousand feet to the plateau, then worked his way around the base of the mountains, carefully skirting the numerous small villages. He was very anxious to see his friends once again. His life had been lonely enough that he prized the few people whom he could count on such as Zilar and her family and Kilihu. He smiled to himself as he pictured his friends. Would they be glad to see him?

The night came when he finally reached Abalom's village. He slipped through the darkened streets, silent except for the barking of dogs that signaled his passing. Abalom's home, too, was dark when he arrived there. He stepped to the doorway, rapping softly on the sill. Startled voices came from within, accompanied by a soft scurrying. Then he heard the slapping of sandals on the hard dirt floor. The doorway curtain parted to reveal the blurred and indistinct shape of Abalom.

"Who is it?"

"Moroni," he said softly.

At the sound of his name, a squeal of delight came from inside the house. "Moroni!" Abalom quickly ushered him inside where Zilar hugged him warmly. She was so excited to see him. Lighting a lamp, and over Moroni's protests, she immediately began preparing a meal. He was so grateful. It was wonderful to be with them again. He sat back and relaxed, pleased to just sit and watch Zilar as she expertly fixed the food. After they had eaten the three friends sat and talked until the eastern sky grew rosy with the light of the coming sun. Then Zilar insisted that Moroni lie down for a few hours of sleep.

He was awakened by a commotion outside. He raised up on one elbow, blinking his eyes to adjust to the semi-darkened room. Without warning he was knocked back on the bed, pinned there by two strong arms encircling his neck. He thought he had been recaptured by Mishnor and his warriors, but then he heard peals of laughter coming from the doorway. He craned his neck to see over the person who was holding him so firmly on the bed. Namah was silhouetted in the doorway, laughing merrily. Moroni got his hands under the man's bare chest and pushed him straight up. Looking down at him, his face wet with tears, was Kilihu. They embraced once again, this time with Moroni also shedding tears of joy at seeing again this friend who had been so loyal to him.

It took several weeks for Kilihu and Namah to make their preparations to accompany him. It was a time of restocking supplies, preparing packs, obtaining water gourds, regaining strength, and enjoying sweet friendships. His friends insisted on seeing the plates and they "oohed" and "aahed" at the delicate engraving. Even though they couldn't read the inscriptions, they were obviously impressed by the fine workmanship and the spiritual messages which Moroni read them. Each evening became a special time when he would read favorite passages to his friends.

The delay also gave Moroni an opportunity to obtain more gold for plates. He still hoped to inscribe some of Mormon's letters and sermons for the Gentiles, and the whisperings of the Spirit informed him that there would be more to write.

Zilar and Namah worked on the packs, carefully stitching and re-stitching the leather so that it would withstand the long journey ahead. As Kilihu and Namah made preparations for leaving, Zilar was saddened. She tried to be cheerful but it was difficult as she thought of her only child leaving—perhaps never to return. Knowing the importance of Moroni's mission, however, she was prepared to sacrifice her own feelings in order for that mission to succeed.

Though reluctant to leave, the time came when Moroni felt they should depart. Spring had come to the land and Moroni knew that the Land Northward would be breaking out in blossoms. If they left later the deserts would be too hot for them to travel through.

Zilar and Namah clung to each other for a long time, reluctant to say that last goodbye. Moroni and Abalom clasped arms, parting as dear friends. They knew they would meet again, even if it were on the other side of the veil. Kilihu also said goodbye to his parents-in-law. These good people had taken him in and had made him feel as welcome as if he were truly their own son.

As darkness blanketed the village they started off, turning to wave one last time to the two figures standing arm in arm before the peasant's hut.

They made good time traveling north on the plateau. By morning they found a grove of trees many miles north of the Temple City where they could camp. They needed the rest. Namah was not used to walking and had worn several blisters on her feet. Moroni made a plaster of some datura bark and applied it to her sore feet. It was good to have his friends along, and Kilihu was a great help in carrying the plates, but Moroni could see that he would not be able to set such a fast pace. It would take some time for Namah to toughen her feet.

After leaving the plateau, they climbed eastward over a large mountain range. They were now far enough away from their enemies to feel that they could travel safely during the daytime.

It took several weeks for them to get over the mountains, and then they caught their first glimpse of the almost interminable desert through which they must now travel.

It was on this desert that Moroni had found Kilihu and saved his life. They stood there, looking over the desert, thinking back. For a moment they relived that time of agony and joy which had so changed the lives of them both. Moroni, ever open to the whisperings of the Spirit, knew it was not happenstance that he had come upon the hapless Kilihu. It was the will of the Lord that the two of them meet and work together.

Now Kilihu turned to Namah, and with arm outstretched explained once again his rescue from certain death. Namah looked gratefully at Moroni, then returned her eyes to the vastness of the desert scene before them.

Crossing the desert in the past had seemed almost routine for Moroni but this time was different. Each day dragged on with the copper sun burning down unmercifully upon them. Water holes that he had used his last time through the desert were now dried up. They struggled forward, each step becoming more difficult.

Moroni was concerned about Namah. His own skin was hot and dry to the touch and his lips were dry and cracked. It was difficult to talk because his tongue was swollen. Namah stumbled often, but Kilihu put his arms around her and they continued on. Moroni could tell that Kilihu was tiring under the load he was carrying but he never complained. Moroni tried to take a turn carrying the plates, but Kilihu just shook his head and smiled to indicate that this was his task and that he would not share it.

Moroni's skin blackened from the sun and he became as dark as his Lamanite friends. After a week of facing the unbearable sun and hot sands, Moroni finally decided that they should travel only at night until they came to more friendly terrain. That helped. And they traveled more slowly, conserving as much strength as possible. Even in his misery, Moroni appreciated the beauty of the night sky. Stars had never shone so brightly; familiar stars to guide them on their way. And even with no moon the landscape was bright enough for them to navigate around obstacles and to thread their way through the tall cactuses.

Moroni was so thankful for the whisperings of the Spirit. Through that still small voice they were able to avoid danger, and then were directed to the few water holes available. The food they had brought with them was long gone so they snared rabbits and quail and, occasionally, a slow armadillo. They were able to harvest some seeds but their greatest treats were ripe, luscious, purple fruit from the prickly cactus.

For four long weeks they battled their way through the inhospitable desert. Then water holes became more frequent with an occasional stream for them to bathe in and to refresh themselves. Cottonwood trees replaced the desert cactus, and soon they crossed the rolling hills signalling the end of the desert.

The rest of the journey to the Capitol City was routine. They crossed large rivers, sometimes floating across on logs, other times using the canoes of friendly tribes. In each village Moroni taught the people, telling them of their Father in Heaven and of Jesus Christ. His love and kindness were apparent to all they met, and he and his friends were received with superstitious awe.

This great land with its sweeping landscapes and vast distances continued to amaze Moroni. He thought of the many prophecies on the plates which told of this land. It truly was a land of promise. He taught the people the promise that Nephi had made concerning their seed, that ". . . *the Lord God hath covenanted with thy father that his seed should have* [this land] *as the land of their inheritance"* and that their descendants would never be destroyed.

It had been but a short time since Moroni had abridged the writings of Ether. He remembered vividly the Lord's promise concerning this land:

"Behold, this is a choice land, and whatsoever nation shall possess it shall be free from bondage, and from captivity, and from all other nations under heaven, if they will but serve the God of the land, who is Jesus Christ." [53]

Moroni never tired of reading the plates. He often shared their teachings with Kilihu and Namah. The time in the evening when they sat to rest and read the plates was the favorite time of the day for all of them. They shared excitement as they heard of the Lord's dealings with Lehi and his associates. They sorrowed together as they heard of their people turning from the Lord. When Moroni read of Samuel the Lamanite, Kilihu and Namah shed tears of joy—to think that their people had become even more righteous than the Nephites.

As they read of the Savior's visit to this land after his resurrection, their joy was full. Again and again Kilihu would ask Moroni to read of the Savior's visit and teachings. Namah's favorite part was when the Savior blessed the little children. She had Moroni read it so many times that she memorized the words:

"And he took their little children, one by one, and blessed them, and prayed unto the Father for them. And when he had done this, he wept again; and he spake unto the multitude, and said unto them: Behold your little ones. As they looked . . . they saw the heavens open, and they saw angels descending out of heaven as it were in the midst of fire; and they came down and encircled those little ones about, and they were encircled about with fire; and the angels did minister unto them." [54] The compassion of the Savior always touched Namah's heart.

The three travelers, footsore and weary, finally reached the Capitol City on the "father of waters." They had traveled over eighteen hundred miles on foot, most of it through very inhospitable terrain. The journey had taken them five months, from late spring to early fall.

Moroni's arrival in the Capitol City signaled a time of rejoicing for the people. They were pleased to have the Pale One back with them. It seemed to Kilihu and Namah that the entire city lined the streets to welcome him. They were totally amazed at the homage paid to their friend. He had been welcomed in the villages along the way, but nothing like this. Moroni was pleased to be back. It saddened him, though, to see how much the people had forgotten of what he had taught them.

Staying through the winter gave him a good opportunity to reteach the people. Every day he walked through the snow to the assembly in the council house where he carefully reviewed each doctrine, teaching them faith, repentance, baptism, and the Gift of the Holy Spirit. Then he would start all over again, remembering the counsel his father had given him many years before: to keep it simple and repeat it often.

Kilihu and Namah were also busy. Kilihu hunted with the warriors, bringing in venison and buffalo for their meat supply. They tanned the hides and dried the meat, all in preparation for their eastward journey in the spring. From the hides Namah made leggings and boots and coats to keep out the winter chill. Moroni taught Kilihu the art of goldsmithing, showing him how to turn a lump of gold into a fine sheet as thin as the bark paper they wrote on.

The deep snow of winter finally gave way to the mud and buds which prefaced the spring. Moroni chafed anxiously. Spring was his favorite time of the year and his heart swelled with the joy of living as he watched new buds forming on the trees. Spring to him was a time of renewing, a time of rebirth. He likened it to an annual resurrection of the earth from its winter death. Having lived in the tropics most of his life where there was no perceptible change between one season and the next—except for the amount of rainfall—he appreciated the spring even more. He enjoyed all of the seasons: summer with its long gentle days; fall with its beautiful colors and harvest; winter with its quiet snows; spring with its exuberance. But spring was still his favorite.

When the last ice floe melted in the river, Moroni knew it was time to leave. He watched anxiously for the trading ships, waiting for the one which would take them eastward to the land of the Senecas. One day while teaching in the council house of the Puants, he was interrupted by an excited Kilihu. "They are here! They are here!"

The traders from the south had arrived. Some of them would surely be traveling eastward. The next days were exciting ones for the three travelers. After unloading their wares, the traders split into smaller groups, some heading north to the city called Sacred, some heading up the West River, and one group going up the river to the east. Moroni arranged passage with this latter group, and they were almost on their way.

They bid a fond farewell to the people of the Capitol City. The people were sad to see him leave. They lined the streets as he passed through on his way to the river. As he watched the Capitol City receding in the distance as the river took them downstream, he realized that this was the last time he would see the city.

Their journey followed the same course as his earlier visit to the Seneca nations. Down the "father of waters" to its juncture with the East River and up the river as far as the boats could take them, then overland to a wide plateau, arriving in the rolling hills south of an immense body of water.

They had traveled from the high plateaus of the land of Tula, through mountains and deserts, across the great plains, along mighty rivers, and through verdant forests in order to reach this particular spot. As they stood at the base of a beautiful, forested hill, the three dropped to their knees in thanksgiving. This was the hill where Moroni would turn over the plates.

It was the hill of his vision. The journey had taken them one-and-a-half years. They had traveled over three thousand miles, transporting the plates and the breastplate from the Hill Cumorah to this unknown hill [which would become known to millions as "Cumorah"]. This was to be Moroni's last earthly home.

Chapter 18

Mission Completed

Moroni, old, tired and feeling his eighty-two years, lay quietly under the rabbit-fur blanket. His body ached and occasionally his knees would quake as a chill ran through his weakened body. Ayloo, his Seneca nurse, put her hand under his neck and raised his head. He could smell the venison broth even before she spooned it into his mouth. It was hot and tasted good. He was content. He knew the time was near when he would rejoin his family and friends, and he was ready. He had fought a good fight.

After eating his meagre fare, he lay there reminiscing about his life. Of course there were some regrets, but he had truly attempted to serve the Lord to the best of his ability. It had now been eighteen years since he, Kilihu, and Namah had brought the plates to this place. The plates were now safely buried in the hill, ready for the restoration of the gospel.

He was very thankful to the Seneca people who had taken him and his friends under their care and protection. They had provided him with this bark house in which to live, and had provided him with servants to care for his needs. He had traveled to each Seneca village, preaching the word and enjoying the opportunity to teach the people.

When at home, he had spent most of his time inscribing on the plates. He hadn't always known what to write, so he had asked, and the whispering had come to him to record the ordinances of the Church. He wrote down how the Holy Ghost had been bestowed by the Twelve, and then wrote concerning the ordination to the priesthood of those who were worthy. He recorded the prayers that had been given to him for administering the sacrament, both bread and wine, and then discussed how the Church had functioned.

Revelations through the Holy Spirit came almost daily. Often he would greet his friends with a shining countenance and fiery eyes. They would know he had received more revelations or had again talked with the Savior or one of his angels. His friends stood in awe of these moments. Moroni knew that, to them, it was still very much a supernatural mystery. After such a visitation, Moroni would take his stylus and a gold plate which Kilihu had prepared and retire to a private place to write. What he wrote on the plates they did not know, as he never talked of it. Once he did mention something about "sealed records" but he realized that just puzzled them even more.

To Moroni, life was beautiful and pleasant. He didn't really like the bitter-cold winters, but his needs were taken care of, he had his friends, and he was in almost constant communication with the Holy Spirit.

Kilihu and Namah were happy, also. Namah had her first baby, a black-haired husky boy, and Kilihu was a very proud father. They asked Moroni to give it a blessing, which he did. They named the boy, Ammoroni, in honor of him. Kilihu spent most of his days hunting and trapping with his Seneca friends, providing food for the four of them, plus obtaining furs which could be used for trading.

The time came when Moroni once again needed more gold for the plates. None was available among the Senecas, so Kilihu volunteered to travel downstream to the Capitol City to obtain more so the work of writing could continue. He loaded a barge of furs for the journey, and with three Seneca warriors, started off. Moroni reluctantly watched him go. It was only after he was long gone down the river that Namah confided to Moroni that she was expecting another child. Tears came to his eyes as he realized her willingness to sacrifice in order for him to continue to write. He knew how difficult it was for her to be left alone, so during the weeks of Kilihu's absence he spent much more time with her and Ammoroni.

He carefully guarded the plates, keeping them in a safe place except when he wanted to read or study them. As often as he could he would walk up on the side of Cumorah, sitting and meditating. Sometimes he would again see visions of the future. He felt he was never alone when he was on the mountain.

How joyous everyone was when Kilihu returned. He had traded furs for gold, but had also made other purchases. Standing close to Namah, who was very obvious now in her pregnancy, he reached into the folds of his fur cape and pulled out a beautiful gold amulet. It was shaped like a fawn deer and hung from a length of sinew. With loving care he placed it around Namah's thin neck. She reached up a hand, touched it, and clasped it to her breast. It was a tender moment, and all three had tears welling in their eyes.

Ammoroni was impatient for attention, tugging at his father's hem. Kilihu picked him up and threw him into the air, catching him and sweeping the ground with him. Ammoroni squealed with delight, asking to be thrown up again and again. Kilihu reached once more into his robe, this time pulling out a toy for Ammoroni. It was an intricately carved statue of a prairie bison, feet apart, head down, looking as if it were ready to charge. The massive front shoulders and tawny mane were done in exquisite detail. Even Moroni, a craftsman himself, was impressed. It was carved from heavy dark wood which had been polished to a bright lustre by the loving hands of its creator. Ammoroni was delighted. Up to now his only toys had consisted of a small bow and arrow which his father had made for him, and some knee bone from a deer which he had used as play animals. It was a time of joy and gladness for all.

The time came for the delivery of Namah's second baby. It was a lovely little dark-eyed girl—the image of her grandmother, Zilar. Kilihu was overjoyed. Moroni was again asked to pronounce a blessing on the baby. She was given the name of Zilpan. It was such a pleasure for Moroni to have Kilihu and his family with him. He enjoyed them as if they were his own children and grandchildren.

Soon after Zilpan was born, Moroni noticed that Namah became more and more restless. Something was troubling her, and Moroni instinctively knew what it was. Her loyalty and love for him was in conflict with her desire to return to the home of her parents. One day when Kilihu was hunting, Moroni approached her about it. "Namah," he began. "It makes me sad to see you unhappy."

She looked at him in surprise. "Unhappy?" she said. "I am not unhappy."

Gently Moroni put his hands on her thin shoulders. "It is no secret, my daughter, that you are lonesome for your parents."

She buried her head in his shoulder, her voice erupting in loud sobs. "Oh, I am so mixed up," she sobbed. "I want to stay with you, but Abalom and Zilar have not even seen their grandchildren. I know not but what they have died already, but I so long to see them once more."

Moroni held her tightly to him, giving her comfort. Her body jerked convulsively against him as she sobbed. It was the first time Moroni had really seen her cry. He stood there waiting for the storm to pass. In time her shaking stopped and she pushed away from him. Looking up into his face with eyes that were now red-rimmed, she asked, "Moroni, you are as a father to me. What should we do?"

"I don't know, my daughter," he replied. "It has been over ten years since you left your parent's home. If I figure correctly, this will be your mother's sixtieth year. She and Abalom are no longer young." He smiled to himself. He was now seventy-five and still going strong. "If you are to see them while they live, you had better soon return to their home."

"But what if they have already died?" she asked, her tear-stained face smudged where she had wiped it with her bare arm.

Moroni smiled again, this time with a look of detachment. "I will inquire of the Lord."

Namah embraced him. "Oh, Moroni, I don't want to leave you."

He held her away from him so he could look into her eyes. "The Lord will give us guidance."

That evening the family gathered around the little fire in the bark house. It was comfortable and warm, even though a wind raged outside. He held little Zilpah on his lap. She snuggled close, enjoying the warmth and comfort of Moroni's big lap. Ammoroni played with his toys at their feet, pretending to be a mighty warrior stalking his foe. Kilihu and Namah waited expectantly, trusting in Moroni's judgment, knowing that he had asked the Lord.

A pang of doubt hit him and he thought, Could it be that after all of this time I am to be a lonely man once again? Zilpan was now asleep on his lap. He continued gently rocking her back and forth. He gazed at the fire, leaping and dancing, casting prancing shadows on the wall. Looking up, he said, "The Spirit has whispered to me that your parents still live, Namah."

There was a drawn-out silence. Namah was relieved, but then she asked, "But what are we to do?"

"My children, that is a decision that only you can make," Moroni said.

During the next few weeks he tried very hard to avoid influencing the decision to be made. After careful thought, accompanied by fasting and prayer, Namah and Kilihu decided it would be best to go back to the high plateau of Tula and see Namah's parents once again. They felt they could stay long enough for Abalom and Zilar to enjoy their grandchildren, and then they could return and live with Moroni.

Moroni was sad, but he did not show it. He was glad that they could go, but he knew they would never return. It was too far. The round trip would take several years, and with small children . . .

All during the winter they made preparation for the journey, and when spring came and Zilpan was two years of age, they departed. It had been a sad and poignant goodbye.

It had now been seven years since they had gone, and as he lay with his memories his eyes once again filled with tears. He wondered what had happened to his friends. He had inquired often of the Lord, and the Spirit had whispered that they were no longer on the earth—that he was the last surviving Christian.

These last seven years had been devoted strictly to completing and protecting the records. With crude hammer and chisel he had fashioned a box of stones near the top of the hill. Using knowledge from his youth, he burned some lime and made cement to hold the box together. He then covered the sides with dirt topped off with sod. Only the very top of the box showed above the ground. Inside the box he placed two long flat stones to keep the breastplate and plates off the floor. For the top of the box he chiseled a large stone which lay nearby. He left the top naturally rounded, but methodically chiseled off the bottom until it was flat and would sit snugly on top of the box. He levered it into place after placing the Urim and Thummin into the box. It was not yet time to put in the plates. He still had inscribing to do.

Each year he carefully inscribed more plates to go into the sealed portion of the book, which now was larger than the portion that he and Mormon had worked on. He was about out of gold plates, having only one plate left. He knew that he would finish his work with that plate. He carefully inscribed his father's sermon that he had carried around with him all these years. He had referred to it often and the bark paper had been replaced several times as he had rewritten it. He felt it was his father's greatest, and he thrilled as he inscribed it onto the plates. It spoke of faith, hope, and charity. It ended with this fervent testimony:

"Charity is the pure love of Christ, and it endureth forever; and whoso is found possessed of it at the last day, it shall be well with him. Wherefore, my beloved brethren, pray unto the father with all energy of heart, that ye may be filled with this love, which he hath bestowed upon all who are true followers of his Son, Jesus Christ; that ye may become the sons of God; that when he shall appear we shall be like him, for we shall see him as he is; that we may have this hope; that we may be purified even as he is pure. Amen" [55]

He inscribed two of Mormon's letters that had been written to him when he presided over the Church in Desolation. One of them dealt with the purity of little children—that they needed no baptism until they were of an accountable age. After he had inscribed the letter, he reread it. Mormon had summarized the principles of the gospel in one paragraph. He read and reread the passage. It was one he had committed to memory many years before and had used it often in teaching the people:

"And the first fruits of repentance is baptism; and baptism cometh by faith unto the fulfilling the commandments; and the fulfilling the commandments bringeth remission of sins; and the remission of sins bringeth meekness and lowliness of heart; and because of meekness and lowliness of heart cometh the visitation of the Holy Ghost, which Comforter filleth with hope and perfect love, which love endureth by diligence unto prayer, until the end shall come, when all the saints shall dwell with God." [56]

The second letter from Mormon told of the evil happenings of the Nephite and Lamanite nations. It was a sad letter, and the last one his father had written to him. The end of the letter was written assuming that Mormon might never see his son again in the flesh. Moroni read it again and thanked the Lord that he had been able to spend those last choice years with his father. The letter ended:

"My son, be faithful in Christ; and may not the things which I have written grieve thee, . . . but may Christ lift thee up, and may his suffering and death, . . . and his mercy and long-suffering, and the hope of his glory and of eternal life, rest in your mind forever. And may the grace of God the

Father, whose throne is high in the heavens, and our Lord Jesus Christ, who sitteth on the right hand of his power, until all things shall become subject unto him, be, and abide with you forever. Amen" [56]

Moroni smiled. His father could surely say things in an eloquent way. As he read the passage again, he was exultant. Christ *had* lifted him up! Filled with this sweet spirit, he embarked on his last writing. He had such a great love for the Lamanite people. For the past thirty years he had lived among the descendants of the Lamanites in the Land Northward. He had a solemn wish that he could have touched the hearts of those in the lands of Bountiful and Desolation. He wrote a message directed toward the Lamanite people:

"Behold, I would exhort you that when ye shall read these things, . . . that ye would remember how merciful the Lord hath been unto the children of men, from the creation of Adam even down unto the time that he shall receive these things, and ponder it in your hearts."

Then he pled with his Lamanite brethren:

"And when ye shall receive these things, I would exhort you that ye would ask God, the Eternal Father, in the name of Christ, if these things are not true; and if ye shall ask with a sincere heart, with real intent, having faith in Christ, he will manifest the truth of it unto you, by the power of the Holy Ghost. And by the power of the Holy Ghost ye may know the truth of all things." [57]

He bore his testimony to the divinity of Jesus Christ and of the gifts of God. He thought back over his own life and how the Lord had showered the gifts of the Spirit upon him. He had healed the sick, raised the dead, calmed the seas, prophesied the future, spoken in tongues, understood the languages of all the people with whom he had come in contact, and had been ministered to by angels. All of these gifts were of the spirit and had come about through his faith. He listed each of the gifts and said:

"And all these gifts come by the Spirit of Christ; and they come unto every man severally, according as he will. And I would exhort you, my beloved brethren, that ye remember that every good gift cometh of Christ." [58]

He again spoke of faith, hope, and charity, reaffirming what Mormon had written so many years before:

"Except ye have charity ye can in nowise be saved in the kingdom of God; neither can ye be saved . . . if ye have not faith; neither can ye if ye have no hope. And if ye have no hope ye must needs be in despair; and despair cometh because of iniquity. And Christ truly said unto our fathers: If ye have faith ye can do all things which are expedient unto me." [59]

As he wrote, he saw in vision the people who would be reading the book, and he spoke directly to them, exhorting them to remember the things they read, telling them that the Lord would show them that *"that which*

I have written is true. " As he neared the end of his writing, his words soared on wings of oratory. Words flowed through his stylus. He wrote:

"And awake, and arise from the dust, O Jerusalem; yea, and put on thy beautiful garments, O daughter of Zion; and strengthen thy stakes and enlarge thy borders forever, . . . Yea, come unto Christ, and be perfected in him, and deny yourselves of all ungodliness and love God with all your might, mind and strength, then is his grace sufficient for you, that by his grace ye may be perfect in Christ; and if by the grace of God ye are perfect in Christ, ye can in nowise deny the power of God. " [60]

He closed his writing with his personal testimony:

"And now I bid unto all, farewell. I soon go to rest in the paradise of God, until my spirit and body shall again reunite, and I am brought forth triumphant through the air, to meet you before the pleasing bar of the great Jehovah, the Eternal Judge of both quick and dead. Amen. " [61]

He was finished. He had fulfilled the mission the Savior had assigned to him. He was now ready to hide the plates, but a nagging feeling kept coming to him. *"Wait, Moroni."*

Once more he knelt in prayer. What is it, Lord? Is there more to write? Thy will be done.

The spirit whispered to him. *"Write a title page for the book. I will tell you what to write."*

He once again picked up the stylus. As the spirit whispered to him, he wrote. It was on the left side of the last plate of gold. There was only room enough for two paragraphs.

THE BOOK OF MORMON

An account written by the hand of Mormon,
upon Plates taken from the Plates of Nephi.

Wherefore, it is an abridgment of the record of the people of Nephi, and also of the Lamanites—Written to the Lamanites, who are a remnant of the house of Israel; and also to Jew and Gentile. . . . also to the convincing of the Jew and Gentile that JESUS IS THE CHRIST THE ETERNAL GOD, manifesting himself unto all nations. . . . " [62]

After finishing, he waited, wondering if there were more. The Spirit whispered: *"That is all. Well done, Moroni. You have completed the work."*

With shaking fingers he gently put the thick stack of plates into the box, propping them up on the stones on the bottom. It took all of his remaining strength and left him exhausted. The plates were heavy. He guessed that they weighed more than one-fourth of what he weighed. He lay there beside the box, building up his strength. Then with great effort, breathing heavily, he levered the large cap rock onto the box. Inch by laborious sweaty inch he moved the rock into place. With his breath coming in gasps, he mixed some mortar and filled in the crack around the top. The job was done and Moroni fell back, completely spent.

He managed to crawl down off the hill that night and there Ayloo found him. She had helped him back into his bed and here he was. He had a peace about him that he had never felt before. He had completed the work.

He lay there, his breathing ever more shallow, feeling a heaviness around his heart. Suddenly in his consciousness he heard a voice: *"Moroni. Moroni."*

He looked up. A light was shining in his eyes. His face became radiant as he heard a voice from the heavens: *"Come unto me, my son."*

He raised his arms, reaching toward the voice, and in peace and contentment, his eyes closed for the last time in mortality.

PART V

Paradise

Moroni was engulfed by a loud buzzing. It was very uncomfortable, but then he felt himself moving rapidly as if through a long dark tunnel. There was no sensation of time or space, but suddenly he found himself floating above the bed in the familiar bark house where he had lived for almost eighteen years. Below him, lying on the cot, was a body which he recognized as his own. The body was old and wrinkled, but it had been the home for his spirit for eighty-three years. Distractedly, he thought that he should be sad now to leave it, but instead he felt joy and anticipation.

Ayloo, his Seneca nurse, rocking back and forth in the traditional Seneca attitude of mourning, was keening a wailing lament. It seemed that he spent only a few moments looking at his body and then suddenly he was whisked towards a bright, warm, glowing light. The closer he got to the light, the brighter it became. As he came out of the darkness he saw that the light was really a person—a person dressed in Nephite armor. "Father," he cried as he recognized Mormon.

His father had come to meet him and escort him to Paradise. Father and son embraced hungrily. Moroni pulled back, looking his father up and down. Mormon was dark-haired, full-chested, robust, in the prime of life. Moroni was surprised at his youthful appearance. He was also surprised when he understood what his father was thinking before he spoke the words.

"My son," Mormon began. "I am so proud of you. For these many years I have watched your every move. I have been near you in everything you have done."

Moroni nodded. "I have felt your influence. So many times thoughts just seemed to come into my mind—things I had heard you say to me in my youth. I almost felt as if you were holding me by the hand in my endeavors." He was still very curious about this spirit world he was entering. "Are you able to go back to the earth and visit those you have left behind?"

"Yes, my son," Mormon replied. "I received special permission to be your guardian spirit. I have encouraged and watched you as you completed your mission on the earth."

Moroni squeezed his father once again. "Thank you."

"Come, there is much to do and see."

They turned, walking together down a little-traveled path through a tall, almost primeval, forest. Moroni looked upwards at the tall trees which pointed their tops at an iridescent sky. It was almost as if he hadn't left the earth, except that everything was so much more beautiful. Long trailing vines, replete with flowers, lined the path. Never had Moroni seen such colors. Instead of all living things being green, as on the earth, the vegetation was various shades of gold and scarlet, muted wtih shades of pink and lavender.

A sweet feeling of calmness pervaded this place—a feeling of peace that he had never felt before. It was as if all care and worry were totally discarded. It was a peace brought forth by knowledge and surety. One no longer had to rely on faith. The future was here!

As they came out of the forest, a vista of great beauty opened before them. To their right was a beautiful aquamarine lake, mirroring the forest which surrounded it. Across the lake and to the left was a group of large, white buildings, more magnificent than any buildings he had ever seen. Coming closer to the buildings, Moroni saw large concourses filled with people.

One group, waiting on the fringes of the crowd, detached itself and ran towards him. As they neared, he recognized them. It was his loved ones! There were Armora, Merena, Sophrista, and his sons, Gidgiddonah and Moronihah. Kilihu and Namah were there with parents and grandparents, Abalom, Zilar, Palorem and Tabor. All were fair-skinned and in the prime of life. There were five he didn't recognize. It suddenly dawned on him; there were no older people and no children. Could it be? . . . The five he didn't recognize, they must be! Yes! Now he recognized his children, Bilnor and Greta. His children were now adults.

He was so excited! He ran to meet them. As they came together, he threw out his arms, hugging one another, feeling their love and excitement in return. Tears flowed freely. He held Armora close. After over forty years of being apart he didn't ever want to let her go. It was such a joyful reunion. He found out that one of the other young men was Sophrista's betrothed, and the other two were Kilihu and Namah's children, Ammoroni and Zilpan. They had all preceded him to Paradise.

They walked arm-in-arm towards the cluster of buildings. Mormon, in a hushed voice, said, "Look!"

Looking where Mormon was pointing, Moroni saw a large group of men, all dressed in shining white robes, coming out of a magnificent large, golden-spired building—obviously a temple. It was a temple more grand and glorious than any he had seen on earth. The men stopped at the bottom of the steps, visiting with one another in muted voices. There was something about them that was different from all of the others Moroni had observed so far in Paradise. Then it struck him. There whole bodies were radiant, glowing with a heavenly illumination. One of the men was even more holy and transcendent than all of the others. Moroni immediately recognized Him. It was the Savior! He looked up, saw Moroni, and smiled, beckoning him over.

Moroni hurried to His side and dropped to his knees. The Savior gently lifted him to his feet. Smiling, he said, *"Moroni, my son. Welcome to Paradise."* With his hand on Moroni's shoulders, he guided him forward until he was facing the other men. Most were bearded. All had an ethereal beauty of countenance. He glanced around the group, not knowing what to expect, but feeling from them a great outpouring of love.

The Savior continued, *"Moroni, I want you to meet some of your fellow prophets who preceded you."* He went from one to another in the group, pointing and calling each by name. *"Moses, Elijah, Nephi, Ether, Mosiah, . . ."* On and on the list went, people whom Moroni had read and heard about since his childhood. All of the great prophets from the brass plates and from the plates he and Mormon had abridged! He was overawed and overjoyed. He solemnly shook hands with each one. He glanced over his shoulder at Armora and his loved ones who watched with shining eyes.

His mind came back to what the Savior was saying, *"All of you have observed how faithfully Moroni has carried out his mission."* All nodded, looking at Moroni with kind and respectful eyes. Turning back to Moroni, the Savior continued. *"Here you will have a continuation of that mission. We still have much to do in teaching the righteous about the Gospel. Moroni, your special mission will be to prepare for the restoraton of the Gospel on the earth. You will play a significant role in that restoration. While here you will gain knowledge and understanding of that role. You will work directly with Elijah and Moses who will also have major roles in the restoration."* Moroni glanced at Elijah and Moses, who smiled back and nodded in affirmation.

Seeing him glance at Armora, the Savior smiled. *"We will have plenty of time to discuss that. Right now, go with your family. Get acquainted with Paradise. We will talk later."* The Savior turned back to the group of prophets and Moroni walked quickly back to his family and friends.

Time in paradise was irrelevant. There was no need for sleep, so people could work and play and study continuously. Moroni spent much time with his family, getting caught up on the news, visiting with grandparents and other ancestors, listening to family and friends as they talked of their last days on earth.

He was impressed at the orderly manner in which everything seemed to be happening. Everyone seemed to have something to do. He observed ladies making new white robes for those just entering. Others were gathering genealogical data, some were studying from the great discourses and histories. Many were involved in missionary work with those spirits who were in the spirit prison. He observed that many new buildings were under construction and many of the people were involved in these projects. Everything seemed purposeful—perfectly organized with the people being industrious and busy. They were self-thinking and self-disciplined.

Most of the people were dressed in white. Moroni had been given a new robe soon after meeting the Savior. He noted that some of the people were dressed in earthly clothing. When he asked, he was informed that they were dressed in such a way that when they met their relatives who were leaving earth and entering Paradise they would be recognized.

There were few children or elderly people. Again, he was informed that only those in need of being recognized would still appear as children or old people. Other than those few exceptions, everyone appeared in the prime of life. Those who had been scarred or had lost limbs were now whole. He chuckled. Even his grandfather, Mormon, who had been completely bald, now had a beautiful full head of hair. He looked at his own hands where for so long the scars of his near death had been so dominant. They were now clear and unblemished.

He enjoyed his family so much. They spent hours discussing what they had done since he had last seen them. He didn't have to inform them of his actions, as they had observed him and had been totally aware of all he had done. How glad he was that he had lived righteously! What would it be like to meet loved ones and have them know of all the evil thoughts and actions one had done on the earth? That would not only be embarrassing, but it would be devastating! One wouldn't be able to face others. Moroni wondered if that was what the first judgment was—people who isolate themselves in a prison of their own making rather than face loved ones who know what one has been thinking and doing.

In addition to being with his family, Moroni loved to associate with the great prophets. It amazed and humbled him that they considered him as their equal. He sat at the feet of Moses, he visited with Elijah and Noah. He met Adam. Most of these great prophets had resurrected bodies. They looked just like the spirit bodies, except for the heavenly glow which came from them. It was a celestial illumination which seemed to emanate from within, causing a luminescence to surround them.

He took every opportunity to follow the Savior, listening to His every word. He thrilled as he listened to Alma and Ether. He stood in awe as he felt the great spirituality of the Brother of Jared. As he thought about it in one of his quiet moments, his existence since entering the Spirit World had been one of a continuous feast—a feast of spirit food unsurpassed in his prior understanding. In addition to meeting personally with the great prophets and patriarchs, Moroni spent a great deal of time in the library.

He found that every record which had ever been written on the earth was duplicated here, including all of his own and Mormon's writings.

Some of his favorite time was spent listening to the heavenly choirs. The four women he loved most dearly; Armora, Merena, Sophrista, and Greta all sang in the choir. Music formed a major part of the spirit world, and Moroni was glad. Each day the choir sang in the plaza before the great temple. They sang praises to the Savior and to Heavenly Father. There were also heavenly orchestras and marching bands.

Years came and went unrecognized in Paradise, except as people had contact with the earth which continued through its annual cycles. In Paradise it was always spring. There was no dying, therefore, no need of renewal. On the earth, he observed the continuation of evil, the wars, the wicked combinations which Lucifer kept encouraging.

With prophetic eyes, he knew that the time of the restoration was close at hand. It was the time he had spoken of when he had written on the plates: *"Behold, look ye unto the revelations of God; for behold, the time cometh at that day when all things must be fulfilled."* [63]

It was so exciting to him to know that the time was near at hand. He observed the work of Calvin, Luther, and the other reformers. As they arrived in the spirit world Moroni visited with each of them to hear from their own lips about conditions on the earth. He studied and prepared himself for his role in the restoration. Often, he would be involved in seminars with the great prophets. Occasionally, the Savior Himself would teach the seminars—giving him greater depth of understanding concerning the plan of salvation.

One day he received a summons to appear in the temple. He had often been in the temple for meetings and programs, but this was the first time he had been invited to the upper rooms where the very throne of God was! As he walked into the temple he was again amazed and awed by its grandeur. The beauty of it defied all description. The workmanship was perfect and the construction materials exquisite. Each feature was wrought in intricate detail. The floors seemed to be solid gold and the walls and ceilings glowed with an ethereal, heavenly light.

Great paintings by heavenly artists lined many of the walls. The stairway, long and winding, seemed to lead into the very heavens. Along one side was a jade-colored banister supported by a balustrade of what appeared to be hand-carved oak. Each baluster was a carved figure of one of the great prophets. Moroni recognized Adam, Enoch, Noah, Abraham and others. They all appeared lifelike. Nearer the top, he was amazed to see carvings of his father and himself. He felt honored and pleased to be included in such a great listing of prophetic figures and leaders.

On the stairs he joined others who had also been summoned. Many of them he recognized as great leaders in Paradise. He also recognized several of the prophets of the promised land. He was extremely pleased when Mormon joined him. Some of the men whispered quietly as they filed into the large council room. Moroni could hear the question in their voices.

He looked around as he entered the great chamber. A huge chandelier dominated the vaulted ceiling, casting light and a rainbow of colors down upon the assembly. The heraldic choir sat in front, singing soft prelude music. When everyone was seated, they burst into a triumphant hymn of praise. As they did so, the eleven apostles of the Master filed in and took their seats in the first row immediately beneath the pulpit. From the other side of the room filed the nine disciples of the Master from the promised land. They took their seats in the row just below the row of apostles. Missing were the three disciples who had ministered to him so often. From personal experience he knew of their decision to remain on the earth until the Savior's second coming. He felt a pang in his heart as he thought how much they had meant to him. Their support and spiritual strength had pulled him through many a crisis.

Next to come in was Adam, the father of the race. Here in Paradise he was known as Michael. He stood at the pulpit, and as soon as the choir had finished its hymn, he said in a quiet but firm voice, "All arise."

As the congregation arose, the choir burst into a great swelling hymn of praise. Moroni listened to the words, "Praise ye the Lord, the God of all Creation. Praise be the Lord, the Ruler of all Nations. . . ." Moroni lost interest in the rest of the words as he saw a tall, handsome white-haired figure mount the podium, followed by the Savior. Moroni's heart seemed to skip a beat. It must be the Father, Elohim! He was so excited that his breathing became shallow, his heart was in his throat, his skin covered with goosebumps. The choir ended the hymn and sat down. Michael extended his arms and motioned the congregation to be seated. Moroni's mouth was dry and he could sense the excitement and anticipation of those around him.

Solemnly, Michael began. "You have been called here for a special purpose. Each of you, in your own way, has been valiant in keeping the commandments, in fulfilling your own special mission, and in defending the faith. You were not only valiant during your first and second estates, but have been anxiously engaged in furthering your knowledge and continuing your mission here in Paradise. The Father . . . (he paused in deference to Elohim) . . . presides at this meeting, but he has asked me to conduct it. I am privileged to do so."

Moroni sat entranced as Michael continued. His eyes often strayed to the two mighty figures seated behind Michael. He had difficulty believing that he was in their holy presence. Michael talked of many wonderful things, giving promises yet to be fulfilled, telling of blessings yet to come. He then turned the meeting over to Elohim, the Father—the God of all Creation.

Elohim stood for a moment, looking over these, his valiant children. He spoke: *"My sons and daughters, you have proven yourselves beyond any question. You are to be exalted, but there is much left to do."* Moroni listened, enthralled. The sweet melodious voice rang forth across the congregation like a bell, pealing forth the message of faith and love. He ended his few remarks by saying, *"And now, my children, you are ready for another change in your progression—a change you have been anticipating."* He smiled a joyful smile. *"My only begotten Son will tell you."* He sat down. Not a sound broke the spell of the Father's words.

The Savior stood. Moroni could feel the intake of breath from the entire congregation. Mormon reached over and squeezed his leg. The Savior was beloved by all and at this time there came again to their hearts the whispering of the Holy Spirit, testifying to each of them of his divinity. He began his message by recounting to them what had happened thus far in their existence. He spoke of the pre-earth life where they had lived without care as the spirit children of the Father. He told of the council in that First Estate when they had voted to go to the earth to receive a body.

He continued: *"Each of you in this room was chosen before you were born to be leaders and prophets. Then each of you was born to the earth during its various dispensations. You fulfilled your calling and completed your mission satisfactorily. Since your rebirth to Paradise, you have also faithfully carried out your duties. It is the Father's will that each of you now receive your resurrected body."*

A hush fell upon the congregation. Their resurrected bodies! They would now have resurrected bodies like Adam and Alma? And the Savior! A whispering passed through the congregation. "Praise the Lord! Hosanna! A resurrected body!" Those on the stand already had their resurrected bodies, but now . . . they were overcome as they looked at each other in that holy place.

The Savior sat down. Michael was again conducting the meeting. Moroni felt a burning within his body as the ceremony continued. The process of change from a spirit body to a resurrected body happened so fast that many were not even aware of it. For Moroni it was a very sacred experience. He felt of his resurrected body. It didn't feel any different, but as he looked around the room he again noted the aura that now surrounded everyone present. As they filed from the temple that day, there was a new feeling, a new sense of freedom. The resurrected body was purified and was not the restrictive being that his earth body had been. Moroni had the same freedom as those who were beings of spirit, but he now had the additional growth potential that his reunited body and spirit gave him.

He knew himself to be ready for the next phase of his mission.

Chapter 19

Teacher to a Prophet

As a resurrected bring, Moroni had even greater freedom and opportunities than he had had as a disembodied spirit. He had the same freedom of movement, but he was not now restricted to the Spirit World. He was able to spend much more time on earth, observing what was happening there.

With interest he watched as colonists came in great numbers to the promised land—the land they called America. It saddened him when he saw how they mistreated the Lamanites—the Indians as they called them—as they pushed their frontiers into the new land. The revolution of the colonists against oppression thrilled him.

He joined with other spirits and resurrected beings who, in great numbers, surrounded the delegates at the constitutional convention, guiding their decisions. He noted with satisfaction the presence in the convention of great thinkers and statesmen, such as Pericles, Cicero and John Locke. Moses, the great law-giver, presided over the assemblage of spirits and resurrected beings. The Lord had marshalled his greatest lawmakers to guide and inspire the writing of the Constitution of the United States.

During the same period of time, Moroni noted the births of those who had been designated as the lineage through whom the prophet of the restoration would come.

A son, Joseph, was born to Asael and Mary Smith on July 22, 1771. Five years later, just four days after the signing of the Declaration of Independence, July 8, 1776, a baby girl was born to Solomon and Lydia Mack. Moroni watched through the years as their lives came together, intertwined, and they were married. He smiled at the way the Lord prepared certain people to accomplish great tasks upon the earth, and then prepared conditions in such a way that they could accomplish them.

He remembered reading the words of Lehi as he cited the prophecies of Joseph concerning a choice seer who the Lord said would come through his lineage. Lehi had quoted Joseph's prophecy:

"Behold, that seer will the Lord bless; . . . and his name shall be called after me; and it shall be after the name of his father. And he shall be like

unto me; for the thing, which the Lord shall bring forth by his hand, by the power of the Lord shall bring my people unto salvation. " [64]

Now Moroni saw that prophecy come to pass. As children were born to Joseph and Lucy, he waited for the chosen one. On December 23, 1805, a son, Joseph, was born. The spirit whispered, "This is he." The prophecy was now to be fulfilled. Moroni's work was now at hand. The Savior had given him the assignment to be a guardian angel to the young Joseph. It was his responsibility to give spiritual help and guidance; to ever be near when Joseph needed uplifting. Moroni was prepared. For centuries he had read and studied and prepared himself for the great day which was coming. The Lord had personally orchestrated this day, preparing the earth for the restoration. All of the political and religious movements for centuries had been leading to this moment. Moroni was excited about having a major role to play in the drama.

He helped prepare Joseph's parents for the part they would play. They would initially be their son's chief supporters. Moroni also nurtured and helped young Joseph over the rough spots of youth, influencing him where he could. It was a labor of love, and though there were many disappointments, Moroni felt a great satisfaction in what he was doing. He developed a great love for young Joseph.

Moroni knew that it was important that Joseph be ready for the Lord's word at the same time that the Lord was ready to give it to him. At last that day came. The Savior called him forth: *"Moroni, the time has come for the restoration of the gospel. All conditions are ready."*

Moroni watched carefully as young Joseph was caught up in the religious revivals of the day. He applauded him as he questioned many of the things which were said. He cheered him on as he opened the Stick of Judah, the modern-day Bible, to find answers to his questions. It didn't require much help on his part to have Joseph find the passage that James had written so many years before: *"If any of you lack wisdom, let him ask of God, that giveth to all men liberally, and upbraideth not; and it shall be given him"* [65]

For his first real attempt at praying, Moroni guided Joseph to a secluded grove of trees where he could pour out his heart. Joseph knelt in prayer. All was going according to plan. Moroni knew that Joseph would have a major test to undergo before he could receive any manifestation from God. Satan, eager to thwart the work of the Lord, would attempt to overpower him. Moroni prayed that the youth would have enough strength to withstand the power of the adversary.

Joseph was seized by Satan and completely overcome. He was thrown to his back and almost lapsed into unconsciousness. He exerted his energies and prayed mightily to be rescued from this awful unseen power. Moroni wasn't able to give him any help, but he encouraged him. Satan had lost.

Joseph had passed the test! Moroni watched as a pillar of light came down from heaven. In that pillar were the Father and the Son. The moment of the restoration was here. Moroni listened as the Father introduced the Savior, and as the Savior told Joseph of his mission. He was proud of the way Joseph handled himself.

After that first great and glorious vision, Moroni continually watched over Joseph, helping him as he gained wisdom and maturity, sorrowing with him as he was persecuted by the so-called religious leaders of his day.

For almost three years Moroni worked closely with Joseph. He was an unseen presence, but a decided influence on Joseph's behavior. Everything that happened was directed toward the time when Joseph would receive the plates from Moroni. My heart is full, he thought as he contemplated the preparation that had gone into this part of the restoration. Here is the person I wrote about so many hundreds of years ago. Now it is time to meet him face to face.

Joseph was kneeling by the side of his bed, praying that the Lord would forgive him of his sins and would give him some sign that He was still with him. Then the command came: *"Go to him."*

Moroni transmitted himself to Joseph's room. He appeared there in his full, resurrected glory. As the room brightened around him, Joseph cowered onto the bed.

"Do not be frightened, Joseph," Moroni began. "I am a messenger sent to you from the presence of God. You have been chosen by the Lord to perform a great mission here upon the earth. Through that mission your name will be known for good and for evil among all nations of the earth."

"But who are you?" Joseph responded. He still appeared to be somewhat frightened and his voice quaked slightly as he spoke. He asked, in a puzzled voice, "And why has the Lord chosen me for such a mission? I am but an unlearned boy."

"I am Moroni," he answered. "I lived upon this continent over fourteen hundred years ago. I, too, was called as a youth to help with the Lord's work, as was my father before me. The Lord often calls upon the young to aid him because they are still teachable and humble. If you accept this calling, I have been chosen by the Lord to be one of your teachers."

Joseph propped himself against the headboard. He was obviously overwhelmed by what was happening, but he listened raptly as Moroni continued.

"During the last part of my life, I wrote of the Lord's dealings with my people. These records were combined with the records my father had compiled concerning the former inhabitants of this continent. These inhabitants are, and were, a branch of the House of Israel which left Jerusalem prior to the coming of the Savior to that land."

This seemed to be a little too much for a seventeen-year-old boy to comprehend all at once. Joseph had a questioning look on his face when he finally asked, "But what became of the people you are telling me about?"

"Many of them were destroyed because of their wickedness," Moroni answered. "Those who remain are known by you as 'Indians.' "

Joseph, looking less frightened, but still very curious, asked, "But why are you telling me all of this?"

Moroni smiled. "Let me remind you that the Lord has chosen you as the one to restore the fulness of His gospel to the earth. You have a great responsibility. The record of which I have spoken contains the gospel in its fulness. The book, written on plates of gold, is buried near here. If you remain worthy, it will be your responsibility to bring forth that record and publish it for all mankind to read."

"But I am unlearned," Joseph repeated. "How would I be able to read ancient records?"

"Hidden with the book are two stones in silver bows, fastened to a breastplate. These stones, along with the power of God, give a person the power to translate. They were used by prophets of old who became known as 'seers.' The Lord has had them brought here, with the plates, to be used in translating the ancient records. That will be your responsibility and calling."

As Moroni spoke, he could see that Joseph listened intently. He was a serious youth and Moroni was proud of him for accepting his calling in such a manner. Joseph now seemed to comprehend the purpose of Moroni's visit, so Moroni continued.

"Joseph, there are certain scriptures which will help you to understand your mission. You are to memorize them and ponder them in your heart. The Holy Ghost will help you recall all that I tell you. The Lord will make the meaning of the scriptures clear to you."

Moroni spent much time teaching from the ancient scriptures, giving quotes from the books of Malachi and Isaiah. As he spoke of the "rod that would come forth out of the stem of Jesse," he paused and looked at Joseph. "You are that rod, Joseph." He then quoted from the book of Acts and the book of Joel, both of which prophesied concerning the last days. After quoting from Joel, he said, "Joseph, the fulness of the gentiles will soon come. You will be very much involved in ushering in that time."

He ended his session with the boy prophet by telling him, "Joseph, when you receive the plates of which I have spoken—and by the way, the time is not yet when you shall get them—you may not show them to any-one—neither the plates nor the breastplate with the Urim and Thummin—unless I give you specific commandment to do so. You are not to even let them out of your hands unless they are secured by lock and key. There are many who would desire to have them, to destroy the work of the Lord. Listen carefully, Joseph, as this is very important. If you do not heed this warning, you will be destroyed."

The Holy Ghost then opened a vision in Joseph's mind showing him the place where the plates were hidden. As he was involved with this vision, Moroni withdrew himself.

The Lord had instructed Moroni to so impress the message on Joseph's mind that he would never forget it. He didn't leave Joseph to ponder for very long. In but a few moments he appeared to him again, repeating almost verbatim what he had said before. Then he added, "Joseph, great judgments will soon come upon the earth. There will be great desolations caused by famine, and the sword, and all forms of pestilence. The people need to repent so they will be ready for these things that will come on the earth during this generation."

As he gave these instructions, Moroni marveled at the youth before him. The Lord had said that Joseph had been prepared from before the foundations of the earth, and that he was a prophet of the same stature as Abraham and Moses; that he was to be God's annointed prophet, seer and revelator on the earth.

When he had finished the instructions the second time, Moroni again left Joseph's room—but again for only a few moments. Once more he returned and rehearsed all that he had said before, adding, "Joseph, because of the financial situation your family is in, Satan will tempt you to use the gold plates for riches. You have already suffered the buffetings of Satan and know his power. The Lord has forgiven you your errors in judgment. Remember, though, that the temptations you have had in the past are as nothing compared with what you will now face. Be careful, my brother, to have no other desires in obtaining the plates than to fulfill the purposes of the Lord and to glorify Him. You must not be influenced by any other motive than that of building up His Kingdom, otherwise you will not be able to obtain the plates."

Once again Moroni left Joseph to ponder his message. His visits had taken all night and Moroni watched to see how Joseph would handle what he had heard. Joseph got up as he normally would, ate a meagre breakfast, and went out into the fields with his father and Alvin, his brother. It was harvest time and they were reaping barley. Moroni noted that Joseph had a hard time staying up. Alvin, seeing how slow he was, came over and said, "Joseph, we must not slacken our hands or we will not be able to complete our task." [66]

Joseph tried valiantly, but in his tired state he was unable to keep up. The scythe became heavier and heavier in his hands. Moroni felt sorry for him, struggling as he was. Finally, father Joseph, seeing how pale Joseph was and thinking he was ill, told him to go to the house where his mother could doctor him. Moroni watched as Joseph started for home. On the way, he tripped crossing a fence and lay there, unconscious.

Moroni called to him. "Joseph. Joseph."

He awakened as Moroni appeared above him. Once more Moroni went through all the training given to Joseph the previous night, repeating it verbatim so as not to be misunderstood. When he had finished, he said, "Joseph, go to your father and tell him what you have seen and heard. The spirit will bless him that he will understand and believe you. I will wait for for you at the place where the records are hidden."

Again Moroni transmitted himself back through the veil and watched Joseph as he returned to his father and told him all that had transpired. Father Joseph in a trembling voice, said, "Joseph, what you have seen and heard comes from God. Go and meet the angel now as he has told you."

Moroni waited on the hillside for Joseph, next to the stone box he had fashioned so many years before: a place of poignant memories. Joseph arrived shortly and must immediately have recognized the spot from his own vision since Moroni did not reveal himself. Joseph looked around, sized up the stone, searched until he found a pole of the right size to use as a lever, and after removing the dirt from around the stone, used the pole to move it. Watching him, Moroni sensed his excitement and expectation.

The stone slid away and there they were—the plates and the breastplate just as Moroni had left them. Joseph stood there in awe for a moment, then attempted to reach in. At that instant Moroni stepped forth. "Wait, Joseph."

Joseph was startled, jumping backward, away from the box. He looked up at Moroni, apparently wondering if he had sinned. Looking kindly at him, Moroni said, "The time for bringing forth the plates has not yet arrived. There is much preparation ahead for you. Meanwhile, meet me at this spot a year from this day and I will give you more instructions."

Nodding in obedience, Joseph took one more longing look at the plates, picked up the lever, and moved the stone back over the box. When it was properly secured he straightened out the dirt to look natural again, stuck his hands in his pockets, and morosely started down the hill. Moroni watched him go, understanding his disappointment, but knowing the wisdom of the Lord's plan.

During the year, Moroni continued to teach Joseph, showing him in vision what his own life had been like. Joseph was excited about seeing the ancient inhabitants of America. He asked questions about how they dressed, how they traveled, the animals he rode, their cities, their buildings, their warfare, and their religious worship. Moroni was glad to have such a willing pupil.

A year passed. Joseph once again came to the hill to see Moroni and the plates. Moroni again did not reveal himself. Joseph waited a few moments, found a stick, and once again uncovered the plates. For a moment he stood there, undecided, then impulsively reached in and lifted out the plates. Moroni read his thoughts. He intended to take the plates home with him. He felt that he was now worthy.

Then Moroni was aware that another thought struck Joseph. "What if there is something else of value in the box?" He put the plates on the grass and turned back to the box. Moroni shook his head sadly. Joseph was human. He had given him explicit instruction to never set the plates down unless they could be locked up. Moroni took the plates. After Joseph had worked the lid back on the box, he turned back to where he had left them. They were gone! Moroni knew that his heart was filled with fear and dread. Joseph knelt and prayed. He asked, "Why were the plates taken from me?" He knelt there for some, pouring out his heart. When Moroni felt that he had shown enough contrition, he appeared once more. He stood there, arms folded, looking sternly at the sorrowing youth.

"Joseph, you take your calling too lightly. Why is it that you treat the plates so carelessly?"

Joseph shuffled his feet and looked at the ground. He could not look at Moroni. "It is true that I was careless." He thought for a moment before continuing, then with understanding said, "It is hard to behave as an adult when one thinks so much like a child." He looked disconsolate. "But what has happened to the plates?"

"Open the box," Moroni suggested.

Joseph eagerly pried off the lid, breathing a sigh of relief when he saw that the plates were inside. Thinking he was still prepared to take them, he started to reach into the box. To stop him and to teach him another lesson, Moroni charged the air around the plates with a bolt of electricity. When Joseph contacted that electrical field he was hurled backward with a great force.

Moroni withdrew, watching Joseph from beyond the veil. He slowly picked himself up from the ground and looked around. Now comprehending that he was not to have the plates yet, he took the lever and replaced the lid. Moroni watched again as the forlorn youth trudged back down the hill, weeping with bitter disappointment. It was difficult for him not to interfere, but he had had to learn for himself the virtue of patience. It was a virtue that the young Joseph needed also to learn.

Moroni decided that being a guardian angel and teacher was not an easy task. On several more occasions Moroni had had to reprimand Joseph for carelessness or frivolity. He was a fun-loving youth and sometimes cut up. It wasn't quite the image that Moroni expected in a future prophet of God. One day in mid-winter Joseph was passing by the Hill Cumorah when Moroni stopped him, "Joseph," he called.

Joseph dismounted from his horse and walked to where Moroni was standing. He was surprised to see him and said happily, "Moroni, it is so good to see you."

Moroni loved this young man and it was difficult to be stern. However, it was important that Joseph be prepared to carry the heavy burdens that would come upon him. "Joseph," he began, "Why is it that you shirk the Lord's work? Do you not know how important this work is and what role you must play in it? My heart is troubled when you treat this mission so lightly."

It was a strong rebuke, and for a moment it appeared that Joseph almost reacted in anger. Then he ducked his head. "I suppose that I am a foolish youth and am not worthy of the trust the Lord has placed in me. I really have tried to keep the commandments."

"It is true that you have avoided temptation, but what have you been doing to prepare yourself for your sacred calling? What studies have you attempted? What activities have you engaged in which would strengthen your faith and give you moral courage so that you can face the adversary and his legions? How much time have you devoted to prayer?"

Moroni paused to let the words sink in. "Joseph," he said in a kindly voice, "I have grown to love you as a brother. Your potential is great but know this: The restoration of the Gospel will come forth at this time and if you are not worthy to be the prophet of that restoration then someone else will be called."

To impress him with the seriousness of his calling, Moroni called on the Spirit for a manifestation. The heavens opened and the glory of God shone around them and then rested on Joseph. As quickly as it had come, it was gone. In its place Joseph beheld the prince of darkness, even Lucifer, with his hosts of evil spirits. That scene also quickly faded, and Joseph and Moroni were once again alone. Facing Joseph, Moroni said: "Joseph, all this is shown to you: the good and the evil; the holy and the impure; the glory of God; the power of darkness that ye may know hereafter the two powers and never be influenced or overcome by that wicked one." [67]

Joseph was silent, awed by what he had seen. The impression was deep. "Joseph," Moroni added, "let me say once more that you are a chosen vessel of the Lord. Prepare yourself! Don't be light-minded or frivolous in your actions. Conduct yourself as a prophet of the Lord." With those parting words Moroni withdrew himself.

During the next months he watched over young Joseph, observing that now he was beginning to wear the mantle of a prophet.

Now it was time to meet once again at the Hill Cumorah. It was a thrill for Moroni to see Joseph's new maturity. He no longer was impatient to get the plates. He was ready to receive instruction. Moroni taught Joseph, teaching him of the plan of salvation, tutoring him in the skills of working with people, preparing him in the leadership skills he would need in order to lead a mighty people.

He was pleased with Joseph. He was like a sponge, absorbing everything that Moroni taught him, asking questions and developing insights. The brotherhood between the mortal prophet and the resurrected being became one of strength and unity. Moroni quietly praised Joseph, saying, "My friend, you are truly developing the characteristics you will need as a prophet of the Lord."

Joseph grasped him with one hand, placing the other on his shoulder. "Thank you, Moroni. I sit at your feet, learning from you. Whatever I am now or will become, I owe a great deal to you."

During this year Moroni did not manifest himself to Joseph. He was now prepared to learn from others. He knew that Joseph was in good hands.

The time came for the third annual meeting at Cumorah. It was September and Joseph faithfully appeared on the twenty-second as he had been instructed to do. "Greetings, my friend," Moroni said. "It is good to see you once again."

Joseph was bubbling with enthusiasm. "Oh, Moroni, I have so much to tell you. My heart is so full. I have learned so much and know how much more there is to be learned."

Moroni smiled. "I am thrilled at your progress. Your learning is obvious, but tell me what has happened."

"I'm sure you know a great deal of what has happened during this year." He told Moroni of being visited and instructed by Abraham and Moses, Isaac, Elijah, Adam, Noah, and Enoch. Even Mormon had appeared to him to instruct him. He smiled joyfully. "Sometimes I wondered if I could absorb any more, but through the help of the Holy Spirit I was able to do so. It has truly been a heavenly education."

Moroni nodded in agreement. "That is true. In this one short year you have learned more about God and the history of mankind than most men learn in a lifetime."

The two visited for hours. When it was time for Joseph to go, Moroni gave him a final warning. "Joseph, remain humble and teachable. You will continue to receive many marvelous manifestations." Then, looking into the future, he added, "This will not be an easy year for you. There are those who will do anything to make your life miserable, but if you remain faithful you will be protected from harm. We will meet here again next year at this time, and if you remain worthy, you will obtain the plates."

The two friends embraced. Moroni noted the tears in Joseph's eyes and that when he walked off the hill, he walked with confidence.

The final year of Joseph's probation passed quickly. He was subjected to much persecution, but he handled it well. The invisible Moroni stood at his side, strengthening, but not interfering; guiding, but not directing. Joseph's education continued, with the hosts of heaven giving counsel and training.

When he approached for the final time the place where the plates were hidded, he was surprised to see the box open and Moroni sitting on the lid.

He was holding the plates and the Urim and Thummim on his lap, slowly turning the leaves—recalling again the work of crafting and writing each plate. He looked up. As Joseph approached, he stood and handed the plates to him. Joseph received the plates in silence, hefting their weight, thinking of the great responsibility which was now his—not only protecting the plates from all who would destroy them, but of translating them and publishing their truths to all the world.

Moroni said: "Now you have the record in your hands, and you are but a man. Therefore, you will have to be watchful and faithful to your trust or you will be overpowered by wicked men; for they will lay every plan and scheme that is possible to get it away from you, and if you do not take heed continually, they will succeed. While it was in my hand, I could keep it, and no man had power to take it away, but now I give it up to you. Beware, and look well to your ways, and you shall have power to retain it." [68]

Joseph looked at Moroni. "I promise you that I will be faithful." His voice broke, but he continued, "I will protect these plates with my very life. I know how much they mean to you. I will care for them and protect them and translate them by the power of God." He spoke with conviction and power.

Moroni said, "Thank you for that assurance. The hosts of heaven are depending on you. I will be near you, but from this time forward you are on your own. I cannot help you. I will not see you until it is time for me to receive the plates from you. Goodbye, Joseph."

"Goodbye, my angel friend," Joseph said. He turned and walked down the hill. Moroni watched him go into the night's darkness, feeling confidence in Joseph's new-found maturity. Then he wept for his friend and for the sorrows he knew were just beginning.

When next he appeared to Joseph, it was not a pleasant occasion. Joseph had given Martin Harris part of the completed manuscript and it had been lost. Moroni had taken back the Urim and Thummim—stopping the translation. Joseph was distraught, suffering the torments of the damned. He found no rest; there was no peace of conscience. He felt so guilty and heartsick that he was even fearful of approaching the Lord.

Moroni appeared, standing in Joseph's room, arms folded, the Urim and Thummim held in his folded arms. "Joseph," he began, "I have brought back the Urim and Thummim."

"But why?" asked the despondent and tearful Joseph. "I do not deserve it. I have violated my trust. I am a doomed man."

Moroni knew the agony in Joseph's heart, "Here, Joseph, take it. The Lord has asked me to give it to you. You are to put it on and then write the revelation He will give you."

Joseph took the Urim and Thummim and through them received a revelation concerning the lost manuscript.[69] As soon as he finished transcribing the revelation, Moroni again appeared. Joseph looked up with red-rimmed eyes. His cheeks were sunken, his complexion sallow. Moroni's heart went out to him, but he had a sacred assignment to carry out.

"Joseph, I must take back the interpreters and the plates. You were told what would happen if you violated the trust placed in you. The Lord loves you, but rebukes you. Read and study carefully what you have written. Prepare yourself once again to complete the mission you have begun. I warn you once more to yield not to temptation." With that warning, he took the plates and left the sorrowing prophet alone in the room.

A few days later, because of Joseph's contrite heart, Moroni was able to restore to him the plates and the interpreters. The lesson had been a bitter one for Joseph to learn, but Moroni knew that a lesson learned in adversity is never lost.

A year later the book was completely translated. It proudly carried the title on its cover: BOOK OF MORMON. Moroni was thrilled that the work could now come forth. He knew that, through this book, his father's name would be known to all nations and peoples. He was anxious for it to be disseminated, but there was one more task.

Moroni had taken the plates back into his possession upon completion of the translation, but now he had a special assignment: to manifest himself and the plates to three special witnesses whom the Lord had designated. Since Joseph had asked him to also show some of the Nephite relics, Moroni had obtained the sword of Laban and the director which Lehi had received in the wilderness.

Joseph and the three witnesses prayed long for a manifestation, but because of Martin Harris's transgression, Moroni held back. Finally Martin seemed to realize what was happening, and he withdrew from the others. After Joseph and the two remaining witnesses had prayed at length, Moroni appeared to them in all of his glory as a resurrected being. He placed the Urim and Thummim with its breastplate, the Liahona, and the sword of Laban in front of them. Then, standing in the air, he carefully turned the leaves of the golden book he held in his hands. After showing them the sacred engravings, he turned to David Whitmer and said, "David, blessed is the Lord, and he that keeps his commandments." [71]

Then, while Moroni stood holding the plates, the voice of the Lord spoke from the heavens behind him, saying: *"These plates have been revealed by the power of God. The translation of them which you have seen is correct, and I command you to bear record of what you now see and hear."* [71]

When the Lord finished speaking, Moroni took everything he had brought and disappeared. Joseph sought out Martin Harris and after they had prayed together, Moroni appeared to them. He knew the gravity of the situation, but he had a hard time to keep from smiling as Martin jumped up and down shouting, " 'Tis enough! 'Tis enough! Mine eyes have beheld; mine eyes have beheld! Hosannah be the name of the Lord!" [71]

Moroni appeared once more to Joseph, just to say goodbye. It was tempting for him to give counsel concerning his future, but that would only distract from the great role Joseph was going to play. He had suffered the trials and persecution while translating the plates. The book was now at the publishers and the work was moving forward. Moroni could see down through the years when this noble man would seal his testimony with his blood, much like Morman had done. As for now, all Moroni could do was to wish Joseph well.

"I go back to the spirit world, my friend. Know that our friendship transcends time and space. I will look forward to the time when you join me in Paradise."

The two friends embraced once more. "Thank you, Moroni. You have been more than a friend. I look forward to an eternal association with you."

With that thought, the mortal prophet and the immortal and resurrected angel parted. Moroni's mission was completed.

Epilogue

Moroni, his mission completed, had earned his rest. Even so, he continued his quest for knowledge. He observed the earth with great interest, especially the growth of the restored Church. He followed the life of his friend, the Prophet Joseph, as he led and developed the Church.

After the martyrdom of the Prophet, he joined with the other hosts of Paradise as they welcomed him with great rejoicing and acclamation to the Spirit World. He and Joseph spent long periods talking of their experiences and sharing philosophy and knowledge. Moroni continued his role of teacher to the Latter-Day-Prophet, sharing with him some of the knowledge he had gained in the Spirit World. He thrilled with him when the Prophet received his resurrected body.

Life in Paradise was sweet and beautiful. It was a fitting interlude between earth life and the joy of Celestial life. Seeing temples built on sites he had dedicated was especially pleasing to Moroni. The temples gave to millions of people the blessings that few had enjoyed during his lifetime. He was secretly pleased when he saw the golden image of himself raised to the topmost spire of the Salt Lake Temple. He watched as that statue became the unofficial symbol of the Restored Church, decorating book covers and spires of temples around the world.

Armora had squeezed his hand. "It is a fitting monument to one who has given more than a lifetime of service to the Master."

Primary children sang of him:

"An angel came to Joseph Smith, and from the ground he took
A sacred record hidden there; a precious Holy Book." [72]

Adults in church meetings throughout the world sang,

"I saw a mighty angel fly, to earth he bent his way,
A message bearing from on high to cheer the sons of day." [73]

He listened as voices in chapels around the world sang praises to him. Tears came to his eyes as he listened to the mighty Tabernacle Choir singing "An Angel From on High." [74] The hosts of heaven enjoyed it so much that even the heavenly choirs picked it up. It was Armora's favorite song.

An angel from on high, The long, long silence broke,
Descending from the sky, These gracious words he spoke:
"Lo, in Cumorah's lonely hill
A Sacred record is concealed.

Sealed by Moroni's hand, it has for ages lain
To wait the Lord's command, From dust to speak again.
It shall again to light come forth,
To usher in Christ's reign on earth.

It speaks of Joseph's seed and makes the remnant known
Of nations long since dead, Who once had dwelt alone.
The fulness of the Gospel, too,
It's pages will reveal to view.

Moroni was touched by all of this recognition. But that which meant the most to him—the crowning touch of all—were the few simple words of the Savior, Him whom Moroni loved and served above all: *"Well done, Moroni, thou good and faithful servant."*

Notes

1. Alma 29:1
2. Ether 12:4, 6-13
3. Moroni 7:40, 41
4. Mormon 3:2
5. Moroni 6:2, 3
6. Mormon 6:19
7. Helaman 13:9
8. Mormon 6:17-22
9. Mormon 6:20-22
10. Mormon 7:2-8
11. Mormon 8:1-3
12. Mormon 8:4, 5
13. Reference 10, p. 28, 29
14. Moroni 8:11, 12
15. Moroni 7:30
16. Reference 10, p. 28, 29
17. Reference 25, p. 20
18. Moroni 6:7
19. Mormon 8:6
20. Mormon 8:7, 8
21. Mormon 8:8
22. Mormon 8:10, 11
23. Mormon 8:12, 13
24. Mormon 8:14
25. Mormon 8:22-24
26. Ether 12:23-25
27. Ether 12:26-28
28. Ether 12:37
29. Mormon 8:34-41
30. Mormon 9:1-5
31. Mormon 9:11
32. Mormon 9:13, 14
33. Mormon 9:19
34. Mormon 9:20-25
35. Mormon 9:28, 29
36. Mormon 9:30-37
37. Ether 1:1-6
38. Ether 2:9, 10
39. Ether 2:12
40. Ether 4:4-7
41. Ether 4:11-19
42. Ether 5:1-6
43. Ether 8:22
44. Ether 8:25, 26
45. Ether 12:6
46. Ether 12:7, 8
47. Ether 12:9, 27
48. Ether 12:28
49. Moroni 7:42-47
50. Ether 12:33, 34
51. Ether 12:39, 41
52. Ether 15:34
53. Ether 2:12
54. 3 Nephi 17:21-24
55. Moroni 7:47, 48
56. Moroni 8:25, 26; 9:25-26
57. Moroni 10:3-5
58. Moroni 10:17, 18
59. Moroni 10:20-23
60. Moroni 10:31-33
61. Moroni 10:34
62. Title Page, Book of Mormon
63. Mormon 8:33
64. 2 Nephi 3:14, 15
65. James 1:5
66. Reference 24, p. 79
67. Reference 34, p. 198
68. Reference 22, p. 60
69. Reference 31, Sec. 13
70. Reference 22, p. 75
71. Reference 22, p. 75, 76
72. Reference 35, B-43
73. Reference 36, p. 300
74. Reference 36, p. 342

References

1. Cheesman, Paul R. *Early America and the Book of Mormon,* Salt Lake City: Deseret News Press, 1972.
2. _____. *Great Leaders of the Book of Mormon,* Provo: Promised Land Publications, 1973a.
3. _____. *The Keystone of Mormonism,* Salt Lake City: Deseret Book, 1973b.
4. _____. *These Early Americans,* Salt Lake City: Deseret Book, 1974.
5. _____. *The World of the Book of Mormon,* Salt Lake City: Deseret Book, 1978.
6. Crowther, Duane S. *Life Everlasting,* Salt Lake City: Bookcraft, 1967.
7. Farnsworth, Dewey. *The Americas Before Columbus,* Salt Lake City: Sounds of Zion, 1981.
8. Fox, Robert Barlow. *Behold I am Moroni,* Salt Lake City: Granite Publishing, 1976.
9. Hammond, Fletcher B. *Geography of the Book of Mormon,* Salt Lake City: Bookcraft, 1960.
10. Hansen, L. Taylor. *He Walked the Americas,* Amherst: Amherst Press, 1963.
11. Hemingway, Donald W. *An Introduction to Mormon, A Native American Prophet:* Publishers Press, 1978.
12. Hunter, Milton R. *Christ in Ancient America,* Salt Lake City: Deseret Book, 1972.
13. _____. *Great Civilizations of the Book of Mormon,* Salt Lake City: Deseret Book.
14. Kirkham, Francis W. *A New Witness for Christ in America,* Salt Lake City: Utah Printing, 1967.
15. Lambert, Roy. *The Weight of an Angel.*
16. Lundstrom, Joseph. *Book of Mormon Personalities,* Salt Lake City: Deseret Book, 1972.
17. Matthews, Robert J. *Who's Who in the Book of Mormon,* Salt Lake City: Deseret Book, 1976.
18. Palmer, David A. *In Search of Cumorah,* Bountiful: Horizon Publishers, 1981.
19. Pierce, Norman C. *The Great White Chief and the Indian Messiah,* Norman C. Pierce, 1971.
20. Priddle, Venice. *The Book and the Map,* Salt Lake City: Bookcraft, 1975.
21. Silverberg, Robert. *Lost Cities and Vanished Civilizations,* Chapter 5, Chichen Itza of the Mayas.
22. Smith, Joseph Fielding. *Essentials in Church History,* Salt Lake City: Deseret News Press, 1950.

23. *Teachings of the Prophet Joseph Smith,* Salt Lake City: Deseret Book, 1974.

24. Smith, Lucy Mack. *History of Joseph Smith by His Mother,* Salt Lake City: Bookcraft, 1979.

25. Sperry, Sidney B. *Book of Mormon Compendium,* Salt Lake City: Bookcraft, 1968.

26. West, Jack H. *The Trial of the Stick of Joseph,* Sacramento: Rich Publishing, 1976.

27. _____. "What Caused the Collapse of the Maya," Ch. 12, *Mysteries of the Past,* American Heritage.

28. _____. "Maya Travels in Central America," *Wonders of the Past.*

29. Moody, Raymond A. *Reflections on Life After Life,* New York: Bantam Books, 1978.

30. _____. *Book of Mormon,* Church of Jesus Christ of Latter-day Saints.

31. _____. *The Doctrine and Covenants.* The Church of Jesus Christ of Latter-day Saints.

32. _____. *The Pearl of Great Price.* The Church of Jesus Christ of Latter-day Saints.

33. *The Holy Bible.*

34. _____. *Messenger and Advocate,* 2:1, Oct. 1835, p. 198.

35. *Sing With Me,* Songs for Children, Salt Lake City: Deseret Book, 1970.

36. _____. *Hymns of the Church of Jesus Christ of Latter-day Saints,* Salt Lake City: Deseret Book, 1974.